Redemption

REDEMPTION

The Two Lives of
HARRY BROOKS

BROOKS EASON

NEW YORK
LONDON • NASHVILLE • MELBOURNE • VANCOUVER

REDEMPTION

The Two Lives of Harry Brooks

Published in New York, New York, by Morgan James Publishing. Morgan James is a trademark of Morgan James, LLC. www.MorganJamesPublishing.com

Scripture taken from the KING JAMES VERSION (KJV), public domain.

Proudly distributed by Ingram Publisher Services.

"Tupelo MS historic First Methodist Church 412 Main Street"
Copyright 2011 Thomas R Machnitzki
https://creativecommons.org/licenses/by/3.0/deed.en

Morgan James BOGO™

A **FREE** ebook edition is available for you or a friend with the purchase of this print book.

CLEARLY SIGN YOUR NAME ABOVE

Instructions to claim your free ebook edition:
1. Visit MorganJamesBOGO.com
2. Sign your name CLEARLY in the space above
3. Complete the form and submit a photo of this entire page
4. You or your friend can download the ebook to your preferred device

ISBN 9781631957482 paperback
ISBN 9781631957499 ebook
Library of Congress Control Number:
2021945569

Cover Design by:
Rachel Lopez
www.r2cdesign.com

Interior Design by:
Chris Treccani
www.3dogcreative.net

Morgan James is a proud partner of Habitat for Humanity Peninsula and Greater Williamsburg. Partners in building since 2006.

Get involved today! Visit MorganJamesPublishing.com/giving-back

For Harry, who overcame

For there is not a just man on earth, who doeth good, and sinneth not.
Ecclesiastes 7:20

Amazing grace, how sweet the sound
that saved a wretch like me.
I once was lost, but now am found,
Was blind, but now I see.
"Amazing Grace"
John Newton

PROLOGUE

Most biographies and works of historical fiction are about famous people or famous events, but this book is about neither. It is instead about a fascinating man who committed grievous sins in the first half of his life and hid them from the world in the second, when he otherwise lived a virtuous life.

The man was my grandfather, Dr. Henry Felgar Brooks. Identical twins Margaret and Marjory, the last of his ten children, were born minutes apart in March 1921. Margaret, whom my sister and I called Mama, was my wonderful adoptive mother. Dr. Brooks, who went by Harry, was a gifted preacher of the Word of God. During the Great Depression, he served as the senior minister of the church where I was baptized two decades later, the First Methodist Church in Tupelo, Mississippi.

This book necessarily contains elements of fiction because Harry died nearly eighty years ago, and many details of his life, including the secrets he kept to himself, died with him. But the core of the book is the unvarnished truth based on historical records. Notes at the end detail what I know to be true in each chapter and how I learned it. The notes are preceded by an introduction explaining choices I made for parts of the book that I don't know to be true.

I never met Harry, who died nearly fifteen years before I was born, though I learned some things about the second half of his life from Mama. Until recently, however, I knew nothing about the first half of his life because she knew nothing about it either—or at least nothing that was true.

But one afternoon, in the spring of 2019, my education about the first half of Harry's life began. I was at my desk working on *Fortunate Son*, my memoir about my adoption and discovery of my birth mother's identity, when my phone rang. The caller identified himself as Lee Cheney from Fresno, California. Lee said he had learned that he was my first cousin. He knew I was adopted and said he was adopted too. Like me, he had discovered the identity of one of his biological parents. His birth father was Edwin Brooks, Mama's older brother. Harry was thus Lee's grandfather too—biological in his case, adoptive in mine. Shortly after Lee was born in 1956, he was adopted out of our family. When I was born a year later, I was adopted into it.

That I had a new cousin in California was not the most intriguing news I learned from Lee. Starting with our first call and continuing over the months that followed, he shared with me an extraordinary story he'd learned through a year-long search of census reports, old newspapers, genealogical records, and other historical documents. It was the story of the first half of Harry's life, the story Harry took with him to the grave. Part of the story is the false birthdate etched on Harry's gravestone in Carlton, Texas, which is fourteen years later than the real one.

When Lee told me the story he'd learned, I knew I wanted to write it. With his blessing, I have now done so. I owe an enormous debt of gratitude to Lee, without whom I never would have learned the story you're about to read.

Seated on the bottom step: Andy Anderson
First row: Ethel Land Brooks, Marjory Brooks, Margaret Brooks
Second row: Harry Brooks, Danny Brooks
Third row: Edwin Brooks, Triss Brooks Soles, Elizabeth Brooks Anderson,
Edgar Lee Anderson

CHAPTER ONE

APRIL 29, 1937

◁《⊙☉》▷

TUPELO

The parsonage was a beautiful white clapboard home a hundred feet west of the sanctuary. Broad steps rose to a wide covered porch that looked out over Main Street. A swing hung from chains on one side of the front door; two rocking chairs sat on the other. Harry was inside, seated behind the walnut desk in his study, putting the finishing touches on his Sunday sermon. Behind him were bookshelves filled with Bibles, books about theology, works by his favorite authors, including Twain, Dickens, and Emerson, and a collection of famous speeches. Harry often reached for a volume to find a reference to use in a sermon. Even alone behind closed doors, Harry neither took off his coat nor loosened his tie. He was not a casual man.

It was late in the afternoon on the last Thursday in April, the 29th, a date Harry would never forget. He rose from his chair to close the blinds. The massive oak trees that had provided shade on the west side of the parsonage were no longer there. Like nearly all of the trees on West Main Street, they had not survived the devastating tornado that destroyed much of the city a year earlier.

Something had seemed different when spring arrived this year, and it took Harry a while to realize what it was. It was the silence. The trees outside the parsonage were gone, and so were the birds. Harry considered birds one of the most glorious of God's creations. In the spring, he listened to the mating calls of male cardinals and watched robins scratch in the grass for worms. He admired the industry of Carolina wrens as they built nests for the new families they would soon have. When he needed a break from his work, he would walk to the open window of the study, watch and listen to the birds outside, and tilt his head the same way they did. Sometimes, one would detect movement in the study and stare back at him.

When he had the time and energy, Harry would drive the family Plymouth west of town and walk alone in the woods along the sunken Natchez Trace, listening for the call of barred owls as dusk came on. He was good at imitating them, and they would often call back in response. One evening, an owl swooped down to investigate and glided past on its silent wings only a few feet away. Harry loved pileated woodpeckers and thought their call was the wildest sound in all of nature. When he heard one in the woods outside Tupelo, he was reminded of a different place and the most exciting time of his life, when he was a younger man and could walk farther and faster.

When the birds came alive in the spring, Harry saw them as evidence of the hand of God. Birds, like all that God had created, were a miracle. In the Sermon on the Mount in the book of Matthew, Jesus reminded his followers that God feeds the fowls of the air. God still feeds them, Harry thought as he looked through the open window, *just no longer outside my study.* The silence reminded him of his time in Pittsburgh three decades earlier, of the three long years he spent without seeing or hearing a single bird.

Harry was a good writer. He had a talent for a turn of phrase and was pleased with how this week's sermon had come together. He was a gifted speaker as well. More than two years earlier, shortly after moving to Tupelo to become the minister of the First Methodist Church, he was chosen from among all the town's preachers to deliver the invocation when

President Roosevelt came to town. A massive crowd estimated at 75,000, more than ten times the population of the city, gathered in and around the high school football field on the corner of Church and Jackson Streets to hear the president speak.

The reason for Roosevelt's visit was to congratulate Tupelo on becoming the first community in America to be powered with electricity generated by the Tennessee Valley Authority, a New Deal agency that was building hydroelectric dams on rivers across the South. The success of the TVA provided a rare glimmer of hope in the midst of the Great Depression. After Harry's prayer, the president rose from his wheelchair and gripped the lectern. Despite his polio, he always stood when he spoke. He looked out at the ocean of faces and smiled. His first words were, "I shall not make a speech to you today." He then proceeded to make one.

A year and a half after FDR's visit, Tupelo was struck by the fourth deadliest tornado in the nation's history. Nearly 300 residents were killed, more than a thousand were injured, and much of the town was destroyed. Church Street School, just to the south of the football field, was reduced to rubble. Two weeks after the storm, Harry wrote a moving essay about Tupelo's recovery from the tornado and how the tragedy had brought the people of the town closer to God and to one another.

Harry returned to his desk and the sermon. The subject he had chosen was a delicate one, at least for him. It was the biblical admonition for Christians to confess their sins not only to God but also to each other. He had chosen three passages of Scripture from his worn King James Bible to make the point. The first was James 5:16: "Confess therefore your sins one to another, and pray for one another, that ye may be healed. The supplication of a righteous man availeth much in its working." The second was Proverbs 28:13: "He that covereth his sins shall not prosper: But whoso confesseth and forsaketh them shall obtain mercy." And, finally, Psalm 32:3: "When I kept silence, my bones wasted away through groaning all the day long."

Harry drew on the three verses to support the theme of his sermon. He would explain to the congregation that the grace of God and the road to salvation may not require Christians to acknowledge and confess their sins to one another, but doing so is necessary to achieve peace and contentment in this life. Making a secret confession to God is not enough. The sinner must also confess his sins to those he has sinned against and from whom he has concealed his wrongdoing. He must seek forgiveness not only from God but also from them.

Harry then considered another famous passage. Though it was not from the Bible, it was often in his thoughts. In *Table Talk*, a book nearly three centuries old, English scholar and author John Selden was quoted as saying that preachers tell their congregants to "do as I say, not as I do." For Harry Brooks, it was ever thus. He sighed and put down his fountain pen.

There was a knock on the door of the study. Harry said to come in, and the door opened. There stood Margaret, one of the twins. The children were under strict instructions never to interrupt Harry while he was working on a sermon. He wondered what could warrant this exception to the rule. Margaret had an odd look on her face. She did not accept his invitation to come in but instead stood in the doorway.

"Yes?"

"There's a lady at the door."

"Who is she?"

"I don't know; Teresa or Tressa, something like that. Her last name is Soles. She says you're her father."

Harry's heart skipped a beat.

"Where is she? Is anyone else home?"

"No. Mama and Marjory went to the grocery store. Danny's at school getting ready for graduation. I asked the lady to wait on the porch. Who is she, Daddy?"

"How should I know? You stay here till I get back."

He motioned to his chair and waited for Margaret to sit. After he left and closed the door behind him, he took a deep breath, then walked to the front of the parsonage. At long last, after all these years, it was time to confront his troubled past. He opened the door, and there she was.

"Triss." It had been three decades, but there was no doubt.

"Father."

"You never called me Father."

"I haven't called you anything in thirty years."

He reached to embrace her, but she pulled away.

"I'm sorry."

"I'm sorry? That's it? Thirty years, and that's it?"

"I don't know what to say. I made a terrible mistake. I suffered the consequences."

"*You* suffered?"

"I'm sorry. How is your mother? Please tell me she's well."

"Dead. In the ground more than twenty years. She never got over it."

He took another deep breath. "And Katherine?"

"Dead too. Year before last. Consumption. I'm the only one left. I can't believe what you did."

"I can't believe Katherine is gone. She was just a child."

"She was a child when you left. Almost forty when she died."

"I'm terribly sorry, Triss. All men are sinners."

"Some worse than others."

"I want to make it up to you. What can I do?"

"Make it up to me? After what you did and how you left?"

"I had no choice about leaving. There was nothing left for me there."

"Just two daughters who adored you. Or at least two daughters who had adored you."

"But I wasn't permitted to see you."

"I would have seen you. I was a grown woman."

"But I wasn't allowed."

"So you didn't try."

"My wife doesn't know about you."

"I bet there's a lot she doesn't know. I know about Ethel. She and I were born the same year."

"You have a right to be angry. Why did you come? What do you want?"

"All I want right now is to hear what you have to say. Then I'll decide. I think I want to spread the news. I want your wife and your children—it's strange to call them that because you already had a wife and children—but I want them to know what you did and who you are. And not just them. I want the members of your church to know the truth about the man who stands in their pulpit and lectures them about sin. I want the whole world to know."

"You can't do that, Triss, I beg of you. We need to talk, but it can't be here, and it can't be now. Please let me tell you my side of the story. Please get a room for the night." He reached into his pocket. "Here's some money to pay for a room at the Hotel Tupelo."

She pushed his hand away. "I don't want your money. I don't need it."

"Alright, but please get a room at the hotel. I'll meet you there for breakfast at eight o'clock."

"Why? Why should I do anything for you?"

"Don't do it for me. Do it for my wife and children. You have no reason to hurt Ethel. Or Margaret and the others. Margaret's the one who came to the door."

"She seemed nice. What is she? Fifteen? Sixteen? I'm fifty, in case you've forgotten."

"I know how old you are. She and Marjory turned sixteen last month. They don't deserve to be hurt, Triss. Please give me a chance to talk to you before you tell anybody."

"Alright, I'll wait for now. I'll do it for your children and the poor woman who married you, the second poor woman who married you. I already have a room at the hotel."

"Thank you. I truly am sorry. I lost my way, and there was no going back."

"So you ran away. Twice. First to England, then to Texas."

"I'm sorry."

"I'll see you at eight."

Harry watched as Triss descended the porch stairs and turned east on the sidewalk. A black Buick Limited was waiting at the corner of West

Main and Green. The driver got out and opened the back door for her. She climbed into the back seat, and the car pulled away. Harry then returned to the study and found Margaret sitting on the edge of his leather chair. She waited for him to speak. He didn't, so she did.

"Who is she, Daddy?"

"We can't discuss it right now. I can't talk to you about it, and you can't talk to anybody else about it. Not yet anyway." He looked at her. "Do you hear me?"

"Yes, sir, but why?"

"Because I can't talk about it yet. I will, but not now. And you can't mention it to your mother or Danny. Not even Marjory. Do you understand?"

"Yes, sir."

"Thank you. Leave me alone now, please. I have a sermon to finish."

CHAPTER TWO

1799

《◎ ②》

LIVERPOOL

John and Mary Brooks stood on the dock and looked out on the River Mersey. It was the first time either of them had seen the river or the city of Liverpool. They were waiting to board a packet ship with their five sons, who were lined up on the rail between them. The oldest, also named John, was nine. Robert, Thomas, and William were eight, six, and five. The youngest, Joseph, was three. The family's belongings were in the bags behind them. Their destination was America; their plan was to start a new life there.

John, who'd been told of cheap, fertile land in the new country, was excited. Mary, who'd heard horror stories about spending months in the steerage compartment of a packet ship, was frightened. Provisions were limited and conditions deplorable. Seasickness and more lethal ailments were common. As Ralph Waldo Emerson later wrote, "The road from Liverpool to New York, as those who have traveled it well know, is very long, crooked, rough, and eminently disagreeable." But John had assured Mary that the journey would not last long and they would arrive safely before the end of summer. The weather in Liverpool added to his natural optimism about what lay ahead. It was warm and sunny, with a light breeze coming off the river.

John was an Englishman through and through and had never thought it would come to this. He had grown up on his parents' farm and then volunteered for the army, in which he'd served with distinction in the French Revolutionary War. He was rewarded with a knighthood for his courage, but he'd found that being a knight didn't put food on the table. As a result of recent events, he had reluctantly concluded that there was no future for him and his family in his native land.

John's parents had died when their house burned to the ground the winter before. If his father had ever written a will, it was lost in the fire. Because there was no will, and because English law was based on the doctrine of primogeniture, John was entitled to no interest in the family farm. James, his older brother, inherited it all. James told John that he could continue to work on the farm and would be treated fairly, but he smiled when he said it. James had a cruel streak, and the two brothers had never gotten along. John liked what he had heard from those who'd spent time in America. He decided to sail across the Atlantic with his family and start a new life in the new country that had been at war with his own less than two decades earlier. Mary was reluctant, but she deferred to her husband.

In truth, John would miss his dog far more than he would miss his brother. George, named for the king, was a handsome fox terrier, though he'd never been asked to hunt a fox. He was bright and loyal and was treated like a member of the family. He was born between the births of Robert and Thomas, and John and Mary referred to him as their third son. But son or not, dogs were not allowed in the steerage compartment of a sailing ship, and George had to be left behind. James promised to take care of him, but John wondered if James could be trusted. He also wondered if James's children, who took after their father, would be kind to George.

On the day they left the Brooks farm, after John, Mary, and the boys loved on George for the last time and exchanged awkward goodbyes with James and his family, John climbed to the seat of the wagon, took the reins, and headed west on the road to Liverpool. Just after they'd topped the first hill, John heard a gunshot. He jumped down and ran back, fearing the worst. James saw him coming and howled with delight. "I knew it. I knew I could get you." He fired another shot into the air, repeating what he'd just done. George stood off to the side, unharmed. John said nothing. He shook his head and returned to the wagon, more convinced than ever that leaving was his only choice.

A slave ship was unloading in the berth next to the packet ship. In the second half of the eighteenth century, Liverpool had surpassed London and Bristol and become the slave-trading capital of Britain. Shipbuilders in the city designed and built "slavers" for transporting Africans captured and sold into slavery by other Africans. The ships were constructed with special features, including a high wall on the main deck with spikes on top to prevent uprisings and keep the peace. The male slaves were kept on one side of the wall; on the other were the women, the children, and the crew. The ships were loaded in Liverpool with textiles and other trade goods manufactured in and around the city. When the ships set sail, they headed south to the west coast of Africa, where the trade goods were swapped for human cargo. Packed with as many slaves as they could hold, the ships took the Middle Passage across the Atlantic to the southeastern coast of the United States or islands in the Caribbean, where the slaves who survived the journey were sold to the owners of sugar and cotton plantations. The ships then returned to Liverpool, were loaded again, and repeated the clockwise journey.

Although Liverpool's economy depended on the slave trade, most of the Englishmen who profited from it had never owned a slave. Slavery was still legal in England, but few of the Africans transported on the slave ships wound up there. But on rare occasions, slaves were brought on the final leg of the journey to the ships' home port and came ashore in Liverpool. John and Mary and their five sons stared as a line formed to walk up the gangplank from the ship. At the front was a white man with a pistol, at the back one with a bullwhip. In between were eight Africans, four men and four women. Their hands and feet were bound with shackles, and they were chained together. They were emaciated, filthy, their clothes in rags. A woman stumbled and was helped up by the man behind her.

This was another first for John and Mary. Neither had ever seen a slave, or any native of Africa for that matter. Their thoughts as the line filed past them and moved slowly away reflected their different views about leaving England. John thought he would have been like a slave in some ways if he had stayed and worked for James. Not in the worst ways—he couldn't be sold or separated from Mary, and there would be no chains or whips—but his labor would have been owned and his life controlled by another man. Mary thought about what lay ahead of them, not what they were leaving behind. They were about to make the same journey the Africans had just made, crossing the North Atlantic in the steerage compartment of a sailing ship. She watched them until they were out of sight, wondering what she would tell her sons about what they had just seen.

The first part of the journey was pleasant, at least during the day. The late spring weather was warm and clear, the seas fair, and the family spent nearly all their waking hours on deck. It was a grand adventure for the boys. They watched the sailors climb the masts to hoist and furl the sails and dreamed of becoming sailors themselves. The ship rounded Anglesey Island off the northwest coast of Wales, sailed south to the point where the Irish and Celtic Seas converge, then went into port in Queenstown on the south coast of Ireland to take on more passengers and cargo. The passengers who'd boarded in Liverpool were permitted to go ashore for several hours. For Mary and the boys, it was their first time to set foot on the soil of a country other than England. Ireland would become part of Great Britain less than two years later, but it was still independent in 1799. John gathered his sons around him and announced that they would be in America, their new home, when they next walked off the ship.

The only difficulty was at night. Conditions in steerage were as bad as Mary had feared and were bound to get worse. It was damp, dirty, crowded, and dark. When the hatch was closed, the only illumination came from a single lamp that was fueled by fish oil and produced more smoke than light. Sanitation was poor, and the addition of the Irish passengers made quarters even tighter.

After they were in the North Atlantic, a storm came, and the seas were rough. For three days, passengers were not allowed on deck. The danger of being swept overboard was too great. They huddled in the dark, many of them seasick. The air was foul. The timbers of the hull creaked as the ship dipped and rose. Mary, who had never been to sea, was reminded of the Old Testament story of Jonah, who was cast by mariners into the sea to keep their ship from breaking apart. She was also concerned about the boys. She did not want to trouble John but, in a rare moment when all five were asleep, she spoke up.

"I'm worried about the boys, John. Robert hasn't kept anything down for two days, and Joseph keeps waking up screaming."

John reached over and patted her leg. "I know it's bad, but Robert and Joseph will get better. The weather will clear."

She put her hand on his and smiled. "I hope it clears soon. We could all use some sunshine."

"It will, I'm sure of it. This too shall pass. It always does. And before we know it, we'll be in our new home." He inched closer to her, and she laid her head on his chest.

The weather did get better, as did Robert and Joseph, and they all returned to the deck during the day. Conditions in steerage were wretched, but at least it was only at night.

But after a week of good weather, another storm came, and they were again barred from going on deck. The passengers did their best to clean up the vomit and other human waste, but the smell never went away. On the first night after they were restricted to steerage, John was awakened by a rat scurrying across him in the darkness. On the second, with all the boys asleep, John again put his hand on Mary's leg.

"I'm not well," he said.

"What is it?" John never complained.

"I believe I have a fever."

Mary put her hand on his forehead. He was burning up. "You do. Anything else?"

"I'm weak. I don't know if I can stand. I have a terrible headache."

"I'll get someone."

"Who? There's no one to get."

"There might be. I'll try."

Mary walked toward the ladder, careful not to step on the passengers sleeping on the floor, and heard a hacking cough behind her. It was John. She could barely make him out when she turned to look but could see his hands pressed to his temples. She climbed the ladder and pushed on the hatch. She found it unlocked, opened it, and pulled herself up. The ship was pitching violently in the heavy seas. She stumbled to the rail and made her way forward, where she found a member of the crew at the helm. She had to yell to make herself heard over the gale.

"My husband is very ill. I need someone to come below to see about him."

The sailor shook his head.

"Can you hear me? My husband is sick. He has a high fever."

He looked at her for the first time. "There's no one, ma'am."

"Is there medicine on board I can give him? Anything?"

He shook his head again. "If it's just a fever, he'll recover."

"That's not all. He's too weak to stand. He has a cough and a terrible headache."

The sailor had heard these complaints before. He turned and faced her. "I'm sorry, ma'am. I'm sure he'll be alright. You need to go back down now. It's not safe for you up here in this storm."

"I'll go, but if you hear of anyone on board who may be able to help, please come below and find me. My name is Mary Brooks. I'm very worried."

"Yes, ma'am. I will."

As she made her way back toward the stern, she heard another voice. A man had joined the sailor at the helm. Mary climbed back down the ladder after pulling the hatch closed and heard a noise on the deck above her. She climbed back up and pushed on the hatch again. It was locked.

The days that followed were a nightmare. Word spread that other passengers in steerage were ill. The sick included both young and old, though the adults were much sicker. John got worse instead of better. He often woke up drenched in sweat, but the fever never broke for good. He became weaker and began having abdominal pain. Mary made him drink water, but he would eat nothing. She tried to go up on the deck again to seek help, and other passengers did as well, but the hatch stayed locked. They cried for help and banged on the hatch, but no one came.

On the second day after John became ill, Mary had a fever too, and by the next day she was too weak to care for him or the boys. That night, when the others were asleep, she motioned for the two oldest boys to come to her side.

"I'm very tired. I need you to take care of your brothers."

They looked at her, frightened. "Yes, ma'am," Robert said.

"You need to make sure they eat and drink plenty of water. And stay as clean as they can. I'm going to try to sleep now. I'm sure I'll be alright. I'm just tired."

The next day, the hatch opened briefly, and sunshine streamed in. The storm had passed; the ship was no longer pitching. A sheet of parchment drifted down from the deck. Then the hatch was closed, and they heard the lock turn. A man about John's age named Melchior Entling reached down and picked up the sheet of paper. He read it to himself and shook his head, then walked to the port side of the ship, banged on the hull, and cleared his throat. After the passengers became quiet, he spoke.

"This letter that has just been dropped to us from the deck is from the captain. It's addressed to all the passengers in steerage. Let me read it to you. 'We believe at least one passenger in steerage has typhoid fever. There may be others. Whatever your number, you have our sympathy and prayers. But there is nothing we can do. There is no doctor on board, no nurse, and we have no medicine. Typhoid fever is very contagious. We cannot allow you to come on deck and put the crew at risk. If the crew becomes too ill to sail the ship, we will not make land and will all perish.'"

Entling stopped, took a deep breath, and continued. "'If someone in steerage should pass away, please wrap the body in a blanket and bring it to the base of the ladder. One person should climb up, knock three times on the hatch, then go back down. A member of the crew will open the hatch and allow a maximum of five people to come on deck to bury the departed soul at sea. There is no minister on board, but a young man in the crew who studied in seminary has agreed to read from Scripture and say a prayer. Those who come up must remain in the stern and descend to steerage as soon as the service ends. I am sorry for your troubles. May God be with you. Yours most sincerely, Captain Abington.'"

John had been delirious with fever at times, but he was calm now. He leaned back and smiled, then rolled over on his side, pulled Mary close, and whispered to her, "It's in God's hands now."

The first of the passengers to die was an elderly man named Edmund Smith from Manchester. He was sailing to America to join his son, daughter-in-law, and granddaughter in Philadelphia. He had told the other passengers how excited he was about the prospect of seeing them after being separated by an ocean for five long years. His eyes lit up when he talked of his beautiful granddaughter. Jones had no family on the ship, so Entling and four other men agreed to take his body up to the deck and cast him into the sea.

They wrapped Smith's body in his blanket, as instructed, and brought him to the base of the ladder. Entling climbed up, knocked on the hatch, then descended. The hatch soon opened, and two sailors came into view. One was holding a pistol. They saw the body, and Entling requested permission to come up. One of the sailors said, "Not yet," then closed and locked the hatch again. They returned shortly and granted permission. With Entling holding one end of the blanket and another man the other, they brought Jones's body up and laid him beside the hatch. The three other men followed.

The sun was bright, and they waited for their eyes to adjust. They had not seen the sky or the ocean in nearly two weeks. When they gained their bearings, they saw a line of five soldiers halfway down the deck, all armed with muskets. Three steps in front of them, a young man stood holding a book. It was a King James Bible. He nodded at them solemnly and said, "My name is Frederic Williams. It is my honor to read from Scripture and say a prayer for the departed. What was his name?"

"Edmund Smith," answered Entling, "a fine man. Thank you for your reading, but if you don't mind, please let me pray. I knew the man."

"Certainly," said Williams. "I will first read from the book of Ecclesiastes, the seventh verse of the twelfth chapter. 'Then shall the dust return to the earth as it was: and the spirit shall return unto God who gave it.' And now two verses from the Gospel according to John. First from chapter eleven. 'Jesus said unto her, I am the resurrection, and the life: he that believeth in me, though he were dead, yet shall he live.' And from chapter three, verse sixteen. 'For God so loved the world, that he gave his only begotten Son, that whosoever believeth in him should not perish, but have everlasting life.'" Williams closed the Bible, looked at Entling, and nodded again.

Entling nodded in return and ran his fingers through his hair. He looked down on the body wrapped in a blanket and closed his eyes. "Let us pray. Dear Lord, I did not know Edmund Smith long, but I believe I knew him well. He was a good man, a kind man, a man who loved his family. He told me of his beautiful granddaughter Henrietta and how much he missed her. Please take Edmund into Your care and hold him close until he is reunited with Henrietta and her parents when they too enter Your kingdom. In Jesus' name we pray, Amen."

Two of the men then lifted the blanket, carried it to the rail, and let it slide into the sea. They watched the body that had been Edmund Smith drift past the stern until it was out of sight. The five then returned to the open hatch to descend. Entling, the last to go down, nodded once more to Williams, and this time Entling smiled. When he reached the floor, he saw the latch above him close and heard the lock turn.

Two more passengers died the next day, a man and a woman. Each left a surviving spouse and two children. Word had spread of Entling's prayer from the day before, and he was asked to perform the same service again. He led one family to the deck in the morning, the other in the afternoon. Williams read the same verses he had read the day before, and Entling asked God to take care of the surviving spouses, who would now have to raise their children alone.

John's delirium worsened. He thrashed and moaned, frightening the boys. But the next morning, he was quiet. Mary was feeling no worse, and she hoped they were both recovering. When she tried to rouse John, however, he was unresponsive. She also noticed blood on his sheet. Another passenger whose brother had died of typhoid years earlier had told Mary that intestinal bleeding was one of the most dangerous symptoms of the disease and often meant that death was near. She held John's hand and talked to him through the day, but he said nothing. She told him over and over that she loved him. Once she thought he squeezed her hand, but she wasn't sure.

Mary slept fitfully, fearing the worst. When she awoke in the morning, she laid her head on John's chest, listening for his heartbeat. There was none; he was gone. She began to sob, but then she felt a pat on her arm. It was William.

"What is it, Mama? Is something wrong with Papa?"

Mary sat up, took a deep breath, and put her hand on William's shoulder. "Please bring your brothers. I need to talk to all of you."

He was back with the other four in less than a minute. All five looked frightened. The older boys could see that their father was not breathing. The little ones were confused. Mary pulled Joseph into her lap. "Your Papa has gone to live with God in heaven," she said. "He will not live with us now. But some day we will all go to heaven too, and when we do, we will all be together again. Until then, we must all love each other and take care of each other." Tears ran down her face, but she managed a smile. "John, please go find Mr. Entling, tell him what has happened, and ask him to come to me." John nodded and walked away. She hugged Joseph, then helped him to his feet. William, Thomas, and Robert stood in line and hugged her in turn. She was weak but squeezed them as hard as she could.

John returned shortly with Entling. "Mrs. Brooks, I am terribly sorry for your loss. John was a fine man."

"The finest," Mary said, and started sobbing again. Entling put his hand on her shoulder and waited for her to collect herself. When she did, she told the boys she needed to talk to Mr. Entling alone. When they were out of earshot, she spoke. "I understand that five of us are allowed to go on deck for the funeral. Is that correct?"

"Yes, ma'am. Five."

"I feared this was coming, and what to do has been in my thoughts. I want William and Joseph to stay below. They're too young to understand, and I don't want them to see their father's body dropped into the sea." She began weeping again, and Entling waited. "If you could be so kind, I would ask you to go up with John, Thomas, Robert, and me and say a prayer for my husband and for us. Will you do that?"

"Of course, ma'am. I will be honored. But will you be able to climb the ladder?"

"I will have no choice. And Mr. Entling, I would like you to know something. John had grown very fond of you before he became ill. He enjoyed the time the two of you spent together."

"Thank you for telling me that. I was very fond of him as well. Now, if you'll permit me, I'll wrap him in his blanket and find someone to help me carry him to the ladder."

Before he began, Mary leaned over, embraced her dead husband, and kissed him on the lips for the last time. Then she rolled away, closed her eyes, and began to cry again.

After Entling and another man had taken John's body to the deck, the three boys went up first, in order of age. Young John led the way. They saw the men in a line facing them, holding muskets by their sides, and another man alone, holding a book. Mary could barely stand, much less walk or climb, but with Entling in front and the other man behind, they managed to lift her through the hatch. She leaned on Entling for support.

When the sailor in the middle of the line saw her, he raised his musket and aimed it at her. "The woman is ill. She cannot be on the deck. Take her back down now."

Entling spoke evenly. "This man," he said, pointing down at John's body, "was her husband."

"I don't care if the man was Christ himself. She cannot be on the deck. Take her down immediately, or we will have to shoot her. Those are our orders." He looked to either side. The other sailors' muskets remained at their sides. They looked down at their feet.

While still supporting Mary, Entling positioned himself between her and the sailor with his musket raised. Several moments passed, then Entling spoke again. "Mr. Williams, you may proceed with your reading from the Word of God."

Williams started with the verse from Ecclesiastes, then turned to the Gospel written by the disciple who shared a name with the dead man on the deck. Before he resumed his reading, Williams looked up at Entling. "I don't know who you are, but you are a brave man." Then he looked back down and read the two verses from the book of John.

Then it was Entling's turn. He said, "Let us pray," and all on the deck bowed their heads and closed their eyes, all but the soldier whose musket was still aimed at Entling. "Dear God, last night we lost a fine and caring man, John Brooks. His wife Mary and their sons will miss his love and guidance, and the days will be hard. But they can rest in peace with the assurance that their kind husband and father has now entered Your kingdom, the kingdom of heaven, and that someday they will join him there. Please take care of his family in the trying times ahead. Let them know Your love and fill them with Your spirit. Watch out for them as they enter a new country and start a new life. And watch out for this ship and these sailors, that they may bring us safely into port." Entling now lifted his head, opened his eyes, and fixed them on the sailor looking at him, "And finally, please forgive the sailor who raised his musket. He was only doing his duty as it was given him to do. In Jesus' name we pray, Amen."

This time, three men nodded: Entling, Williams, and the sailor with the musket. Entling asked John to support his mother and then, with help from Robert and Thomas, slipped their father's body into the sea. Entling watched as the body disappeared in the wake of the ship and said, "John Brooks, I'm glad I knew you."

Mary was worse the next day. Her symptoms were following the same course as her husband's. She noticed fresh blood on the sheet. At mid-day, she felt a hand on her arm and opened her eyes. It was Robert. "Mama, I think Joseph is sick. He says his head hurts. He feels like he has a fever."

Her eyes opened wide. "Bring him to me."

She felt Joseph's forehead. He didn't feel warm but, with her own fever, she couldn't be sure. She asked him what was wrong. He said he was tired and his head hurt. All the boys had avoided the fever so far, but this was bound to happen. She turned to Robert. "Please find Mr. Entling and tell him I would like to speak to him."

Entling soon appeared, just as he had the day before. When the boys had left them, he nodded and waited for Mary to speak.

"Mr. Entling, you have been a Godsend to us. You risked your own life yesterday to save mine. It pains me to do this, but I must ask you for something else. I don't know where else to turn."

"Anything, Mrs. Brooks."

"I believe I am dying. I am now bleeding, just as John was the day before he died. I am not concerned about me. If I die, I will soon be with John again. But the boys. My five little boys. I'm afraid of what will happen to them."

"If something happens to you, Mrs. Brooks, I will see that they are taken care of. I can't take them, but I will find good people who will."

She smiled and reached for his hand. "I know you will. I know you're a man of your word."

"Thank you."

"The baby, Joseph, I'm afraid he has the fever. His head is hurting, and Robert says he's warm to the touch. I felt him but couldn't tell."

"I will check on him. I'm sure he'll be fine. Children don't seem to get as sick as—"

"Their parents do." She finished his thought, smiled, and closed her eyes.

"I will look after him. He's a good boy."

"They're all good boys. All different but all good. It's funny, I always wanted girls, but God had other plans. Thank you, Mr. Entling. John was right about you." He squeezed her hand, turned, and went to look for Joseph.

Mary thought of Jonah again. She was ready to be cast into the sea, but she couldn't leave her boys. She wondered if she should talk to them, tell them what to expect, not to worry, that Mr. Entling would take care of them. But she died in her sleep and never got the chance. When Entling again made his way to the deck to bury her at sea, the sailor who had raised his musket was again in the middle of the line. When he saw that it was the same boys who had come up to bury their father two days before, he hung his head. Then he looked up, met Entling's eyes, took off his hat, and bowed to the man who had offered to give his life for a dying woman. After Williams read the now familiar verses, Entling said a prayer for Mary and her sons. Later, after returning to steerage, he said one for himself, that he might do right by them.

Entling knew he couldn't take all the boys. Truth be told, he shouldn't take any of them. The house that he and Elizabeth lived in alongside the Delaware River in Trenton was tiny, and they already had three children. How could he return from England with a fourth? They could barely feed their own, much less one more. Entling's goal was to keep the boys together, and he identified men who might be willing to take them all. These were kind men, all of them. He knew that from their harrowing journey across the North Atlantic. But he found no one able and willing to take all five boys.

Over the course of the next week, Joseph began to improve. The older boys took care of him with help from Entling and several women who had taken an interest in the family. Late one afternoon, the hatch opened, and another letter drifted down to the floor. This time, for the first time in two months, it was good news. The ship would reach New York the following day. A cheer went up.

Entling had thought he had more time to make arrangements for the boys, but now he had very little. He rounded up the men he thought could be trusted to raise them and asked for privacy. The other passengers moved away, and the men sat in a circle. Thirty-four adults and three children had died from the fever, but the Brooks brothers were the only children who had been orphaned. All the others on board had at least one surviving parent. Entling had gone on deck to pray for nearly all the victims, all but the few who had at least five family members who wanted to be there.

"We need to decide what to do with John and Mary's sons," Entling began. "I promised Mary I would find good homes for them, and it's a promise I intend to keep. The boys have no relatives in America. They have lost both of their parents, and they shouldn't have to lose each other too. I wish I could take them all in, but Elizabeth and I have a small house and three children of our own. Is there anyone among you who can take all of them? I know it's a great deal to ask, but I'm asking. They're good boys."

The group was silent until James Cooper, who was headed to Massachusetts after the ship landed, spoke up. "I wish I could take them all, Mr. Entling, but five little boys? All less than ten years old? It's impossible. Where would they sleep? How would I feed them? If you can find homes for the other four, I will take Robert. I have been teaching him mathematics. He's a bright boy."

Cyrus Allen, who had a small tobacco farm in Virginia and had lost his wife on the journey, was the next to speak. "I am willing to take Thomas, who has the makings of a fine young man, but even that will be a hardship. Only a rich man could take in five young boys. We wouldn't be in steerage if we were rich."

Several of the others nodded. Then Entling spoke again. "Thank you, gentlemen. Can any of you take more than one?" Again there was silence. "Must the brothers all be separated from each other?"

Geoffrey Harrison, who was the youngest of the men, chimed in. "This is a terrible tragedy for the boys, but the way I see it, it's far better to take one that I can support than two or three that I can't. I am headed north to my brother's farm outside Albany. I'll be sleeping in the barn until I can build a place of my own. I am willing to take John. He's old enough to earn his keep on the farm. I don't know what my brother will say when the two of us appear, but his name is John too, and he has no sons of his own. We'll make do."

The last to volunteer was a gaunt man named Roger Davies who planned to live with family members who'd come to America a decade earlier and settled in the countryside west of Baltimore. "I am willing to take William. I have only me to support. I will find a way to support him too."

Entling was disappointed that the boys would be separated but satisfied that he had kept his promise to Mary. Good men he trusted had agreed to take four of her sons. Before any of them could have second thoughts, Entling decided to declare the matter resolved and end the meeting. "So then it's settled. I will take Joseph. I made Mary a special promise that I would look after him. Elizabeth will think I've gone mad, but she's a kind woman. She will understand. Mr. Harrison, Mr. Davies, Mr. Allen, Mr. Cooper, thank you very much for your kindness. As for the rest of you, please keep us in your prayers. Now, gentlemen, let's go find the boys and tell them about their new lives."

The older brothers took the news in stride. After what they had been through, there was little that would upset them. They were sad that they would be separated from their younger brothers, but they were relieved that they would all be taken care of. John asked to explain the plan to William and Joseph. He crouched beside them and told them they would have new families and make new friends and would all see each other again soon. John was not yet ten years old, but he sounded like a grown man as he assured his little brothers that all would be well.

The next afternoon, on the dock in New York Harbor, the five men stood off to the side as the brothers hugged and said goodbye. They were bound for five different states along the Atlantic Seaboard, stretching more than 500 miles from Massachusetts to Virginia. They had lost their parents, and now they were losing their siblings. They never saw each other again.

Joseph would not turn four until September. In less than a year, his grandparents had died in a fire, he'd left the only home he'd ever known, his father had died, then his mother, and now his brothers were gone too. He was in a new country, riding on the seat of a horse-drawn buggy with a man he hardly knew. Entling tried to comfort him on the road to Trenton. "My wife's name is Elizabeth. She is beautiful, and she loves children. We have three. Won't she be surprised when she sees that I've brought her a fourth? You will now have something you've never had before–sisters. Mary is seven; Alice is five. And you will no longer be the youngest. Henry turned two while I was in England. He had not yet learned to talk when I last saw him. If he still doesn't know, you will have to teach him."

Entling looked down at Joseph and smiled. Joseph looked straight ahead at the road winding through the woods. He did not smile, but he reached over for Entling's hand, which was holding the reins. When he found it, he did not let go.

CHAPTER THREE

1863

‹© ›»

SPRINGFIELD TOWNSHIP

The three-year-old orphan who landed in New York in 1799 planned his own funeral in Pennsylvania more than sixty years later. Joseph Brooks and his wife Dorothy met with their pastor John Amos after the doctor said nothing more could be done and time was short. Joseph was in the four-poster bed he shared with Dorothy. She and John were in chairs on either side. Joseph had several requests for his funeral. He wanted John to read verse sixteen from the third chapter of the Gospel according to John the Apostle. The verse was the favorite of the man who had raised Joseph, and it was Joseph's favorite as well. He also had one song request, "Amazing Grace," and he said to John, "I want every verse to be sung, and I want them sung loud. Tell everybody to sing at the top of their lungs. I want God to know I'm coming."

"I will tell them, Joseph, but God will already know."

"I suppose He will, but tell them anyway. I also want you to remind my family of the debt of gratitude we owe to the Entlings. You know about that. And another thing: So you won't embarrass yourself by laughing out loud when you see me in the casket, you should know that I will be buried in my favorite Prince Albert coat and high hat."

John, who had been taking notes, looked up at Joseph and smiled. "You'll be buried in a hat?"

"That's right. I believe I look my best in a high hat. This is the last time anyone on Earth will see me, and I want to look my best."

"I've never known anyone to be buried in a hat, a high hat or any other. Can you do that?"

"I don't know about anyone else, but I can."

"Not to be indelicate, Joseph, but you're a tall man. If you wear a high hat, how will you fit in the coffin?"

Dorothy spoke up. "They're making one longer than usual." Joseph smiled and nodded. He'd thought of everything.

"Alright then, you'll wear your Prince Albert coat and your high hat. No one at the funeral will be more elegantly attired. And I will tell everyone to sing loud and make a joyful noise." John would miss Joseph terribly.

"Good. Then we're all set."

"Not quite. Your plan is all well and good, but there's a problem we need to discuss."

"The problem is that I'm dying. What could be a bigger problem than that?"

"I understand your perspective, but there's another problem we'll have after you're gone. It's the question of location."

"Location of what?"

"Your funeral. There's not a church in the township that will hold all the people who will come. Not even the church we built with your money."

"I guess I should have given more."

"Wouldn't have helped. Croesus himself couldn't have built a church big enough. There's barely one that will hold all your family. How many children do you have again? I can't keep up."

"Thirteen," said Dorothy. "Fifty-eight grandchildren, with two more on the way. And the great grandchildren have started coming in droves. I can't keep up either."

"And that's just your family, Joseph. Your friends will all want to come. All the people you've helped along the way. And you founded the township. Every public official for miles around will show up."

"Politicians? Can't we stop them from coming? Seems blasphemous."

"Nothing stops politicians. And there's no church here that will hold everybody. There's not even one in Pittsburgh."

"My funeral will not be in Pittsburgh. You may be surprised to hear this, John, but I've thought about the matter of location. I've always prided myself on being a problem solver, and I've solved this one. My funeral will be outside, on God's green earth. It will be right here on our front lawn. Nobody can say they weren't allowed to come. And I will be buried beside my two grandsons right here in the family plot. The pallbearers will be grateful that they won't have far to carry me."

"You're right about the pallbearers." Joseph was a big man. He weighed well over 200 pounds. "But an outside funeral? I don't think so. It would be neither proper nor respectable."

"And just where did they have funerals before there were churches, John? Outside, that's where. And that's where mine will be. God made Springfield Township more beautiful in the autumn than any church built by the hands of man. More beautiful than the Sistine Chapel."

"But what if it rains?"

"Postpone it a day. I'm not going anywhere."

"But I've never performed an outside funeral. I've never even heard of one."

"Then my death will give you two firsts in your life. An outdoor funeral for a man wearing a high hat. And I expect you to outdo yourself. I want you to give me a first-class send-off. Understood?"

"Yes, sir, Mr. Brooks."

"I'm dying, John. Don't make it worse by calling me Mr. Brooks."

"My apologies, Joseph."

"Apology accepted. You now have your assignment, and Dorothy has hers. I've asked her and our daughters to feed our guests well. I guess they'll even have to feed the politicians. No one has ever left our farm hungry, and I don't want them to start on the day of my funeral. So while I'm busy dying, Dorothy will be busy cooking."

"She's a wonderful cook, that's for sure."

"That she is. You can tell that from looking at me. And one more thing: There is to be no sadness, not on my account. I've had a wonderful life, and it's about to get even better."

"Amen to that." John stood, bent down and kissed Joseph on the forehead. He then turned and walked out the door so they wouldn't see him cry.

◀◦▶

It was the first week of October. A crowd of hundreds was gathered on the sweeping lawn outside the farmhouse. It was a beautiful, cloudless day—no postponement had been necessary—and the surrounding hills were ablaze with every shade of red and gold. There were oaks and chestnuts, maples, beeches, and hickories. Joseph had been right; it was more beautiful than any church hewn by mere mortals.

There was a chill in the air, and a platoon of Joseph's grandsons kept a half dozen campfires going around the perimeter. Tables were piled high with food, and Joseph's sons and grandsons had brought every chair in the house out to the lawn. Though many of the mourners had come with their own, there were still not enough. Young men stood off to the side, and children played in the back.

One of the young men was Milton Brooks. His wife Eliza, who was pregnant with their second child, sat at the end of one of the rows of chairs. Milton, who stood beside her, was one of Joseph and Dorothy's many grandchildren. He was the oldest son of their second son, Henry. Henry's older brother was named John for their grandfather who died on the terrible voyage from Liverpool.

One of the youngest of the children playing in the back was Henry Felgar Brooks, Milton and Eliza's first child. The choice of a name when he was born was easy because his two grandfathers were Henry Brooks and Henry Felgar. But there were already so many Henrys in the family that Milton and Eliza decided to call the baby Harry. He was born on New Year's Day 1862 at their home in nearby Salt Lick Township. On the day of his great grandfather's funeral, Harry was not yet two years old.

Eliza and Milton asked another couple to keep an eye on Harry so they could walk to the front to pay their last respects. Eliza's father Henry was an undertaker and coffin maker. He had stopped by to see Eliza and Milton after work a few days earlier and told them he was building a coffin eight feet long for Joseph. He didn't tell them the reason for the extra length, but now they saw why. They smiled at each other when they saw Joseph in his coffin, looking grand in his high hat.

After everyone had finished feasting on the dinner on the grounds, John Amos walked to the lectern he had brought in a wagon from the church, looked out on the huge crowd, and raised his hands for quiet. "We will begin this celebration of the life of Joseph Brooks with the hymn that he requested. Those of you who knew Joseph well will not be surprised that he chose 'Amazing Grace.' Nor will you be surprised by the instructions he gave me. We are to sing all the verses, and we are to sing them loud. Joseph said he wanted God to know he was coming.

"But before we sing, brothers and sisters, I want you to consider two things about God's amazing grace. First, when Joseph said he wanted God to know he was coming, God already knew. Second, it doesn't matter how loud we sing because Joseph is already there. He is already home. But let's sing loud anyway. Please join me in singing of the amazing grace that has brought Joseph home." The congregants sang all six verses of the beautiful hymn written by a former slave trader, and they sang them at the top of their lungs. When they were finished, John continued.

"Joseph Brooks was what a man should be. He was what we all should be. He worked hard, he loved his family, he was generous to his church and his community. He always did the right thing. Joseph was a good friend to us all. He was a good friend to me. All of us will miss him, and all of us will suffer from his loss. We will miss him, and we will cry. I already miss him, and I have already cried. But then there is this: God's grace, His amazing grace, will be the balm for our grief.

"Joseph was a Christian man, and through God's grace he is now in a better place. He had another request for me today, that I read his favorite verse, John 3:16. 'For God so loved the world, that he gave his only begotten Son, that whosoever believeth in him should not perish, but have everlasting life.' Joseph believed in God's son, and Joseph's life is now everlasting.

"When Joseph asked me to read this verse, I was reminded that it was also the favorite of the man who raised him, the man named Melchior Entling. Many of you knew him. Joseph told me years ago how the verse had become Mr. Entling's favorite and how it had given him comfort when he needed it most. It was on the fateful journey from England that brought Joseph to America more than sixty years ago. He was only three years old. Many passengers on the ship were infected with typhoid fever. Many of them died. A young man named Williams read this verse, John 3:16, more than thirty times as passengers were buried at sea. Two of the burials were for John and Mary Brooks, Joseph's parents. Now, long after it was read at their funerals, it has been read at their youngest son's. It is both fitting and proper.

"Joseph was a grateful man, grateful for all the many blessings in his life, and he asked that I remind his family of the great debt of gratitude that he owed, and that all of you owe, to Melchior and Elizabeth Entling. Joseph was orphaned on the voyage, and then he was separated from his four brothers, never to see them again. He was still recovering from typhoid fever himself. Yet the Entlings, who already had three children, took Joseph in and raised him as their own. They taught him the values that made him the man he was, the man we all loved and admired. Joseph told me more than once that the Entlings saved his life. And had they not saved Joseph's life, his children, grandchildren, and great grandchildren who are gathered here today never would have been born. This is a celebration not just of Joseph's life, but of all of their lives as well.

"In the twenty-eighth verse of the first chapter of Genesis, the very first chapter of the very first book of the Bible, God instructed his people to 'be fruitful and multiply.' Joseph and Dorothy Brooks took the Lord at His Word. Dorothy told me when I met with them last week that she and Joseph have thirteen children, fifty-eight grandchildren with two more on the way, and that great grandchildren have started to arrive. I knew there were many of you, but I didn't know there were that many. And each of you, each of the many descendants of Joseph and Dorothy Brooks, is a miracle. All of you owe your lives not just to Joseph and Dorothy and to Melchior and Elizabeth Entling, but also to God's amazing grace in placing Joseph in their care. All of you are here because of God's amazing grace.

"Those of us who loved Joseph will grieve his loss, and I pray that God will give all of us, but most of all Joseph's family, the strength to carry on without him. But we need not pray for Joseph. He was a man of towering faith, and he is now at home with his heavenly Father. Joseph doesn't need our prayers, and he doesn't need our sympathy.

"I want to close with the last words Joseph shared with me the last time I saw him. He said there was to be no sadness today, not on his account. He told me that he'd had a wonderful life, and it was about to get even better. And I will say to you what I said to him. Amen to that. Amen to that, brothers and sisters."

———◄o►———

On November 19, 1863, six weeks after Joseph Brooks was buried on his farm in Springfield Township, a funeral of a different sort took place more than a hundred miles to the east. In the weeks between the two ceremonies, the leaves of the hardwoods in Pennsylvania had turned brown and fallen. The trees were now bare. The site of the second ceremony was the battlefield at Gettysburg, where more than 7,000 soldiers had been killed in the fighting during the first three days of July. It was the battle that turned the tide in the Civil War and led to the abolition of slavery, the end of the war, and the reunification of the country.

The purpose of the gathering in November was to consecrate the Gettysburg National Cemetery, where more than 3,000 Union soldiers had been laid to rest. The principal speaker was Edward Everett, who had served as Secretary of State, Governor of Massachusetts, and President of Harvard University. Though Everett was regarded as one of the great orators of his time, and though he spoke for two hours, a speech of fewer than 300 words and lasting only two minutes came to overshadow the one he gave. In Abraham Lincoln's brief comments, he stated that "the world will little note nor long remember what we say here." But Lincoln was wrong about that. His Gettysburg Address is regarded as one of the greatest speeches in American history, and his promise that "this nation, under God, shall have a new birth of freedom—and that government of the people, by the people, for the people, shall not perish from the earth" is one of the most memorable passages from any speech given anywhere by anyone.

CHAPTER FOUR

1886

❦

NEWTON COUNTY
WESTMORELAND COUNTY

Henry Clay Land, named for the Great Compromiser from Kentucky, was born and raised in rural Newton County in east-central Mississippi. His wife, the former Mary Elizabeth Williamson, grew up there as well. By the dawn of 1886, the couple had been married four years and lived on their farm outside the community of Garlandville, just north of the line between Newton and Jasper Counties. They had two young children, Florence and William. Mary was now pregnant with their third and was due any day.

Henry was the fifth son born to Fountain and Demarius Land and the third they named for a statesman. Their first, born in 1831, was George Washington Land. Their second, born seven years later, was christened Thomas Jefferson Land. Two of the Land brothers, Thomas and the third oldest, William, were killed in battle fighting for the Confederacy in the Civil War. Thomas Jefferson wrote the Declaration of Independence and was one of the nation's Founders. Thomas Jefferson Land fought for the right of the Southern states to leave that nation and form another one. He died committing an act of treason against the country that was created by an act of treason against King George.

Henry Land was fourteen when Mississippi seceded and had just turned fifteen when Confederate cannons fired on Fort Sumter. He could have joined the Army later in the war, but his parents had already lost two sons and would not allow it.

Mary was even younger when she lost her parents than Joseph Brooks when he lost his. Her mother died shortly after Mary was born and, just months later, her father left home to fight in the war. He served as a major and adjutant general in the Confederate army and fought in the Battle of Shiloh, but Mary never learned what became of him after that. Whatever it was, he never came home.

Henry was late in marrying—he was thirty-five, Mary only twenty-one—and, as was the custom, the couple wasted no time starting a family. Florence was born eight months and twenty-nine days after their wedding. William came along eighteen months later. Now, for the second time in their short marriage, Mary had one on the hip and one on the way.

The couple took the children to church on Sunday evening, January 17, and Mary went into labor the following morning. When she told Henry the baby was coming, he hitched the wagon to their best horse, left the children with Mary, and headed for the Johnson farm a mile away. Clara Johnson served as the community midwife. When she saw Henry coming at top speed, she knew why. She grabbed her bag, climbed onto the seat, and Henry turned the wagon around and headed home. He pumped water from the well and then kept the children occupied while Clara tended to Mary. The labor went fast, and the baby, another girl, made her entry into the world just after noon. They named her Ethel Jane.

Before taking Clara back home, Henry tried to give her a five-dollar gold piece, but she pushed his hand away. "Put your money away, Henry Land."

"Clara, you have delivered all three of my children, and I haven't paid you a cent. I know there is other work you need to be doing. It's not right."

"I seem to recall that you helped Tom and the boys build our barn."

"But there was just one barn, and we've got three children." He tried again to give her the coin.

"I will not take your money, Henry. I won't have you paying me for being a good neighbor."

Henry put the coin back into his pocket and smiled. "Alright then, I won't pay you, but I'll get you a ham. Good neighbors share their food."

Some of the work that needed doing while Clara was delivering Ethel was making lunch for Tom and their three sons. They would be starving when she got home. She didn't refuse the ham. On his walk back from the smokehouse, he stopped by the chicken coop and gathered a dozen eggs. Clara didn't refuse them either.

Tragedy struck the Land family that summer. In early July, William contracted pneumonia. Pneumonia in the summer was rare but not unheard of. There were no antibiotics in the 1880s and no effective treatment. William got worse over the course of a week and died in his sleep.

Deaths of young children were a fact of life in the nineteenth century. Even at the dawn of the twentieth century, more than a decade after William passed away, thirty percent of all deaths in America were of children less than five years old. A hundred years later, the percentage was barely over one. The loss of a child in the 1800s rarely stopped a couple from having more, and it didn't stop Henry and Mary. In the fourteen years after they buried William, the Lands had seven more, including twins Hattie and Carrie but only one boy, Grady. Their last child, Irene, was born on July 1, 1900, when Henry was fifty-four.

Shortly after the turn of the century, Henry and Mary decided to move to Texas. Like John and Mary Brooks when they sailed for America a century earlier, they were drawn by the prospect of farmland that was both cheap and fertile. They sold their farm in Newton County, packed their belongings, and headed west with their nine surviving children. They traveled by train, their livestock in the cattle car behind them, and bought a new farm in Erath County, just west of the town of Carlton. They lived there the rest of their lives. When the family arrived in Texas, Ethel was fifteen.

———◇———

One month to the day after Ethel Land was born in Newton County, Mississippi, two carriages pulled up in front of a large Georgian mansion in Westmoreland County in Southwest Pennsylvania. The home was surrounded by towering chestnut trees. The limbs were bare in February. It was almost dusk, and a light snow was falling. In the first carriage were Harry Brooks and his maternal grandparents, coffin maker Henry Felgar and his wife Catherine. In the second were Harry's two younger brothers, William and Samuel. All five were dressed in their finest. The mansion belonged to Hanna Cochran, John Cochran's widow. The gathering of the two families was for a wedding. Harry was marrying Rose, Hanna's oldest daughter. Harry had just turned twenty-four; Rose soon would.

Harry had lost both of his parents years earlier. His father Milton was killed in an accident on the family farm when Harry was only nine, and his mother Eliza died of cholera seven years later. Harry and his brothers were raised to adulthood by Henry and Catherine, who saw to it that they got a good education.

After watching his father die, Harry made a vow that he would find a way to make a living with his brain and not his hands. He was exceptionally bright, studied hard, and secured a position as a teacher in his native township of Salt Lick when he was only seventeen. He later taught at West Overton and then in the Bridgeport Independent Schools near Mt. Pleasant, forty miles southeast of Pittsburgh. He also attended the University of Kentucky, graduating from its commercial department in only a year.

Harry and Rose met at a church social after his return from Kentucky. She was attractive, her family well-to-do and highly regarded. They owned a manufacturing facility that purified coal to make coke, which was used to make iron. Harry asked Rose to join him for coffee, then for dinner the following week. The two found they had much in common, including birds, books, and religion. They began spending most of their free time together, talking for hours and going for long walks in the woods.

Harry had a pair of field glasses, which he used to spot birds and identify them for Rose. The two seemed made for each other. After several months of courtship, Harry decided to propose. Because Rose's father had died five years earlier, Harry requested her mother's permission to seek Rose's hand in marriage. Mrs. Cochran consented, Harry proposed, and Rose accepted.

The ceremony was small and simple, with only family present. Rose wore the beautiful handmade gown her mother had been married in three decades before. The wedding was conducted by the German Baptist minister of the local church. Harry and Rose stood before one of the home's enormous fireplaces to recite their vows. The newlyweds then took one of the carriages to the train station and left for New York.

The newlyweds had saved themselves for marriage and discovered the pleasures of intimacy on their wedding trip. When they got home from New York, Harry returned to the classroom, and they soon learned that Rose was pregnant. Their first child, a daughter named Tressa, was born in December, less than ten months after the wedding. They called her Triss. Fifteen months later, Rose gave birth to a second daughter, Grace.

Harry's career advanced as the family grew. He soon was promoted to principal of the Bridgeport Schools, where his students and their parents addressed him as Professor Brooks. During his years in Bridgeport, he was also called into the ministry in the Indian Creek congregation of the German Baptist Brethren Church, which later changed its name to the Church of the Brethren. Some years later, he became a Methodist, but he continued to preach. The *Biographical and Historical Cyclopedia of Westmoreland County, Pennsylvania*, published in 1890, described Harry as "an intelligent, industrious, energetic young man of noble ambitions and high aspirations." He was twenty-eight years old, and his life was going according to plan.

CHAPTER FIVE

1897

⟪⟨◉ ◉⟩⟫

McKEESPORT

Harry stared at himself in the mirror. He looked and felt older than his thirty-five years. He tightened his necktie, combed his hair, and returned to the bedroom. The curtains were drawn, the lights were off, and Rose was still in bed. Her eyes were closed, but she tilted her head in Harry's direction when she heard his footsteps. "Rose, you need to get up and get dressed. We need to leave for the church soon."

She opened her eyes and looked at him. "I'm not going." She said it as a fact, not as an argument.

"We have to go, Rose. It's our son."

"I'm not going. You and Triss go on without me." She rolled away from him and toward the wall.

"You have to go too. You're his mother. What will people think?"

Now it was an argument. They had lost another child, another sweet, innocent baby, and Harry was concerned about what people would think. She rolled back over and faced him. "I don't give a damn what people think, Harry. I will not watch another of my children being lowered into the ground. I won't do it. I can't."

"But what will I tell them?"

"I don't care what you tell them. Tell them I can't attend another funeral for one of my babies. That should be enough. If it's not, tell them I don't give a damn what they think."

"Rose, I must insist that you go. You're his mother. You need to be there. Reverend Southwick's words may prove a comfort to you."

She propped herself up on her elbows. "And what will his words of comfort be, Harry? That George's death was part of God's plan? That it was God's plan for that sweet child to suffer in pain and then die? Just like it was His plan for Grace to suffer and die before George did? And for Roswell to die before Grace did? Even though God has allowed three of our precious children to die, will the good reverend tell us that God still loves us? Is that the comfort he will provide?"

"Everything is part of God's plan, Rose. We may not understand it, but it is. And God does still love us." Harry had been taught from childhood that all that happened in the world, both good and bad, was part of God's mysterious plan. Not even the deaths of three children could change his opinion. "You need to go to the funeral. Please get up and get ready. There's not much time."

Roswell was their third child but the first to die. He was only two weeks old. Rose put him down for a nap. Nothing was wrong, he wasn't sick, he just didn't wake up. When she went into the nursery to see about him, he was gone. It just happens sometimes, the doctor said. Among Roswell's many survivors was his great-great-grandmother Dorothy Brooks, Joseph's widow. She was born in the last decade of the eighteenth century, died in the last decade of the nineteenth, and lived to be ninety-four, more than twice the average life expectancy at the time. Not many people live long enough to see the birth of a great-great-grandchild, much less the death of one.

Three years after Roswell's death, Grace was stricken with tuberculosis. She was five. Harry and Rose watched, helpless, as Grace slowly suffocated, her lungs filling with blood. It took her two weeks to die, which was far too long both for her and for those who loved her.

Grace was a beautiful child, full of life, and recovering from her death had been difficult. Harry and Rose both went through times of depression, but they were able to lean on each other for support. Then, two years later, Rose had another baby, George, and life got better. But just two days ago, death had come again, and this time it had claimed that baby, who had just turned two. A week after his birthday, George developed a severe case of diarrhea. The doctor said the cause was something called enteritis. Had he been older and stronger, he probably would have survived, but he became severely dehydrated and couldn't be saved. And now his mother wouldn't go to his funeral.

"I am not going, Harry. I cannot go through it again. Please leave me in peace."

"You have to, Rose. You need to be there for Triss."

"No, she doesn't, Daddy."

It was Triss, standing in the doorway. Though it was June, she was in her winter Sunday dress, the dark gray one. She was only ten years old, but she knew not to wear her yellow spring dress to her brother's funeral.

In truth, Roswell's death had little effect on Triss. She was only three then, and he died in his sleep. Her parents were sad, but life soon returned to normal. She barely remembered him. But the deaths of Grace and George were much different. She and Grace were inseparable. They were together every minute, playing and sleeping together, and then Grace was gone. Her death left a huge hole in Triss's life. But then George came along to fill it. They were eight years apart, and she thought of him as her baby. She was helping her parents raise him and teach him to talk. Now he was gone too.

Perhaps worst of all, both Grace and George had suffered terribly before they died, and Triss had watched them suffer. Harry and Rose tried to spare her, but when Grace was ill, Triss slipped out of her bed in the middle of the night and sat beside Grace, holding her hand, listening as she struggled to breathe, telling her to get better. When George got sick four years later, Triss did the same thing. She had to do something. But it didn't help, and now, for the third time, Triss was an only child.

"Let Mama stay here, Daddy. You and I can go. I'll be fine." Triss was still a child, but life had already turned her into a stoic. "If people don't like it, something's wrong with them, not Mama."

Harry was now outnumbered and gave up. He also knew that Triss was right. If people decided to look down on Rose for being unable to come to yet another funeral for yet another child, that was their problem, not hers. She didn't need to make an appearance for their sake. Harry smiled at Triss, then sat down on the bed and put his hand on Rose's leg. "Alright then, you stay here. If anyone asks, I'll say you're not feeling well and just not up to it."

The sanctuary was almost full when Harry and Triss followed Reverend Southwick into the sanctuary through the side door and made their way to the front pew. When they heard whispers behind them, Triss squeezed Harry's hand, leaned over, and whispered "their problem" in his ear.

Reverend Southwick spoke from the heart, but he said what Rose had predicted he would say. Harry wondered: How could it be God's plan to take three innocent young children from the same family? How could he choose to snuff out their lives that had just begun and break their parents' and sister's hearts? What kind of God would do that? When the congregation sang "Amazing Grace" to close the service, Harry couldn't bring himself to sing with them. But then he reminded himself that the children were now in a better place. The pain from their loss, like all earthly pain, was temporary. One day he and Rose would be reunited with them in God's kingdom.

After George was buried beside Grace in the cemetery behind the church, members of the congregation lined up to speak to Harry and Triss. With but one exception, they offered their condolences, asked Harry to extend their sympathies to Rose, and said nothing about her absence. The exception was Alice Pendergast, the last in line.

No man had ever been brave enough to court Alice Pendergast, much less marry her. Her face was fixed with a permanent scowl. Her life revolved around the church, but she found no joy there, or anywhere else for that matter. And yet every time the doors were opened, she arrived and took the place she had claimed as her own decades before. But though she was there for every service, the message delivered from the pulpit often seemed lost on her. She had heard many sermons, for example, on Jesus's admonition in the seventh chapter of Matthew to "judge not, that ye be not judged." But for the life of her, Alice couldn't bring herself to do what Jesus had instructed. When it was her turn to speak, she stayed true to form.

"I am sorry for your loss, Professor Brooks. Where is Mrs. Brooks?"

"Thank you, Miss Pendergast. She is not feeling well. She was not up to coming."

"I'm quite surprised that she's not here for the funeral of her own son. Quite surprised. She was his mother."

Harry winced when he heard the same words he'd used to pressure Rose to come. "She just wasn't up to it, Miss Pendergast. I'm sure you understand."

"It's a terrible loss, I'm sure, Professor Brooks, but it was her own child. I can't imagine what kind of mother would miss her own child's funeral. I think she should have been here."

Harry cleared his throat. Triss glanced over at him. Alice had judged Rose, and now Harry spoke his mind. "Ma'am, you profess that you can't imagine what kind of mother would miss her own child's funeral, so I'll tell you what kind. Rose is a wonderful mother. She has loved all of her children with all of her heart. She would have gladly given up her own life for any of theirs, but that's not how it works. So now she has lost three of them, three of her precious children, and seeing the third one put into the ground was more than she could bear. That's why she's not here. So, if you will excuse us, Triss and I need to go home to see about her. Triss, as I'm sure you know, is our only child still above the ground. Rose needs her."

They turned to walk away, but then Harry stopped and turned back. "Miss Pendergast, there's something else I want you to know. You think Rose should have been here. Well, I want you to know that I don't give a damn what you think." Triss squeezed his hand, and they turned again and set out for home.

Rose was still in bed when they got there. She hardly looked up when they walked in, said nothing, and asked no questions about the service. In the weeks to come, she rarely spoke or got dressed. Friends brought meals, but she declined to see them. With Triss's help, Harry prepared the other meals. Rose came to the table but just picked at her food.

On the third day after the funeral, Harry and Triss went back to school. He thought it best for them to return to their routine as soon as possible, and he wanted to be anywhere other than that sad house. But Rose had no place to go. When Harry and Triss came home in the evenings, they found her either lying in bed or sitting in the living room. Other than her location, everything was exactly as it had been when they left in the morning. She couldn't bring herself to cook or clean, and she didn't leave the house. Wherever they found her, the lights were off.

Harry tried to be patient, but time wore on, and it became more and more difficult. He'd also lost three children, but he wasn't curled up in a ball staring at the wall. He reminded himself that Rose was their mother, that she was the one who had given birth to them and nursed them, but how long would this last? There was nothing he could do to bring them back, and he got on with his life. How long would it be before Rose got on with hers? She had not been anything like this after they lost Roswell and Grace.

Two months after the funeral, Harry reached for Rose when he came to bed and kissed her on the shoulder. It was his first attempt at intimacy since the funeral. She rolled toward the wall and pushed his hand away.

"No, Harry. Not tonight."

"But when? I miss you, Rose. I miss loving you."

"I can't have another child, Harry. I can't risk it."

"I'll be careful."

"No, Harry." But she rolled back over and put her hand on his chest. "I'm sorry about the way I've been. It's been harder this time. I don't know why."

"It will get better, and I'll be careful."

"No, you won't. You never are. I can't have another child, Harry. Do you promise you'll be careful?"

"I promise."

Harry meant to keep his promise, but he didn't. When Rose realized it, she pushed him away and started to cry.

"I'm sorry, Rose. It had been so long."

"But you promised."

"I'm sorry."

The next day, after Harry and Triss left for school, Rose moved Triss's clothes to the armoire in George's nursery and put clean sheets on the bed he had died in. Then she moved her own things to Triss's room. When Harry came home and saw what she had done, he asked why. Rose said he knew.

But it was too late. Six weeks later, Rose woke up feeling sick. She had suspected, and now she knew. She was pregnant for the fifth time. She never slept in the same bed with Harry again.

The baby, whom they named Katherine Roseanna Brooks, came the following spring, in May 1898. Triss had turned eleven in December. She and Katherine were the first and last of Harry and Rose's five children. The three that had come in between were all dead.

Harry had high hopes that having another baby in the house would lift the cloud of sadness as it had when George was born. But it did not help this time. Rose performed the chores of motherhood–nursing and changing diapers and all the rest–but she did it without joy. It was as if she was afraid to love another child. And she lived in fear. Whenever Triss or Katherine caught as much as a sniffle, Rose was terrified that it would turn into something worse.

Living in the Brooks home was like living in a morgue. Muffled voices, no laughter, no smiles. Triss seized every opportunity to get away and spent the night at the homes of friends whenever she could. Each evening after dinner, when the dishes had been put away and Katherine put to bed, Rose and Harry followed the same routine. She said goodnight, went to her new bedroom, and closed the door behind her. He returned to his study, where he stayed up late reading, usually the Bible. He often returned to the book of Job and the story of the pain God had inflicted on a righteous man. Was God testing Harry as He had tested Job? Could Harry pass the test?

More than a year passed, and there was little change. Harry and Rose were polite to each other and never fought, but they never touched or kissed either. They went about the business of running the house and raising the girls, and time went by. On January 1, 1900, Harry's thirty-eighth birthday, he decided to take up a new practice at night to comfort himself. He bought a bottle of whiskey and hid it in the bottom drawer of his desk. Harry had always been opposed to alcohol, but he found that he enjoyed the effect it had on him. He only drank alone and only at night, but he often drank to excess. On more than a few mornings, he woke up with his head on his desk, an empty glass of whiskey in one hand, an open King James Bible in the other.

Rose and Triss never knew—the study was Harry's refuge—and his work life was unaffected. He was still highly regarded as an educator, and in early 1902 he was approached about running for the position of school superintendent in Uniontown, more than thirty miles south of McKeesport. Harry thought that leaving the home and city where two of their children had died might help Rose, which might help their marriage. He told her about the opportunity, she did not object, and he decided to make his first and only run for elective office.

Unhappy couples often think that relocating to a new city or buying a new home will give them a fresh start and cure all their problems. But it rarely works, and it didn't work for Harry and Rose. Harry won the election, but the move to Uniontown changed nothing about Rose's depression or the state of their marriage. She still slept in a separate bedroom, and she still went there as soon as the dishes were put away and Katherine was put to bed. Harry still retired to his study, and he still drank.

CHAPTER SIX

1905

(⊙ ⊙)

PITTSBURGH

Harry stepped to the lectern, looked out at the congregation, and began.

"Genesis is the first book in the Bible. We've all known that since we were little children. But it is not the first book in the Bible that God gave us. That honor belongs to the book of Job. Job tells the story of a wealthy, righteous man who lost everything–his wife and children, his servants and livestock, his health–only to have it all restored in the end.

"Some biblical scholars believe that God gave us his Word in the book of Job more than 1700 years before Christ was born. If they're correct, that means that Job was written more than 3600 years ago.

"In the thirty-eighth chapter of Job, God refers to three constellations–Orion, Pleiades, and Arcturus. I took the train into this smoky city yesterday. When I finished preparing this sermon on Friday night in Uniontown, where the sky is clear, I walked outside and looked up at the night sky. I stared at the three constellations God spoke of in Job, constellations that were in the sky more than a hundred generations ago. The stars, like the lessons from the book of Job, are eternal."

When Rose had come down for breakfast the day before, Harry had given her a bouquet of roses. It was February the 18th, nineteen years to the day since their wedding. Rose thanked him and patted him on the arm. She then ate in silence and returned to her bedroom. Harry watched as she closed the door behind her. Her sadness is permanent, he thought. She did not come out of her room before he left to catch the train into the city.

Pittsburgh was a booming industrial center by 1905. It had tripled in size in the last twenty-five years, had a population of nearly half a million, and was the tenth-largest city in America. But the growth had come at a cost. Pittsburgh was loud, with noisy factories and clanging streetcars. Burning coal polluted the air, giving the city its identity as the City of Smoke. It was often dark in the middle of the day. Pittsburgh's three rivers—the Allegheny and Monongahela merged in the city to form the Ohio—were cesspools of pollution filled with raw sewage. For more than thirty years, Pittsburgh had suffered the highest mortality rate from typhoid fever in the nation. Harry preferred Uniontown. It was quiet, the air was clean, the water pure. He didn't like going into the city, but he was there now because of an offer he couldn't refuse.

In the late 1800s, Christ Methodist Episcopal Church, located on the corner of Penn and 8th Avenues in the heart of downtown Pittsburgh, was one of the largest churches in the city. But in May 1891, the church was destroyed when a fire burned a whole city block. The congregation soon met to decide what to do. The minutes of the meeting included this sentiment: "We refuse to rebuild in the midst of dirty, filthy Pittsburgh."

The congregation decided to form two new churches on opposite sides of the city, miles away from the factories that lined the rivers downtown. First Methodist Church was built east of downtown in Shadyside, and Calvary Methodist Church was built to the northwest in Allegheny City.

Allegheny City was the wealthiest section in the Pittsburgh metropolitan area and one of the wealthiest in the world. There were more millionaires within a one-mile radius than any other place in America. Nearly a quarter of a million dollars was raised to build the new church. An architect was hired and sent to France. He designed the new church based on a thirteenth-century Gothic cathedral. Nearly 200 stained-glass windows crafted by Louis Tiffany were commissioned for the sanctuary. Three were the largest Tiffany windows in the world.

The church was magnificent, and now Harry had been asked to preach there. Ralph Becker, the minister of the church, was recovering from surgery, and the district superintendent requested Harry to fill in for three Sundays during Reverend Becker's convalescence. Harry loved to preach in beautiful churches, he had never preached in one as beautiful as Calvary, and the honorarium would supplement his modest salary as a school superintendent.

Most of Harry's sermons were from the New Testament, but he knew the book of Job better than any other and believed it had much to offer the modern Christian. After beginning his sermon with the three constellations mentioned in the thirty-eighth chapter, Harry quoted a number of verses from the ancient book and explained how they had been meaningful in his own life. He told the congregation that Job's life of suffering and faith had meant a great deal to him in the years after he and his wife lost three of their children.

Harry began by describing the state of his life fifteen years earlier. He and Rose had been married four years and were very happy together. They had two beautiful daughters named Triss and Grace and a son they named Roswell. Harry had lost his parents years earlier, but his loving grandparents had raised him and his brothers. In comparison to others, he had never truly suffered. But then, over the course of three years, Roswell and Grace had both died. He and Rose then had a fourth child, another son named George, but two years later he died too. Like all men, Harry said, he was a sinner, but he did not believe he had done anything to deserve the unbearable suffering that came with the loss of three children. Nor had Rose. She was a fine woman, a woman of faith. She did not deserve it either. But in the book of Job, Harry said, he had found both answers and comfort.

His first realization was that all people suffer. All of us, even those who are happy and successful, will lose loved ones. Most of us will suffer in pain before we die, and all of our lives on Earth will come to an end. God does not spare us from suffering. That is not His plan. Second, we should not expect to find answers in this life for our suffering. Not all pain is deserved, at least as we understand it. Bad things happen to good people, just as good things happen to bad, and it's pointless to ask why in either case. God knows, but we may never know. We must have faith in God and accept that all things are His will. God is in charge; we are not. He knows what is best; we do not.

Harry said he had also learned that suffering tests our faith in God and, if we pass the test, suffering will make our faith grow stronger. It is easy to keep our faith when all is well, when we have a happy marriage, two beautiful daughters, and a handsome new son. The challenge is to maintain our faith when bad things happen and we are in pain. Through all that he lost, Job kept his faith in God and, in the end, God restored all that had been taken away. The final chapter of the book reveals that "the Lord blessed the latter end of Job more than his beginning," he lived another 140 years, then died, "being old and full of days."

Harry closed the sermon by turning to his favorite verse in the New Testament. "The lesson from the Bible is that God takes care of the faithful," he said. "He may not do for us what He did for Job and restore to us what we have lost, but He does something for us that is even better. Indeed, it is far better. We are all familiar with God's promise in John 3:16. 'For God so loved the world, that he gave his only begotten Son, that whosoever believeth in him should not perish, but have everlasting life.' And so, from Job in the Old Testament to John in the New, we know two things to be true. We know that we will suffer in this life but, if we have faith, we will have a second life, an everlasting life, in God's kingdom. God's promise to the faithful is that we will live forever. Let us pray and thank God for his promise."

After the service, members of the church came forward to shake hands with Harry and thank him for his sermon. The last in line was a lovely young woman with dark hair and eyes. She was by herself. When it was her turn, she stuck out her hand.

"I'm Bess Montgomery, Reverend Brooks."

"I'm Harry Brooks, Miss Montgomery."

"I know that."

"I suppose you do."

"I want to thank you for your fine sermon today and tell you that I'm sorry for your pain. My younger sister died when I was ten. It was very hard for my parents. For me too."

"Thank you. I'm sorry for your loss too. We think of the pain that parents suffer, but siblings may suffer even more because it's harder for them to understand. The loss of her sister and brothers was very hard for Triss, but now she has another sister. Katherine is six."

"It's good that you and your wife were faithful enough to have another child. I appreciate your words today about Job. My fiancé was killed in the mines two years ago. We were to be married two weeks later. I have struggled with losing him and keeping my faith in God. What you told me was very helpful. I wish I could know more about what you've gone through and how you've remained faithful."

"I would be honored to tell you. Would you like to join me for lunch, Miss Montgomery? My train back to Uniontown doesn't leave until three o'clock."

"Would that be proper?"

"I don't see why not. It's lunch with a preacher to talk about how Scripture has helped him."

"Alright then, if you say so. Where shall we go?"

"I know little about Pittsburgh. You choose a place."

For the first half hour, Harry and Bess stuck to the topic she wanted to discuss. Harry told her of the low moments he'd felt after each child's death and how he'd struggled to keep his faith. But then he would go to his study, pull out his Bible, and read the words of Job. He guessed he'd read it from start to finish a hundred times. He knew it by heart. Harry said Job suffered far more than the loss of three children but, in the end,

God took care of him. Harry had faith that God would take care of him too. He would suffer more before he died, he was sure of that, but in the end, God would be there for him. Harry said nothing about Rose. He didn't mention her depression or the separate bedrooms.

After dessert, the talk turned to other topics. When Harry asked about her fiancé, Bess said he was her one true love. She didn't think she would ever fall in love again and figured she would wind up as an old maid. Since his death, she'd gone out with two or three men, but she just wasn't interested. When they asked her again, she made excuses, and they gave up. She hoped there would come a time when she would be interested, but the time had not yet come.

Harry talked about growing up in Salt Lick, playing in the woods with his brothers, and helping on the farm. He told her about the terrible day when his father was impaled by a plowshare and bled to death. Harry was nine years old and vowed that day that he would never be a farmer. From then on, he studied hard and prepared to be a teacher and a preacher. He loved both and couldn't decide which one he enjoyed more.

Bess had liked school but had to go to work when she was fifteen. She started out as a seamstress in a dress shop, Carlisle's, but she learned Pitman's shorthand in her spare time and secured a position at the leading law firm in the city, Knox and Reed. The pay was better and the work much more interesting. She never got bored with working on documents involving the Carnegies, Mellons, Heinzes, and Fricks. The firm demanded strict confidentiality, so she couldn't reveal details, but she got to work on matters involving more money than she could even imagine.

Bess took a sip of coffee, and Harry pulled out his pocket watch. "Uh-oh. I've missed my train."

"I'm so sorry. I've been carrying on and not paying any attention to the time."

"It's not your train, so it's not your fault. And it's nothing to worry about. There's another one at five."

Harry left his watch sitting on the table in front of him. The five o'clock was the last train, and he didn't want to miss it too. Bess's apartment was between the diner and the railway station, so Harry walked her home after they'd talked another hour. When they got to her door, he stuck out his hand.

"Miss Montgomery, it has been a pleasure spending time with you. Worth missing the first train. Very much worth it."

"Thank you. I enjoyed it too, and please call me Bess. Being called Miss Montgomery makes me feel like I'm an old maid already. I was told you will preach again next Sunday. Is that true? Will I see you then?"

"It is true. I've agreed to preach three Sundays while Reverend Becker is convalescing. But I have another idea. My train arrives in Pittsburgh at 5:30 Saturday evening. Would you do me the honor of joining me for dinner? I hate to eat alone. We can eat at the same restaurant, or you can surprise me and choose a different one."

"I don't know, Reverend Brooks."

"Harry, please. I get tired of being Professor Brooks and Reverend Brooks all the time. It's nice to be just plain Harry."

"Alright then, Harry it is. But I don't know about Saturday. Lunch after church is one thing, but dinner is something else."

"But it will still be a meal with a preacher, and we'll still talk about Scripture."

"Are you sure? I'll be having dinner with a married man."

"A married man who's a minister with two daughters."

"Are you sure it's alright?"

"I'm certain. Perfectly proper."

"You're the preacher. If you say it's proper, I guess it must be."

"Excellent. I'll walk here after my train arrives and ring the bell for your apartment at six o'clock sharp."

They shook hands again, and Harry continued to the train station. He smiled when he realized he was walking faster than usual.

For Harry, the week went by at a snail's pace. He couldn't wait to see Bess again. He couldn't recall the last time he'd had such a conversation with a beautiful woman, but he did remember the last time he'd felt this way. It was twenty years ago when he first started courting Rose. He knew it was wrong, but he couldn't help it. After his last class on Friday, he went to the finest men's store in town and bought himself a new necktie. He spent twenty minutes picking it out.

Harry's train the next day was on time, and he walked even faster than he had six days earlier. When he arrived at Bess's apartment, he pulled out his watch. He was fifteen minutes early. He began pacing back and forth, shivering in the cold, waiting until six o'clock to ring her bell. A window on the second floor opened, and Rose stuck her head out.

"What on earth are you doing?"

"Waiting until six o'clock. Our date is at six o'clock."

"We don't have a date. We have an appointment to discuss Scripture. But I wonder if I should listen to a man willing to freeze to death to keep from being ten minutes early."

"I suppose that would be a foolish way to die, wouldn't it?"

"Let me get my coat and come down while you still have a breath left in you."

When Harry helped Bess take off her coat at the restaurant, he saw that she was wearing a beautiful blue dress.

"What a lovely dress, Miss Montgomery."

"It's Bess, remember, and thank you. Clothes are my weakness. They have been ever since I worked at Carlisle's. If I had fewer dresses, I would have more money."

"But money is of no use unless we spend it, and I'm glad you spent some of yours on that dress."

Bess had chosen a nicer restaurant this time, with chandeliers and thick carpets, and they had an even better time. They spoke briefly about the Bible but spent most of the evening telling stories from their lives, both happy and sad. Sometimes they mixed stories and the Bible. Less than a month after her fiancé's death, Bess said, his best friend had tried to kiss her. She said she now found it difficult to trust any man. Harry responded with a verse from the book of Psalms: "It is better to trust in the Lord than to put confidence in man."

Bess asked Harry what his life was like now. How was it after the loss of three children? He told her about Rose and how things had been since George's death. He confided in her about the separate bedrooms, the sadness, and the silence. He'd lost three children and then lost his wife. He didn't mention his drinking. Bess put her hand on his arm.

"You poor man. No wonder you turned to the book of Job. I am grateful that you found comfort there."

"Thank you, but enough of that. Let's talk about something happier. Let's talk about birds. I was looking out the train window today and saw a red-tailed hawk gliding beside us, going exactly as fast as we were. I wondered if the hawk was racing the train. Have you ever seen a red-tailed hawk? Beautiful, majestic birds."

"I don't think so. I love birds, but birds don't like smoke. We don't have many birds in Pittsburgh."

"Then we need to get you out of the city."

"And how would you propose to do that, Harry?"

"I don't know." Harry drummed his fingers on the table. "But seeing birds is good for you. Clean air is good for you too."

The waiter approached. He had their check as well as their coats. Harry had been focused entirely on Bess but now looked around and saw that the dining room was empty. "My apologies, sir, I didn't realize we were the last ones here." He reached for his wallet.

When they got to Bess's apartment, Harry turned and looked at her.

"I had a wonderful time, Bess. You're very easy to talk to."

"I had a wonderful time too." She smiled. "You're very easy to listen to."

"Hey, wait a minute. You talked too, you know."

"I know I did. I was teasing you, Harry. I don't think Professor Brooks and Reverend Brooks get teased very much."

"You're right about that."

"So I guess my prescription for you is more teasing and your prescription for me is more birds."

"It's a deal. I cannot have lunch with you tomorrow. I have a meeting in Uniontown and have to take the first train back after church. But next Saturday, will you join me for dinner again?"

"I would love to."

"Six o'clock again?"

"Or when you get to my apartment, whichever comes first. It will be March by then, but it will still be cold. I don't want a frozen man on my conscience, especially a frozen preacher."

"I won't pace, and I won't freeze, I promise."

Instead of sticking out his hand, he put his hands on Bess's shoulders and pulled her toward him. She turned her face up to his. He was about to kiss her, but then he thought of her fiancé's friend and stopped himself. When he raised his chin and kissed her on the forehead, she laughed.

"You're right, Harry. It was an appointment, not a date."

"Yes, an appointment. And we will have another one a week from today, at six o'clock."

Harry opened the door for Bess, and she stepped inside. But when he tried to close it behind her, she held it open and turned to face him. "Thank you for not kissing me, Harry. I wanted you to kiss me, but I'm glad you didn't."

"You're welcome. I showed great restraint. I believe I qualify for saint-hood." Bess leaned out, kissed him on the cheek, then turned and pulled the door closed behind her. Harry reached up to knock on the door, then pulled back, stuck his hand in his coat pocket, and turned in the direction of his hotel.

With Bess sitting on the third row in the sanctuary, Harry had difficulty concentrating on his sermon the next morning. They spoke briefly after the service and, in case anyone was listening, took care to call each other Reverend Brooks and Miss Montgomery.

After Harry returned to Uniontown, Bess was out of his sight but never out of his mind. He struggled to focus in class. While the students did their lessons, he berated himself for the way he felt. He was an elected school official, a minister of the Word of God, and a married man. It was wrong to want another woman. It was a sin. But sin or not, he couldn't remember wanting anyone or anything as much as he wanted Bess. When he thought about her, and he thought about her constantly, he felt more alive than he'd felt in years.

And though he knew it was wrong, he began to justify his feelings. He and Rose were still married in the eyes of the law, but were they still married in the eyes of the Lord? They lived under the same roof, shared the same meals, and were raising the same daughters, but they had neither kissed nor held each other since before Katherine was born. Their marriage was not what God intended marriage to be. Harry was certain of that.

The Saturday train needed a minor repair and was forty-five minutes late leaving Uniontown. Harry checked his watch a dozen times along the way. When the train finally pulled into the station, he considered running the mile to Bess's apartment but decided that saving a few minutes was not worth appearing at her door panting. He rang her bell at 6:30. The door opened seconds later, and Bess stepped out and threw her arms around his neck.

"Oh Harry, I was afraid you'd changed your mind and weren't coming."

"I'm so sorry. My train was late. I walked from the station as fast as I could. I could have run, but I didn't want to arrive for my appointment with a beautiful woman both late and sweaty."

"You don't need to apologize; it wasn't your fault. And you look very handsome yourself."

"I see that you're wearing another lovely dress, Bess. It looks perfect on you." It was burgundy velvet with cream lace at the neckline and cuffs. The weather was warmer, and Bess wasn't wearing a coat.

"Thank you. It's brand new. I have less money but one more dress than when you last saw me."

"And I have less money but one more suit." Harry tugged on his lapels and smiled.

"Find a photographer and flag him down. We need to pose in our fancy new clothes for the Montgomery Ward catalog."

"Forget about me. They should put you on the cover and change the name. It should be the Bess Montgomery Ward catalog. Where are we dining tonight, Miss Montgomery Ward?"

"I thought we might go to Dimling Brothers on Market Square. It's not fancy, but if you like German, the food is wonderful."

"I'm sure it will be wonderful with you." They linked arms and headed up the sidewalk. "I have a suggestion for tonight. If it's alright with you, I say we stick to happy stories."

"Good idea. I'll start. I've been dying to tell you this. You're not going to believe it, Harry, but on Thursday I met the richest man in America. I was asked to take a cup of coffee to the main conference room. I wasn't told who wanted the coffee, but I walked in, and there he was, Andrew Carnegie himself. He stood up, shook my hand, and introduced himself, like I wouldn't know who he was. He said he was early for a meeting with Mr. Reed. I told him my name, and he asked how long I'd worked at the firm and if I grew up in Pittsburgh. We talked until Mr. Reed arrived. Before I left, he told me to let Mr. Reed know if he could ever be of service to me. He was so nice, Harry. I couldn't believe it."

Harry laughed.

"What's so funny?"

"You're so funny. Naïve actually."

"What are you talking about?"

"Bess, I'd be willing to bet that every man you meet is very nice to you, from Andrew Carnegie to the poorest man in Pittsburgh. At least every man with eyes to see."

She stopped walking and turned and looked at him. "You called me beautiful when I came to the door. Do you really think I'm beautiful, Harry?"

"I don't think you're beautiful, Bess, I know you are. It's a fact, not an opinion."

She pulled him close, holding on to his right arm with both of hers, and they continued up the sidewalk to Dimling Brothers.

As Harry had requested, they stuck to happy stories during dinner. He talked about building a treehouse with his brothers in the woods behind his grandparents' house. He would go there by himself just before dawn, lie perfectly still, and listen to the songbirds. He saw white-tailed deer and wild turkeys, and one morning he watched a red fox stalking a rabbit. Bess was pleased to hear that the rabbit got away. She described the dollhouse her father had made for her and her little sister. They played with it for hours on end and gave names to all the dolls. Bess named her favorite one Mary because she looked so pure. Harry talked about how he loved sunsets and how no two of them were ever the same. Bess said she loved them too but rarely saw one in Pittsburgh because of all the smoke.

Harry believed the main course must have been good, but he hardly remembered eating it. They couldn't decide if they were still hungry but agreed to share a piece of *apfelkuchen*, German apple cake, for dessert. While they were waiting for it to arrive, Harry reached into his coat pocket, pulled out a small box, and handed it to Bess.

"I got you something."

"You shouldn't have, Harry. This is just an appointment, remember. Appointments don't come with gifts."

"It's just a little something, and it was your idea. You even prescribed it."

"What do you mean?" Bess opened the box and pulled out a tiny painted brooch. It was a bird. "Oh, Harry, it's beautiful. What is it? What kind of bird?"

"It's a black-capped chickadee. It's a very small bird, but not as small as the brooch."

"Chickadee. That's a funny name."

"It makes a call that sounds like chick-a-dee-dee-dee."

"I love it, but you said it was my idea. I never said I wanted a brooch."

"Don't you remember? More birds for you, more teasing for the stuffy professor."

"I've never known a man like you, Harry." She pinned the brooch to her dress, then reached across the table for Harry's hand. She was still holding it when the *apfelkuchen* arrived.

Harry and Bess walked back to her apartment with his arm around her waist. This time, when he pulled her to him, he kissed her on the lips. And this time, when she walked through the door, she held Harry's hand and he followed. After they undressed each other, she pulled the combs from her beautiful black hair, and it fell nearly to her waist. He kissed her again and said they would need to be careful. She said no, that she couldn't have children. She lay back on the bed and he lay down beside her.

When Harry awoke the next morning, the smell of coffee was coming from the kitchen, and Bess was standing at the oven. Before he got out of bed, he looked around the apartment. It was tiny but tasteful, with art on the walls and hook rugs on the oak floors. The bedroom had barely enough room for a bed and an oversized pine wardrobe, which was filled to overflowing with Bess's dresses. Harry slipped out of the bed, sneaked up behind Bess, and put his arms around her waist. "I love you, Bess Montgomery."

She leaned back against him and sighed. "I love you too, Harry. I can't believe this is your last Sunday in Pittsburgh."

"This is not my last Sunday. Reverend Becker has had a setback. My engagement has been extended."

She spun around and faced him. "Really? I haven't heard that."

"You haven't heard it because it's not true. But Rose doesn't know that, and she doesn't have to. I won't be preaching in Pittsburgh after today, but I'll be back. I love preaching, but I've found something else here that I love even more." Bess put her arms around his neck, kissed him hard, and led him back to the bed.

CHAPTER SEVEN

1905

《ⓒ ⑨》

PITTSBURGH, WASHINGTON, UNIONTOWN, NEW YORK CITY

PART ONE

The weekends during the next three months were the most exhilarating times of Harry's life. He told Rose his preaching engagement in Pittsburgh had been extended indefinitely. As he expected, she didn't mind that he would be gone every Saturday night and asked no questions. After taking the train into the city on two more Saturday afternoons, he told Rose he'd been asked to conduct a Bible study on Saturday mornings. He began leaving for Pittsburgh on Friday after teaching his last class of the week in Uniontown.

Harry and Bess had wonderful times together. They dined in Pittsburgh's finest restaurants, and he indulged her weakness for fine clothes. She never asked him for anything, but it gave him great pleasure to buy her fine things and see the look on her face when he gave them to her. One Saturday they walked into Carlisle's, her former employer, which had new spring dresses on display. Bess tried on several. Each time she walked out of the dressing room, Harry jumped to his feet and offered his compliments. They settled on a beautiful cream linen pinafore dress with fine lace and puffed, elbow-length sleeves. It was the most beautiful dress either of them had ever seen. He purchased a wide-brimmed hat with ribbons that matched it perfectly. Carlisle's had hats that were adorned with stuffed birds, but Bess said she could never wear a dead bird atop her head.

When spring came, Harry kept his promise to get Bess out of the City of Smoke. He studied the map looking for a small town where nobody knew either of them and they could meet on weekends. He settled on Washington, thirty miles south of Pittsburgh, a booming oilfield town filled with newcomers. He figured two more new faces wouldn't draw attention. Every Friday, beginning in late April, Harry left Uniontown and Bess left Pittsburgh at the same time bound for the same destination. They met at the train station in Washington and took a carriage to the Auld House Hotel, which offered the finest lodging in town. Harry got them the same room every weekend, a corner room on the fourth floor. It had a beautiful four-poster bed and a private bath with a clawfoot tub. After they checked in, they made love, went to dinner, then returned to the room and made love again. They couldn't get enough of each other.

On Saturdays and Sundays, they took long walks in the hills around town, where the new leaves were every shade of green. Harry had taught himself all there was to know about the trees and birds of Pennsylvania, and he loved sharing what he knew of God's creation with Bess. The wood of hickories, he told her, was the toughest of all and had led Andrew Jackson's soldiers to nickname him Old Hickory. The leaves would turn yellow in the fall. He pointed out chestnut trees and recited the first lines of "The Village Blacksmith" by Longfellow. One afternoon they heard a wild bird call that Bess had never heard before. Harry said it was a pileated woodpecker, and he spotted the bird with its distinctive red crest and undulating flight before it landed on the trunk of a dead oak tree. Harry pointed to the bird just as the heads of three immature woodpeckers emerged from a hole in the trunk. Harry and Bess returned to the tree and saw the family again the following weekend, but by the third weekend the fledglings had learned to fly and were gone.

Over dinner, Harry and Bess discussed a wide range of subjects, from politics to music to books. Harry considered himself a Democrat but had voted for Teddy Roosevelt over Alton Parker in November. Bess had supported Roosevelt as well, though women in Pennsylvania were still not permitted to vote. They both found the marches of John Philip Sousa inspiring and preferred American literature to British. They settled on Mark Twain as their favorite author and *Huckleberry Finn* as his finest work. They also loved the short stories of O. Henry. What they never discussed was the future. They were living in the present, focused entirely on each other, and preferred not to think about what might interfere with their perfect life together.

When they were apart on weekdays, Harry wrote Bess long love letters during breaks between classes. He decorated the letters with drawings of the birds they had seen, including the family of woodpeckers, and he often added favorite quotations. Bess had said one night that she regretted that she did not have more formal education. Though Harry was an educator, he was mostly self-taught and knew that formal education was not the only way to learn. In one of his letters to Bess, he cited their favorite author to vindicate his position. Twain had said he never let his schooling interfere with his education. Bess kept Harry's letters in her purse and read them over and over while they were apart.

Harry had never felt about Rose the way he felt about Bess. He was consumed by her, madly in love and deliriously happy. The time they were in bed together was nothing like it had ever been with Rose. Rose had enjoyed intimacy in the early years of their marriage, Harry thought, but she always seemed embarrassed and restrained, as if she were doing something shameful. Her interest waned after Roswell's death, and Harry sensed that she accommodated him only out of a sense of duty. Beginning shortly after George's death, there wasn't even that.

But now he had Bess, who wanted him every bit as much as he wanted her. She was unrestrained, unembarrassed, and adventurous. After they made love, she would lie in bed and stare at him, sometimes saying nothing but sometimes professing her love, not just for Harry but for their lovemaking too. When he got out of bed, she would remain there, face down on the sheets, and he would stand beside her, admiring her beautiful body, her flawless skin and curves. As long as he stood there watching, she remained still. One day she interrupted his trance with a question.

"Do you like your mignon?"

"My mignon?"

"It's French. Mignon is a small, pretty thing. So, do you like your mignon?"

"I love my mignon."

He sat back down on the bed beside her. He loved the touch of her smooth skin. He started at her ankles and gently stroked her all the way up to her shoulders. When he finished, she rolled onto her side, asked, "Do you want your mignon?" and they made love again.

It wasn't just in bed that Bess was different. Rose was a graduate of a prestigious finishing school. She knew the proper way to do everything and was always proper in everything she did. Bess was not that way. She was a free spirit, not confined by conventions. She questioned the rigid rules imposed by those on the top rung of the social ladder. One evening, as she was sitting at the dressing table getting ready to go out for dinner, she looked at Harry's refection in the mirror.

"Harry, you are a minister of the Word of God. Are you troubled by the word damn?"

"That's an odd question. As long as it's not used in the presence of children or to take the Lord's name in vain, I suppose it doesn't bother me. Why do you ask?"

"Because I'm sick of this damn corset, that's why. Is it alright with you if I don't wear the damn thing tonight? Then I won't have to worry about whether there's any room in my damn stomach for my damn food."

Harry laughed, pulled up another chair behind Bess, and wrapped his arms around her. "My mignon, you need not wear a corset for me. In fact, I prefer that you wear nothing at all."

She smiled at him in the mirror. "I prefer that too, but I might get banned from the restaurant. I didn't want you to freeze, and you don't want me to starve."

When Harry was with Bess, life was perfect, the best it had ever been. But there was a problem looming. Rose had grown up in a prominent family. She was accustomed to living well, and Harry had always aspired to live well too. They struggled to make ends meet even with the extra money he made by preaching, and they saved very little. Now Harry wasn't doing any preaching and was spending far more than usual. His weekends with Bess were wonderful, but they were expensive as well. The costs of train fare, hotels, fine meals, and gifts added up. The savings account was now empty, and Harry owed money on accounts all over Uniontown. In the past, he had taken a bottle of whiskey to his study at night because life with Rose was so sad. Now he drank because he was worried and because he missed Bess when they were apart.

Harry needed cash and needed it immediately. He first tried his brothers. William ran a hardware store, and Samuel had taken over the funeral business from their grandfather. The three brothers still owned the family farm in Salt Lick and rented it out to the farmer next door. Harry sent telegrams to William and Samuel and asked if either or both would be willing to buy his share. They'd said they were interested when they were all together at Christmas. Harry figured his one-third was worth at least $5,000, but he would sell it for four. Both brothers responded that they would think about it.

Harry next approached his friend Mart Kiefer, the Fayette County Sheriff, and told him that he'd had some setbacks and needed some cash to tide him over. Mart knew Harry to be a man of his word and said he could spare $475.00. Harry signed a note promising repayment in sixty days, but the loan didn't solve his problems. He used most of it to pay off accounts around town and was soon nearly broke again. He didn't know where to turn.

The following Thursday, there was a knock on Harry's office door. The father of two students in the upper school was there to pay their tuition for the fall term. He asked if he could pay it in cash, and Harry said certainly. After the man left, Harry started to take the money down the hall to the school's bookkeeper, Edith Schneider, but then he stopped himself. He put the money in his pocket, pulled out a notebook, and recorded the names of the students and the date and amount of the payment.

Harry was the superintendent, and parents and pupils often brought tuition payments directly to him. He received a half dozen more payments the following week, and they came in even more often after that. He followed the same practice each time, pocketing the money and making a record of the payment. He began keeping the money for himself even if the payment was by check. He would take each check to the bank it was drawn on and endorse and cash it, explaining that the school needed petty cash. He was a respected elected official of the local schools as well as a Methodist minister. Nobody suspected a thing.

Harry knew it was wrong, but he was powerless to stay away from Bess. He kept going to Washington every Friday to meet her. He kept a record of all the payments and would make good on them as soon as one or both of his brothers bought his interest in the farm. He convinced himself that it would all work out.

But it didn't. Tuition payments were due by the first of June. There were always some stragglers, some parents who had to be prodded, but this year there were far more than usual, at least according to Mrs. Schneider's records. A week after the deadline, she came to Harry's office and showed him a list of those who had still not paid. He said he was sure they would pay soon and instructed her to wait two more weeks before mailing reminder statements. His response surprised her. Professor Brooks surely knew how important it was for budgeting and planning to know how many students they would have in the fall.

Immediately after Mrs. Schneider's visit, Harry sent telegrams to his brothers. He had offered to sell his interest in the farm for $4,000. Now he would take three, but the deal had to be closed within two weeks. William responded that the price seemed fair, but he couldn't do anything until they received their rent payment after the harvest. Samuel didn't respond at all.

Mrs. Schneider put the reminder statements in the mail on Thursday, the twenty-second of June, three weeks after the payments were due. The reaction was immediate. Parents who had phones called the school. Others responded by letter or came in person. Mrs. Schneider spoke to several of them, but most asked for Harry. He told those who had paid him directly that there was obviously some problem with the school's records. There was nothing to worry about; he knew they had paid.

The walls were now closing in. It was just a matter of time, and not much time at that. On Monday afternoon, he sent a telegram to Bess at the law firm and asked her to take the last three days of the week off so they could go to New York City. He wanted to show her Central Park and the Statue of Liberty. He would arrive in Pittsburgh Tuesday evening, and they would take the eastbound train Wednesday morning.

On Tuesday morning, Harry walked hand in hand with Katherine to school. He carried a suitcase in the other hand filled with as much as it would hold. Before they parted ways on the sidewalk outside, he squatted down to her level and hugged her longer and harder than usual. He told her he would be gone for a while, that he loved her very much, and that she should behave and mind her mother and teacher. He watched her until she disappeared inside the building.

Mrs. Schneider knocked on Harry's office door at nine o'clock. He invited her in, and she sat down.

"Professor Brooks, we have a problem."

"I know we have a problem. People who haven't paid their tuition are claiming they have."

"This has happened once or twice in the past, but it's never been like this. I don't believe the parents I've talked to could all be lying. It's too many people, and most of them paid like clockwork before."

"What are you saying? You've deposited all the tuition payments I've given you, haven't you?"

"Of course, but you haven't given me any in weeks."

"Do you think payments have somehow gotten lost? Or deposited to the wrong account?"

"I don't know what it could be. I've asked those who say they paid by check to bring me their cancelled checks."

"Good. That should tell us something. Please let me know the minute you know more."

Four parents were waiting outside Mrs. Schneider's office when she got to school on Wednesday morning. They had all brought cancelled checks, and each check had what looked like Harry's signature on the back. She asked if she could borrow the checks, promised to return them, and apologized for the misunderstanding.

After they left, she walked down the hall to Harry's office. She had great respect for Professor Brooks and found it hard to believe that he could have done anything wrong. She hoped that his signatures were forged, but these looked just like the one she'd seen a hundred times. Maybe the checks had been deposited to the wrong account, but she handled the deposits and had never seen the checks the parents brought her this morning. She knocked on Harry's door, but there was no answer. She opened the door, but the office was dark. She came back four more times during the day, but Harry was never there. At the end of the day, she telephoned Mark Shepard, the owner of the mercantile and president of the school board, and said she needed to meet with him about an urgent matter. He had a prior commitment for the evening, but they arranged to meet in his office at nine o'clock the following morning.

———◄○►———

When Harry arrived in Pittsburgh Tuesday evening, he told Bess about his predicament. He'd been sure he could sell his interest in the farm to his brothers, but when that didn't pan out, he had no way to make good on the tuition payments he'd borrowed. Bess blamed herself for allowing him to spend so much money on her, but Harry wouldn't hear of it.

"You tried to blame yourself when I missed the train the day we met. It wasn't your fault then, and it's not your fault now. I'm a grown man. I knew what I was doing."

"But what will you do, Harry? You're not a thief, but I've learned enough about the law to know you'll be charged as one."

"I'm sure I will if they find me."

"If they find you? You're not going back to Uniontown?"

"Not for a while. I'm going to go somewhere else, find a job, and save enough to pay back what I owe. I'll probably never work in Uniontown again, but surely I won't be prosecuted if I make good on the debt."

"But where will you go, Harry? You won't be safe in Pittsburgh or Washington. They would find out how often you've been to both places from the railroad's records."

"I know. I need to get far away. I'm not sure where I'll go, but I'm thinking of booking passage on a ship to England."

"England? Really? The land of Dickens? And leave me here in dreary Pittsburgh?"

"I can't take you right away, but when I save enough money, I'll buy you a ticket, and you can join me."

"Sounds like you'll have to save all the money you make."

Harry smiled. "With an ocean between us, I'll have no one to spend it on."

"Oh, Harry, I'm so sorry. I feel like this is all my fault. If we had never met, you wouldn't be in this predicament."

"Meeting you, Bess Montgomery, is the best thing that's ever happened to me."

When they got to the train station on Wednesday morning, Harry decided to use his middle name to make finding him more difficult. He bought the ticket in the name of H. B. Felgar. Bess asked if she should use an alias too, but Harry said it wasn't necessary. Nobody knew about their relationship, so nobody would be looking for Bess Montgomery. Harry's office was dark and empty when Mrs. Schneider came looking for him on

Wednesday because he was speeding across Pennsylvania with Bess by his side.

◄○►

Mrs. Schneider was fifteen minutes early for her meeting with Mr. Shepard Thursday morning. She got to the point right away.

"Mr. Shepard, I'm afraid that Professor Brooks has been embezzling tuition payments from the school district."

"Professor Brooks? Surely not. What makes you think such a thing?"

"I find it hard to believe too, but it's the only thing that makes any sense."

"Tell me what you've learned."

Mrs. Schneider then laid out the facts in chronological order. First was the unusually large number of parents who failed to pay tuition by the June 1 deadline. Then Professor Brooks asked her to wait two weeks before sending reminder notices, which struck her as odd. Next came the parents' reactions to the reminder notices she'd mailed a week ago. Many claimed they'd already paid. Some could be mistaken or lying, but surely not all of them. She told Shepard that parents and pupils often paid Professor Brooks directly. He would turn over the payments to her, and she would deposit them, but it had been weeks since he'd given her any payments this year. Mrs. Schneider then showed him the four checks. She wasn't a handwriting expert by any means, but she was familiar with the professor's signature, and the endorsements sure looked genuine to her. She had brought the matter to Professor Brooks's attention on Tuesday. Then yesterday he hadn't come to school at all. She had stopped by again on her way to Shepard's office, and he wasn't there today either.

"This is terrible, Mrs. Schneider. I agree it looks bad, but I think we need to do some more digging. I would like for you to do a couple of things and then meet me back here at two o'clock. First, please take your list of all the parents who haven't paid according to your records and make a notation of the ones who say they have."

"I'm sure some parents have told Professor Brooks they paid, but I don't know who they are."

"Start with the ones who told you. We'll sort out the rest later. And then, go to the banks the checks are drawn on and try to find out if Professor Brooks presented the checks and, if so, whether he deposited or cashed them. If someone else presented the checks, try to find out who it was. And please be discreet. It's possible there is some innocent explanation, and we don't want to start any rumor or damage any reputation unnecessarily. Also, if you have time, please stop by the school again and see if Professor Brooks is there or if he has been."

———◄○►———

Harry and Bess made the most of their brief visit to New York. They spent their two nights at the Algonquin, the fine new hotel on 44th Street. Bess marveled at the beauty of the lobby when they checked in on Wednesday night. The next morning they went to the south tip of Manhattan and viewed the Statue of Liberty at a distance from Battery Park, then took the ferry to Liberty Island to see it up close. After returning on the ferry, they rode the subway that had just opened the previous fall to midtown and strolled arm in arm through Central Park. Bess said she had never seen any place so beautiful.

While walking back to the Algonquin to dress for dinner, they saw a sign outside another hotel offering bookings on passenger ships bound for Europe. While Harry studied the schedule, Bess suggested that he not use his middle name but come up with something that would be harder to trace. He decided to book passage to Liverpool leaving on Monday morning at eight o'clock on the *Carpathia*, the Cunard liner that would rescue the survivors of the Titanic seven years later. He persuaded the landlord to sell him a ticket in the name of H. B. Telfer. He had gone to the university in Kentucky with a young man named Telfer.

Harry proposed that they go to dinner at Healy's on 18th Street. He had read that O. Henry was a regular there. It was later reported that he wrote "The Gift of the Magi" in one of the restaurant's booths. Harry and Bess had a wonderful meal and kept their eyes peeled, but they didn't spot O. Henry. After dinner Harry was going to hail a carriage to take them back to the Algonquin, but Bess stopped him. It was a beautiful night, and she suggested they walk. They strolled up Fifth Avenue and past the theaters in Times Square. Bess said New York made Pittsburgh seem like a county fair.

———◄O►———

Mrs. Schneider returned at two o'clock with the list Shepard had requested and more bad news. She had gone by the school, and nobody had seen the professor. Tellers in the banks confirmed that he had presented the checks. To avoid raising suspicion, she had told them that Professor Brooks sent her because some records had been misplaced and they were trying to determine which checks had been deposited and which had been cashed. She learned that Harry had cashed them all and explained that the funds were needed to replenish the school's petty cash drawer.

Shepard then gave her one more assignment. He asked her to contact those on the list she had not yet talked to, find out if they had paid, and let him know. He thanked her for bringing the matter to his attention and instructed her to keep it strictly confidential. Right after she left, he began placing calls to the other Board members to determine their availability for an emergency meeting. Several were out of town on business and would not return until the following evening. He set the meeting for nine o'clock Saturday morning in his office at the store.

———◄O►———

On Friday morning, Harry and Bess walked to Grand Central Station and caught the train back to Pittsburgh. Along the way, she began addressing him as Mr. Telfer so he would get used to it. They spent the night in each other's arms in her apartment. When they got up the next morning, he asked where she wanted to spend their last day and night together before he returned to New York to board the *Carpathia*. She chose Washington, where they'd had their most wonderful times together, and they headed back to the train station. Harry wasn't thinking about his new name and again used H. B. Felgar when he purchased their tickets. As they climbed aboard, Bess reminded him that he was H. B. Telfer now.

CHAPTER EIGHT

1905

⟨ℂ ℐ⟩

PITTSBURGH, WASHINGTON, UNIONTOWN, NEW YORK CITY

PART TWO

The Board members arriving at Shepard's office grumbled about having to meet on Saturday morning. Two of the men were supposed to be playing golf in the same foursome and teeing off at 9:30. But when Shepard explained why he'd called the special meeting, the other Board members fell silent. For the next twenty minutes, he laid out what he'd learned from Mrs. Schneider and showed the Board the four cancelled checks. The reaction in the room was shock and dismay. Professor Brooks had an impeccable reputation, an unblemished record. Surely there was some explanation.

One member questioned whether Mrs. Schneider could have done it. She was familiar with the professor's signature. She could have forged it, then lied about talking to the tellers. And she could have waited to come forward until she knew he would be out of town. Shepard said he'd thought of that and had contacted two of his friends who were on Mrs.

Schneider's list. Both said they had paid their children's tuition directly to Professor Brooks and had spoken to him after they got the reminder notice. He told them he knew they had paid; there was just a problem with the school's records. Shepard had also stopped by one of the banks and confirmed the teller's story. He said he didn't yet know the full amount of the loss but, from the additional information Mrs. Schneider had provided Friday afternoon, he was certain it exceeded a thousand dollars and might be twice that much.

Another member asked Shepard if he had any idea where Professor Brooks was, where he might have gone. Shepard said he didn't. He had considered going to the Brooks residence but decided not to take further action without the entire Board's approval. A third member asked Shepard if he had a recommendation about what to do next.

"I do. Most of us are businessmen. Harold is a lawyer but not a criminal lawyer. Nobody on the Board is a police officer or a criminal investigator. In my opinion, it's time to alert the authorities and let them take over the investigation and search for Professor Brooks. I believe we have enough evidence to charge him with appropriating public funds and that we should file a criminal information against him today. I move that the Board authorize Harold Watson and me to present the information we've learned about Professor Brooks to Justice Dawson as soon as we adjourn. He lives on my street and is a close friend. Do I hear a second?"

"I second it."

"Thank you. Any discussion? Any questions? Alright, hearing none, we shall now vote. All in favor say aye." The vote was unanimous. Shepard and Watson went straight to the judge.

◄○►

Harry and Bess checked into their regular corner room on the fourth floor of the Auld House. He remembered to use his new name this time and signed the registry as Mr. and Mrs. H. B. Telfer. During their time in Washington, they made full use of the room but nothing else. They planned to take one last walk in the hills outside the city, but they never made it. They were going to have dinner in the restaurant downstairs, then decided to order room service, then did neither one. When they realized it was too late to get anything to eat, Harry said they might just as well have stayed in Pittsburgh.

Before they went to sleep, they talked about all the things they would do when Bess got to England. They would go to London and see Big Ben, the Tower of London, and Trafalgar Square. They would watch the Changing of the Guard at Buckingham Palace. Bess rolled over and put her head on Harry's chest.

"I love you, Mr. Telfer."

"I love you too, Miss Montgomery, but let me be Harry Brooks until tomorrow." He pulled her to him, kissed her, and they made love one last time.

The next morning, Bess was glum. Tuesday was the Fourth of July, and the law firm would also be closed on Monday. She decided to stay in Washington for another night and not rush back to spend the night alone in the smoky, dirty city. Harry went downstairs and paid for one more night. When he returned to the room, Bess tried to pull him back into bed. He said he couldn't, he would miss his train. He promised again that he would send for her, kissed her again, and walked out the door. He changed trains in Pittsburgh and retraced the route to New York he and Bess had taken four days earlier. But this time he wouldn't turn around in New York and head back west. He was bound for Liverpool. He shook his head when he thought about all he had done and was about to do.

———◁○▷———

Justice Dawson came to the door. "Shep, Harold, what a surprise. To what do I owe this pleasure, gentlemen?"

"I'm afraid it's not a pleasure, Your Honor," Shepard said. "May we speak to you in private?"

"Certainly." The judge led them to his study. After his wife brought coffee, he closed the door.

Shepard repeated the story he had just told the Board. The judge asked a few questions to satisfy himself, then picked up the phone. When Sheriff Kiefer answered, Justice Dawson asked him to come to the house immediately. He arrived minutes later, and the judge offered him a chair and again closed the door. "Mart, we've got a serious problem. Shep, please tell Mart what you just told me." He had barely gotten started when Mart interrupted.

"Damn. Damn, damn, damn."

"What is it?"

"The good professor owes me 475 bucks. I loaned it to him."

"You did what? When?"

"Two months ago. The note was due last week. I haven't heard from him, and I've been too busy to pay him a visit."

"Did he say what he needed it for?"

"Just that he had some problems. I didn't ask him what they were. He and I are friends. I figured I could trust him. He's a Methodist preacher, for God's sake.

Mart's first stop was the Brooks residence. Rose came to the door and invited him in. When he asked when she had last seen Harry, she asked why he needed to know, if something had happened to him. Mart said he was not yet at liberty to say, but he had no reason to believe that Harry had been hurt or was in danger. Mart just needed to find him. Rose said she'd last seen him when he left for school Tuesday morning. He'd told her he was going to a conference in McKeesport and from there would go straight to Pittsburgh, where he had standing engagements at the Calvary Methodist Church to teach a Bible class on Saturdays and preach on Sundays. She expected him back Sunday evening.

Mart said he needed to go through the house and, when he saw the living arrangements, asked if she and Harry slept in separate bedrooms. She said yes, but why did it matter? He told her it probably didn't, but he made a mental note that it might. He then said he needed to borrow some photos of Harry, and she gave him a half dozen. As he was leaving, Mart noticed photos of two beautiful young women on a bookcase in the foyer. He asked who they were, and Rose said they were her younger sisters. He said he wanted to take the photos of them too. She asked why, and he said he probably wouldn't need them but would have them just in case. He promised to take good care of all the photos and bring them back as soon as he was finished with them.

Mart then contacted County Detective Alexander McBeth and asked him to pack a bag and meet him at the railway station. Mart stopped by his house and packed a bag for himself. At the station, they learned that Harry had not gone to McKeesport on Tuesday but had taken the train to Pittsburgh. They bought tickets on the next train into the city. When they arrived, they first went to the church, where they found Reverend Becker at work in his office. He said he'd had surgery in February. Harry had preached the next three Sundays, but the reverend hadn't seen him since. He had no explanation for Rose's claim that Harry was still preaching at the church and leading Bible studies.

Mart and Detective McBeth next went to the police station and asked for the Chief of Police, Alan Wilson. Mart had worked with Wilson on investigations in the past and told him what he knew. Mart said he suspected that Harry was seeing another woman, perhaps one he met when he was preaching at the Calvary Methodist Church in the winter. From Mart's experience, that was the most likely explanation for Harry's need for cash and his claim that he was still preaching in Pittsburgh every Sunday. The separate bedrooms were another clue. He asked Wilson if he could spare a few officers for the day to help find the fugitive. Wilson said he could have three, brought them in, and Mart briefed them. He told them who Harry was and what he was suspected of doing, said his full name was Henry Felgar Brooks, and gave each of them a photo of Harry. They agreed to start with the area around the church and move out from there. The chief split up the area into five sections, one for Mart, one for Detective McBeth, and one for each of the three officers. They agreed to meet back at the station at five o'clock.

When they gathered at five, one of the Pittsburgh cops was sitting at the table with a smile on his face. He announced with satisfaction that he knew where Harry was. Based on Mart's theory that Harry was seeing another woman, the policeman had gone into Carlisle's, Pittsburgh's finest bridal and women's store, pulled out the photo of Harry, and asked if anyone in the store had ever seen him. One of the sale clerks recognized him and said that he'd been in with a lovely young lady weeks ago and bought her a fine dress. She said Harry and the woman couldn't keep their eyes off each other. They were obviously in love. The officer asked her to describe both the dress and the young woman. The dress was a fine cream linen pinafore dress with beautiful lace. All the clerks wished they could afford it. The young woman was a beauty with dark hair and eyes. The clerk knew her name because she'd worked there years before as a seamstress. She was a delightful young lady and an excellent employee named Bess Montgomery.

The policeman said he'd stopped by the railway station on the way back to see if any Bess Montgomery had booked a ticket recently. He wanted to make sure she was still in town. He was surprised to find that someone had bought a round-trip ticket to New York City for a Bess Montgomery on Wednesday last and another one to Washington this very morning. The man was named H. B. Felgar, and he'd also bought tickets for himself. Because Mart had told the officers that Harry's middle name was Felgar, the policeman surmised that Harry Brooks and H. B. Felgar were one and the same. If he was right, Harry and Bess were now in Washington, less than an hour south of Pittsburgh.

Mart was pleased with this turn of events. He thanked the officer for his fine work and Chief Wilson and the other policemen for their help, collected the photos of Harry, and announced that he and Detective McBeth would now go to Washington. Before leaving the city, however, they obained Bess's address, went to her apartment, and asked the landlord to let them in. They found an unmade bed where two people had slept the night before and a dress that matched the clerk's description of the one Harry had bought at Carlisle's. On a bedside table was a photograph of Harry with his arms wrapped around Bess's waist. They took the dress and the photograph as well as another one of Bess and headed for the train station. They arrived in Washington at eleven p.m., found a cheap hotel, and agreed to meet for breakfast at seven.

———————◄○►———————

Mart walked into the lobby of the Auld House on Sunday morning an hour after Harry walked out. Mart told the desk clerk who he was, showed him the picture of Harry and Bess, and asked if he had seen either one. The clerk said he hadn't, but this was a new job, and his shift had just started. Mart asked for the registry to see if there was a Brooks, Felgar, or Montgomery staying at the hotel, but there was no one with any of those names. Mart told the clerk where he was staying, asked him to call there and leave a message if he saw Harry or Bess, and continued his search elsewhere. He and Detective McBeth met for lunch and again at five o'clock. Both had found several Washington residents who recognized Harry and Bess from their photos, but nobody knew where they were staying or where they were. Harry and Bess could not be found because he was almost to New York City and she had spent the day reading and napping in the room registered to Mr. and Mrs. Telfer.

———————◄○►———————

The long train ride across Pennsylvania gave Harry time to think, and it was too much time. He had always sinned, as all men do, but his sins until now were nothing like the ones he had committed these last four months. They were not even close. He had committed adultery over and over. He had taken tuition payments that were to be used to educate the children of Uniontown and spent them on his pleasures. He had abandoned his wife and daughters and was about to board a ship for England to escape the fate he richly deserved. He was using an alias to avoid detection.

Harry could hardly believe what he had done and was overcome with shame. He had preached that God's people must read His Word and obey the Ten Commandments revealed in the book of Exodus. And yet he had violated two of those commandments and done so repeatedly. In the fourteenth verse of the twentieth chapter, God had commanded his followers that "Thou shalt not commit adultery." In the very next verse, God had decreed that "Thou shalt not steal." Now Harry had done both. He had tried to justify his sins, but they could not be justified. God did not declare that adultery is prohibited unless your wife has grown cold and you fall in love with a beautiful woman. God did not decree that stealing is a sin unless you call it borrowing and plan to pay it back.

But then Harry thought about Bess, smiled, and admitted something to himself. He was a preacher, but he was also a man. He would do it all over again. He couldn't wait until he could send for her. He couldn't wait until he could hold her again.

Harry had not been able to speak to Triss before he left Uniontown. She was in her final year at the Orontz School in Philadelphia, a finishing school for young ladies of the upper class. Harry and Rose could scarcely afford the tuition, but Rose had attended the school and insisted that Triss attend it too. Most of the cost was covered by the modest inheritance Rose had received after her mother's death.

Triss was always a daddy's girl, and they had become even closer after George died and Rose sank into depression. They would go for long walks in the woods on weekends, and she had come to love birds as much as Harry did. During her three years in Philadelphia, Harry wrote her a letter every week, always on Sunday. He'd continued the practice even after he began seeing Bess. He would go to his study on Sunday night and, before reading the Bible or anything else, would write Triss. He would tell her about all the birds he had seen that week, regale her with stories from the school, and update her on what Katherine was up to. He offered his opinions on the latest political issues and books he was reading. Sometimes he quoted Scripture. Rose was never mentioned; nor were his weekend trips.

It was Sunday again, his day to write Triss, but this letter would be different. On the last hour before the train reached Philadelphia, Harry wrote her a long letter of apology. He was sorry for all the pain of her childhood, the pain caused by the loss of three siblings and by his problems with Rose. He said he was leaving Pennsylvania because of some bad things he had done. She might hear or read about them. There was no excuse for what he had done, but he asked her not to judge him until she heard his side of the story. He was sorry for any pain his misdeeds would cause her. He signed the letter, "Love always, Daddy."

He also wrote a much shorter letter to Rose. He said he had done something bad and was having to leave, but he knew her family would take care of her. He said he was sorry for everything and asked her to tell Katherine that he loved her. He wondered how he should end the letter and decided just to sign his name.

Harry got off at Grand Central Station, mailed the two letters, then found a cheap room near Battery Park. He was running low on cash and had bought the cheapest third-class ticket available on the *Carpathia*. Harry pulled out his wallet and counted the money. He was down to twenty-six dollars. When he left his office for the last time on Tuesday afternoon, he took the notepad on which he had recorded the tuition payments he'd pocketed. After counting his cash, he pulled out the notepad and added up the total. It came to more than $2,000, and this was in addition to what he'd borrowed from Mart Kiefer. He wondered if Mart suspected anything. Harry couldn't sleep and was waiting to board the ship on City Pier A long before the sun came up.

———◁○▷———

Mart decided to make another round of Washington's hotels on Monday morning. A different clerk, this time a woman, was behind the counter at the Auld House. Mart showed her the photo of Harry and Bess and asked if she recognized them.

"Of course, that's Harry and Bess. A lovely couple. They've been stay-ing here every weekend."

"When did you last see them?"

"I was here when they checked in on Saturday. I saw Bess just a few minutes ago. She said she was going out for a walk. I haven't seen Harry."

"Do you know what room they're in?"

"Yes. I don't even need to look at the register. They're in 408. They always book that room."

Mart asked to see the register and saw that a Mr. and Mrs. H. B. Telfer had checked into room 408 early Saturday afternoon. He thanked the desk clerk and strode toward the elevator. Five minutes later, he returned to the desk.

"I knocked, but nobody came to the door. I need you to unlock it for me."

"I'm afraid I can't do that."

Mart pulled out his badge. "Ma'am, I'm the Sheriff of Fayette County. Your guests registered as Mr. and Mrs. Telfer are not married, and their name is not Telfer."

"My goodness. I didn't notice how he signed the register Saturday. I thought they were Mr. and Mrs. Brooks."

"He's Mr. Brooks, Professor Brooks actually. He's a Methodist preacher, believe it or not. Her name is Bess Montgomery. He's a fugitive from the law, wanted for embezzling more than a thousand dollars from the Union-town School District. I will be back in ten minutes, and you will need to unlock their room as soon as I get here. If you see either of them before I get back, don't say a word. Do you understand?"

"I can't believe this. They're so nice."

"He's a thief, ma'am. And he's a married man, and she's his mistress. Do you understand my instructions?"

"Yes, sir. I won't say anything."

Mart walked briskly back to his hotel and returned with the dress and the two photos of Rose's sisters. He and the clerk rode up in the elevator together, she unlocked the door, and Mart looked around the room. The bed was unmade, but it appeared that only one person had slept in it the night before. Bess's purse and suitcase were there, but there was no sign of Harry's belongings. He thanked the clerk, told her he would wait in the room, and again instructed her not to breathe a word. Then he closed the door.

The corner room with the grand bed and tall windows on two sides was finer than any room Mart had ever stayed in. That he may well have supplied the money Harry used to pay for it infuriated him. He took the dress Harry had bought at Carlisle's, folded it neatly, and arranged it on the foot of the bed, then placed the framed photo of Harry and Bess and the two of Rose's sisters face down on the dressing table. He found half a dozen letters from Harry in Bess's purse and walked over to the window to read them in the sunlight. She was his mistress, there was no doubt about that. He didn't know Harry was an artist and admired his drawing of the pileated woodpeckers. He placed the letters next to the photos on the table, sat down in the chair beside it, and waited.

———◄○►———

Bess had decided to go for a walk in the woods before she caught the three o'clock train back to the city. She walked the same route she and Harry had planned to take on Saturday. Along the way, she thought about their last four months together. She had thought she was a good Christian woman, and yet she had carried on an affair with a married man. And he was not just any married man. He was also an elected school official and a minister, and he was now a fugitive from the law. He'd left his wife and children and was fleeing across the ocean using an assumed name. He was on the lam because he'd taken money that didn't belong to him and spent it on her. Bess would go to her grave thinking that Harry was a wonderful man, but it was impossible to justify what he had done. What she had done either.

Bess reached the dead oak tree, the pileated-woodpecker tree. A tiny gray head was peering out of the hole where the woodpeckers had raised their brood. Then a second head appeared. She couldn't identify them, but then their mother did it for her. The mother raccoon appeared from the edge of the woods and scrambled up the trunk to see about her babies. Bess felt exactly as she had the day she met Andrew Carnegie. What she wanted more than anything was to tell Harry. She'd wanted to tell Harry about Mr. Carnegie then, and she wanted to tell him about the raccoons now. She would write him about them as soon as she received his new address.

———◁◯▷———

Bess unlocked the door and walked in, a match flared, and the lamp on the dressing table came to light.

"Miss Montgomery, please come in. Or is it Mrs. Telfer today?"

"Who are you? What are you doing in my room?"

"My name is Mart Kiefer. I'm the Sheriff of Fayette County. Perhaps our friend has mentioned me to you."

"What friend? What are you talking about?"

"I mean our friend who paid for this room. I mean our friend who's been spending my money to entertain you."

"I don't know what you're talking about."

Harry reached over to the table and stood the middle photograph up on its stand.

"This friend, Miss Montgomery. Professor Harry Brooks. The Reverend Harry Brooks. I see from the photo that the two of you are acquainted. Close the door, have a seat on the bed, and take care not to wrinkle your lovely dress. Miss Montgomery, let me tell you something before we begin our discussion about our friend. This will go much easier for you if you don't try to hide anything from me. You're already in enough trouble as it is."

"I've done nothing wrong."

"Oh, I quite disagree with that. You've had an affair with a married man. That's both a sin and a crime."

"You have no proof of that."

"I disagree with that too." He held up the letters for her to see. "Harry's very eloquent and quite an artist–I didn't know that about him–and he obviously has very strong feelings for you. Very strong." He waited for her to respond, but she said nothing. "And it's not just the affair, Miss Montgomery. This lovely dress he bought you from Carlisle's, where they remember you fondly by the way, was very expensive. And our friend bought it for you with stolen money. Do you know what that makes you?" She remained silent. "An accomplice, that's what. Have you ever spent time in jail?"

"Of course not."

"I haven't either, but I'm in charge of the Fayette County jail, and I can tell you it's no place for a lovely young lady like you. So where is our friend, Miss Montgomery? I don't believe he slept here last night. Where did he go?"

Mart struck another match, lit a cigar, and waited.

"I don't know where he is. I don't know where he went."

"Now Miss Montgomery, we both know that's not true. The man who wrote these letters would never leave a woman like you without telling her where he was going. I'll give you another chance. Where is he?"

"He's gone. Long gone. You'll never find him."

"Perhaps not, but I'm sure going to try. Did he tell you he borrowed nearly $500 from me to pay for your affair?"

"No, I've never heard of you until just now. How do I even know you're the sheriff?"

Mart reached into his vest pocket, pulled out his badge, and handed it to her. She inspected it and handed it back.

"Where is he, Miss Montgomery?"

"I'm not going to tell you. You can't force me to."

Mart sighed. "There are ways of making you talk, I assure you. I would prefer not to have to resort to them on a lady like you, but I'm willing to do a lot to find Harry Brooks. An awful lot. But first I will try to convince you that the best thing for you is to tell me the truth. Are you really willing to go to jail to protect a man who stole money from his employer and left you behind?"

"He's going to send for me."

"From where?"

"I'm not telling you."

"I admire your loyalty, Miss Montgomery, but I assure you that our friend is not as loyal as you are." He reached over and stood the closest photo up so that Bess could see it. "Do you know this woman? Have you ever met her?"

"No. I've never seen her. Who is she?"

"I figured as much. Her name is Sara Lancaster."

"Who is she?"

"She's another of our friend's mistresses. She lives in McKeesport. He lived there for a decade, as he may have told you. He doesn't see her as often as he used to, but he still sees her."

"I don't believe you. He loves only me."

"I believe those were Miss Lancaster's exact words. The letters he wrote her are similar too. Our friend is quite romantic. Quite a Lothario too."

Mart reached over and righted the third photo.

"Who is that?"

"Her name is Martha Harrison. She's a beauty, isn't she? She lives between Uniontown and Connelsville, just a few miles up the road from our friend's home. She's his weekday mistress. It's little wonder he stole so much money. It takes a lot to support a wife and two children and keep three mistresses happy."

"I don't believe you. I don't believe a word of it. Harry and I are in love."

"Let me ask you this, Miss Montgomery. Did Harry tell you that he and Rose sleep in separate bedrooms?"

"Why are you asking me that?"

"Harry and I are friends, or at least we were, and I've been to his home. And I happen to know that he and Rose sleep together. I also happen to know that he told Miss Lancaster and Miss Harrison that they don't."

"Why would he tell me that if it weren't true?"

"He stole from his employer, Miss Montgomery. You don't think he would lie to seduce a lovely young woman like you? Let me ask you again: Where is he?"

"I'm not telling you. I refuse."

"You are stubborn as well as loyal. I admire your tenacity. I was hoping to appeal to reason, but it appears that more will be needed. I will try one more time. You have two options. I will give you five minutes to select the first one. If you don't, I will choose the second one for you. That would be truly unfortunate, I assure you. The first option is that you tell me the truth now and promise to testify truthfully if it comes to that. If you do that, I will allow you to go back to Pittsburgh and return to your apartment and your job. But, if you don't tell me the truth now, I will place you under arrest as an accomplice to our friend's crime and for adultery. I will then take you back with me to Uniontown and put you in jail, where I have other methods of interrogation at my disposal."

"What methods? What are you talking about?"

"I think that it's best that you not find out, but I will say this: You *will* talk. Witnesses and suspects in my custody *always* talk. And I would hate to see you suffer for a man who cheated on you, stole the money he spent on you, and left you behind when he knew we were after him. I would hate to see you suffer for a man like that."

Bess thought a minute before she responded. The *Carpathia* had left New York four hours earlier. There was no way they could catch Harry now. She could tell the sheriff the truth, he would leave her alone, and Harry would still get away.

"So I won't be charged with anything if I tell you?"

"If you tell me the truth, you won't."

"What if I tell you the truth and you don't catch him?"

"If I don't catch him, that's my fault. You won't be charged."

"Do I have your word?"

"You do. I'm in charge of this investigation. I decide who gets charged and who doesn't. And for what it's worth, I believe you're a victim of our friend's crimes too. If it weren't for him, you wouldn't be sitting here with me facing the possibility of a long prison sentence."

"Will you agree not to tell my employer? I would lose my job."

"I see no reason that your employer needs to know."

"Alright then, he was scheduled to board a liner in New York this morning. He's already out to sea. You'll never find him."

"What's the name of the ship?"

"The *Carpathia*."

"Bound for where?"

"Liverpool."

"What name is he using? Brooks, Felgar, Telfer, or something else?"

"Telfer. H. B. Telfer."

"Thank you very much, Miss Montgomery. You've been very helpful. I hope you've told me the truth. If I find out you haven't, I know where to find you."

"It's the truth, I promise."

Mart stood up, collected the dress, letters, and photos. "My apologies, but I must take the letters and dress with me. They're material evidence, I'm afraid."

He walked to the door and opened it but then turned around. "One more thing, Miss Montgomery. From everything I know, from what I read in the letters, and from all our friend did and all he risked, I truly believe he is in love with you."

"But the other women. What about them?"

"These two?" He held out the photos. "Lovely, aren't they? But they're not Harry's mistresses. They're his sisters-in-law, his wife Rose's younger sisters. I got the photos when I spoke to her on Saturday. I thought they might come in handy. And, by the way, Harry and Rose really do sleep in separate bedrooms."

"Damn you. You lied to me."

Mart smiled. "It's true. I did. I've found that sometimes I have to lie to get people to tell me the truth. I wish I didn't, but I do."

CHAPTER NINE

1905

《⊙ ⊙》

QUEENSTOWN, LONDON, UNIONTOWN

PROF. BROOKS ON HIS WAY TO EUROPE

And Will be Arrested on His Arrival in Queenstown

USED NAME OF H.B. TELFER

WHEN SAILING FROM NEW YORK ON CUNARD LINER

In the century after the tragic journey on which John and Mary Brooks died of typhoid fever, transatlantic travel improved dramatically. There was now a doctor aboard each ship. Steam replaced sails, and a trip that had taken as long as ninety days could now be completed in less than ten. Electric lights took the place of fish-oil lamps, resulting in better light and no smoke. Open steerage no longer existed. Even passengers who booked the cheapest third-class passage were assigned a cabin with only three others.

Harry had paid thirty dollars for the journey to Liverpool, which included three meals a day and a berth in a cabin he shared with three other men. They were gone most of the time and said very little. Harry became accustomed to his new name because nobody on board knew his old one. He planned to live out his days as Henry B. Telfer.

The weather was clear and the trip pleasant, but Harry was in a bad state emotionally. He was overwhelmed with guilt for what he had done. He thought about his many victims—the schools he'd been elected to lead, the woman he'd married and pledged his life to, the daughters he was responsible for raising. Triss was eighteen, ready to be on her own, but Katherine had just turned seven and was stuck at home with a mother who was so consumed with depression that she could barely drag herself out of bed. He needed to be there. And yet he was here, running from the law on the high seas and using an assumed name to help him escape. Bess was a victim too. He had used money that did not belong to him to court her, then left her behind when he fled. What kind of man would do that?

Harry missed Bess terribly. He was guilty of egregious sins, sins he could scarcely believe he had committed, but he'd done it all because he'd found the love of his life. He lay in his berth at night, thinking of her face and how she looked at him—how she glanced over her shoulder and then looked down when she sensed his eyes on her from behind; how she leaned forward at dinner, smiling, when he talked about going to the woods, listening to the birds, and teaching himself their calls; how her eyes narrowed and she breathed through her mouth when he began to undress her. He wrote Bess a long letter every day telling her how much he loved her and missed her, how he regretted having to leave her behind, how he couldn't wait to see her and hold her again. He planned to mail the letters when the ship docked in Queenstown, the port city on the southern tip of Ireland and the only stop before Liverpool.

———◆◇◆———

Mart realized he would probably never get his money back, but he wasn't giving up on getting Harry back. His mission now was to figure out a way to have Harry arrested and returned to Pennsylvania to stand trial and pay for his crimes. Because Harry was en route to England, Mart knew he would need the assistance of federal authorities. He and Detective McBeth parted ways at the train station in Washington, with McBeth heading home to Uniontown, and Mart taking the train back to Pittsburgh to see the U.S. Marshal. The marshal listened to Mart's story and cabled his supervisor in D.C. The director in turn cabled his counterpart at Scotland Yard in London. After several exchanges, it was all set. Agents would be waiting for Harry when the *Carpathia* docked in Queenstown. They wouldn't take the chance that he would disembark there and disappear in Ireland before reaching Liverpool. Once Harry was arrested, he would be taken to London to await extradition.

When Mart got back to Uniontown, he went straight to see Justice Dawson to recount all he had learned in the last three days. Mart requested authority to take the train to New York and a liner to England and take McBeth with him. They would have Harry extradited and bring him back to stand trial.

The judge frowned. "How much will this cost, Mart? The schools have already lost the money Professor Brooks stole. How much more will be spent to bring him back?"

"I don't know, Your Honor. We will travel third class. But we can't just let him get away. The next thief will think, if he can just make it to New York and catch a ship, he's home free."

"I understand the importance of deterrence, but I also know that it's unwise to throw good money after bad. You sure you're not suggesting this just because he stiffed you on the loan?"

"I'm sure I'll never see my money again, but I don't think we should just wash our hands of the whole matter. He's a thief, Judge."

"He is that. Alright then, bring me a list of expenses so we can see what it will cost. There's no real hurry. It makes no sense to get on a ship until we know he's in custody. For all we know, he might leap off the stern, drown himself, and save us the trouble."

"That would be fine with me, Your Honor. That would be just fine. I'll put together a list."

When the Carpathia arrived in Queenstown at two in the morning, two Scotland Yard detectives were waiting. Because all they had was a name and a description, they decided not to stay on the dock and take the chance that Harry would walk off the ship and slip past them. As soon as the ship docked and the boiler was shut down, they went aboard. They located a steward on the main deck, identified themselves, and asked to see a passenger list. On the second page was an H. B. Telfer along with the number of the third-class cabin to which he and three other passengers were assigned. The detectives directed the steward to lead them there. When they arrived, one of them pulled his sidearm, and the other knocked on the door and commanded the occupants to open it. One of Harry's cabinmates responded.

"Go away. We're trying to sleep."

"This is Scotland Yard. Open up."

"Alright, alright, just a minute."

The agents heard footsteps and saw the lock turn. A man in his underwear rubbing his eyes opened the door.

"Which one of you is Mr. Telfer? H. B. Telfer."

The other three men pointed at Harry, who was in his bunk propped up on an elbow. The man had a full beard but otherwise matched the description the agents had been given. Harry nodded. "I'm Telfer."

"You're actually Brooks, Professor Brooks, and you're under arrest for crimes you committed in the United States. Stand up and turn around so we can handcuff you."

"May I please get dressed and pack my things first? I will go peacefully. There's no need for handcuffs."

"Get dressed. Then we'll cuff you and pack your things."

After he was dressed and handcuffed, Harry sat on his berth while the agents gathered his belongings. He winced when one of them picked up the stack of envelopes addressed to Bess.

"Those are mine. Please give them to me."

"I'm afraid we can't do that, Professor Brooks. We'll need to take them into evidence." The agent put the letters into his coat pocket.

Twenty minutes after they had walked onto the ship, the detectives walked off with their prisoner. They sent a cable to their superior in London confirming that Professor Brooks had been taken into custody, then escorted him to another pier, where they boarded a ship headed across the Celtic Sea to Bristol. From there, they took a train on the Great Western main line to London. When they reached Scotland Yard, Harry was placed in a private cell in the basement. The following morning, a man in uniform stopped by to see him.

"Professor Brooks, I presume."

"I'm not sure professor is still operative, but Brooks is correct."

"Don't spoil it for me, Professor. We usually just get pickpockets and such in here. Rarely a professor, maybe never. Until I'm instructed otherwise by duly constituted authorities, Professor Brooks it will be. I'm Commander Spencer Jameson of Scotland Yard. I'm in charge of the prisoners in custody here."

"I was taught as a child that I should now say that it's a pleasure to meet you, but I can't say that I'm pleased to be here. I will say that I'm sure it would be a pleasure to meet you under other circumstances."

"Fair enough. I understand that you're also a Protestant minister. In the Methodist Church, I believe."

"I'm not sure that's still operative either, but I was a minister before I boarded the *Carpathia*."

"Splendid. I don't recall that we've ever had a professor or a preacher in a cell in this building, and I'm quite certain that we've never had a man who's both. You must have a fascinating story. I wish you were at liberty to share it with me."

"I don't know that fascinating is the correct word for it, Commander. Do you happen to know how long I will be held here? That is, if you're at liberty to tell me."

"I've been told that you will be extradited to Pennsylvania for trial. There's no point in hiding that from you. That means someone will have to come from America to escort you back. Of course, there will also be court dates to attend and paperwork to complete. I'm sure you will be with us for at least several weeks."

"I figured as much. That being the case, could I possibly ask you to do me a favor, Commander? I have brought my Bible, but I would like access to another book or two if that's possible."

"I'll see what I can do. Do you have anything particular in mind?"

"I've thought about that. This was not how I planned to make my first visit to your famous city, and yet here I am. I believe it would be fitting for me to read some books by Charles Dickens while I'm here."

"Most fitting, and I believe it can be arranged. Do you have any specific books in mind?"

"Any of his works will do. I've read them all but none in the last several years."

"I'll bring you some to choose from tomorrow."

"Thank you very much. Under the circumstances, it's far more than I deserve."

———◄○►———

They met again in the judge's chambers. "Congratulations, Mart. You're going to London. Count yourself lucky that the men on the school board and city council are as angry as you are. They'll find a way to pay the expenses for you and McBeth to bring him back."

"Excellent. I can hardly wait to see the good professor and tell him what I think of him."

"For the record, Mart, I wish to register a complaint. I've been a dedicated public servant for lo these many years, and nobody's ever footed the bill for me to go as far as Philadelphia. And yet you, fifteen years my junior, are being sent on an all-expense-paid trip to London. Life's not fair."

"You're right, Judge, it's not. I loaned the scoundrel nearly 500 bucks I'll never see again, and I have to travel third class across the stormy North Atlantic to bring him back."

"Alright then, we'll call it even. I understand that he's being held at Scotland Yard in London."

"He is. McBeth and I will go there and secure an order of extradition and bring him back. The U.S. Marshal in Pittsburgh has outlined the process for me. I still find the whole thing hard to believe. Miss Montgomery is quite beautiful. Spirited too. She was a tough one to crack. I can certainly understand the attraction, but Judge, the man's a preacher."

"It is disappointing, Mart, but let me tell you something I'm sure you already know. Harry Brooks is not the first good man to do bad things because of the charms of a beautiful woman, and he won't be the last. It happened in ages past, it's happening all around the world today, and it will still be happening as long as men and women walk the Earth. Reason, morals, and scruples are no match for the allure of a beautiful woman. It's as powerful and certain as gravity."

"I know you're right, Judge, but I never would have suspected Harry. Never. Is there anything you want me to tell him when I see him? So long as it's not an expression of sympathy or support, I'll be happy to pass it along."

"Yes, I suppose there is one thing. Tell him I hope it was worth it."

———◄O►———

Commander Jameson brought four volumes of Dickens from his personal collection to Harry the next morning and stopped by each day after that to chat with him. They debated Dickens versus Twain and the English parliamentary system versus the American Constitution. Harry told Jameson how his ancestors had come from England to America a century earlier, about the harrowing voyage on which his great-great-grandparents died, leaving five sons to be divvied up among the surviving passengers. Jameson said England was the best place on earth to live, that John and Mary had made a terrible blunder. Harry acknowledged that they probably agreed, at least after they contracted typhoid.

On the tenth day of his confinement, as Harry sat on his bunk reading about the French Revolution in *A Tale of Two Cities*, the door of the room outside his cell opened. It was Commander Jameson, but he was not alone. He announced that Harry had two visitors from Pennsylvania, Sheriff Kiefer and Detective McBeth. Harry stood and walked to the front of his cell to face them. Mart spoke first.

"Well, if it isn't the Honorable H. F. Brooks, now transformed into the Dishonorable H. B. Telfer."

"I'm very sorry, Mart. I will pay you every cent I owe you, I promise."

"Ah, but your promise was to pay every cent you owed me a month ago and on the other side of the Atlantic. That's when and where your note was due. But instead of paying me, you fled the country using an assumed name. I see that you've even grown a beard to disguise yourself. These are not the actions of a man who intends to honor his obligations, Harry."

"But I will pay you back, Mart. I will also pay back what I borrowed from the schools."

"Borrowed, is it? I don't believe that's the correct legal term for what you did with the schools' money. You borrowed money from me, Harry, but you stole it from the schools."

"I borrowed it. I kept careful records. It was always my intent to pay it back."

"We will learn what twelve good men from Fayette County think in due course, but I believe the jury will agree with me that stole is the correct term. To borrow money, you must have permission, which you didn't have, and the jury may not believe you planned to repay it when they learn that you adopted an alias and fled the scene of your crime."

"I had to leave Uniontown to give me time to get a job and save money to pay my debts. It was my only choice."

"And so off to England as Mr. Telfer you went. You'll need William Jennings Bryan to get you off with that story, Harry. Look, I've brought you something. I thought you'd like to see that we made the front page. You also might want to learn how we caught you."

"What is this?"

"It's the July 6, 1905, edition of the *Mt. Pleasant Journal*. That was just three days after you boarded the *Carpathia*. You were in the middle of the North Atlantic, thinking you were free as a bird. But we knew where you were. Speaking of birds, we found your little chickadee, and she sang like a canary."

"What are you talking about?"

"You called Miss Montgomery your little chickadee in one of the letters you sent her. Surely you remember that. And your mignon. The letters were very romantic, I must say. I told Miss Montgomery when I left her that I was sure you were in love with her. And I had no idea you were such a fine artist."

"How did you get the letters?"

"Read the whole article. You'll see. My favorite part of the story is the role of the fine dress you purchased for Miss Montgomery. An enterprising Pittsburgh policeman showed your photo to the sales clerk in Carlisle's who sold it to you. She knew Miss Montgomery and, once we had her name, we were able to track her to Washington. I suspected you were seeing another woman, but if you hadn't bought the dress, we never would have known Miss Montgomery was the one. You would have gotten away scot-free. Your generosity is what got you caught, Harry."

"This says she was a woman of doubtful repute. That's not true. She's a fine Christian lady."

"I'm not the one who called her that, but some might question the repute of even a fine Christian lady who carries on an affair with a man who's not only married but is also an elected public official and a Christian minister."

"This makes her sound like some kind of trollop."

"If it's any consolation, she didn't seem like a trollop to me."

"This says you sweated her. What does that mean? You better not have hurt her."

"I didn't touch a hair on her lovely head, I assure you. The reporter exaggerated. Literary license, I suppose. I just had to persuade her that she should tell me the truth. And she refused for quite some time. Even when I told her she could be prosecuted as an accessory, she wouldn't tell me. I don't think she ever would have told me if I hadn't told her about the other women."

"Other women? There are no other women."

"I know that, and you know that, but she didn't know that. Just like Rose didn't know you weren't really preaching at the Calvary Methodist Church."

"So now Bess believes I was seeing other women."

"Not anymore. I told her the truth after she told me the truth. I think she told me only because she figured we couldn't catch you. She said it was too late because your ship had already sailed. And yet here we are, with me on the outside of the bars and you on the inside. You know the photos of Rose's sisters in the foyer at your house? Lovely girls. I borrowed them when I went to your house to get some photos of you to help us in the search. When I was trying to get Miss Montgomery to tell me where you were, I told her they were your other mistresses."

"So you lied to her."

"I did, and it worked. I was glad I had the photos. Pictures can be very persuasive."

"Is Bess alright? Is she in trouble?"

"We have no plans to press charges against her if that's what you're asking. I told her she could go back to Pittsburgh and return to work. Of course, if her employer learned of her involvement from this article, they may have let her go. Firms like Knox and Reed don't exactly like this kind of publicity, you know."

"I can't believe I got her into this."

"I was shocked when I found out what you did, Harry. There aren't many people I would loan money to, and I loaned you nearly $500. You let me down. You let a lot of people down."

"I know I did. I'm more ashamed than I've ever been."

"So why did you do it? Miss Montgomery is a beautiful woman, I'll grant you that, but look at all you lost, all the people you hurt. How could you do it? How old are you, Harry? Forty?"

"Forty-three. I've asked myself that a thousand times, Mart. All I can say is that she made me feel better than I've ever felt. I've never felt so alive. I couldn't stay away from her. So, what happens to me now?"

"The court here will order you to be extradited, then we'll take you home to stand trial. Commander Jameson says you won't oppose extradition, which will make it easier, but it's still going to take at least two weeks. During that time, Detective McBeth and I plan to see the sights. You cheated me out of a bunch of money, but at least you got me a trip to London."

"At least I did that."

"One last thing: Justice Dawson asked me to tell you something. He said to tell you he hoped it was worth it. So, Harry, let me ask you: Was it? Was it worth it?"

Was it worth it? It had been just over four months since Bess walked down the aisle to the front of the church and introduced herself, but it seemed like ages ago. Harry thought of everything that had happened since then and all he had felt, the shame and the fear but also the joy and the excitement. He smiled. "It was, Mart. I'd have to say it was."

After leaving Scotland Yard, Mart sent a cable to Justice Dawson asking him to inform the mayor and head of the school board that Harry would not fight extradition, but red tape would delay their return. They would sail home in three weeks on the *Teutonic*, departing on August 16. In the interim, he and Detective McBeth would visit points of interest in England. He ended the cable with a personal note to the judge: "He says it was worth it."

————◄○►————

First thing Monday morning, Bess's supervisor appeared and instructed her to go immediately to Mr. Reed's office. Bess had feared this was coming. Word about the article in the *Mt. Pleasant Journal* was bound to get around. Mr. Reed's secretary showed her into his office, offered her a chair, and closed the door when she left. Bess sat and waited for Mr. Reed to appear. She had never been invited to his office. The high ceilings and elaborate moldings reminded her of the lobby of the Algonquin. The walls were raised panels of dark walnut. Bess wanted to walk over to the bank of windows and look down on the river but decided it was best to stay put. Mr. Reed arrived shortly, said good morning, and sat down behind his enormous mahogany desk.

"Miss Montgomery, we have a problem. I believe you probably know what it is. Is what I read in the papers true? About your relationship with Professor Brooks?"

"I'm afraid it is."

"He's a married man, Miss Montgomery."

"I know, and it was wrong, but he and his wife have not had a real marriage for many years. He and I met at church. We were both lonely. I know it was wrong, Mr. Reed."

"The firm's reputation is very important to us and our clients, Miss Montgomery. It is essential that we maintain an excellent reputation in order to provide them with the representation they deserve. I'm sure you understand that."

"I do. I made a terrible mistake."

"We can't afford to have our reputation damaged by one of our employees being written up in the papers for sleeping with a married man. Do you understand that?"

"I do."

"Then you understand that we have to let you go. You've been a fine employee, but we have no choice. Please pack up your belongings and leave as soon as you can. We will pay you through the end of the week."

"I understand, and I regret that anything I've done has damaged the firm's reputation. The firm has been very good to me."

"We try to treat our employees fairly."

"Before I go, Mr. Reed, I'd like to ask you something. Do you recall when you had a meeting with Mr. Carnegie several months ago? He got here early, and I took coffee to him in the conference room."

"I seem to recall that." He recalled it well. When Reed had walked into the conference room, he had seen the gleam in Mr. Carnegie's eye as he looked at Miss Montgomery. She was one of those rare young women who are beautiful but don't seem to know it, who are too naïve to appreciate the power that comes with their beauty and too innocent to take advantage of it. Mr. Carnegie was obviously charmed.

"Mr. Carnegie told me to let you know if there was ever anything he could do for me. I will have to find a new job now, of course. Do you think it would be possible for you to contact him and see if he has any position that I could fill?"

"Mr. Carnegie? Really?"

"He might want nothing to do with me now, but his holdings are so vast there might be a job for me that would not risk damage to his reputation. I could try to get word to him myself, but he told me to come to you."

"I see. Let me think about this and see if there's something that can be worked out. Please go back to your desk. I'll send for you when I have an answer."

Reed did not want to decide Miss Montgomery's fate alone, but firm co-founder Philander Knox was serving an unexpired term in the United States Senate and was unavailable. Reed walked down the hall to discuss the issue with the next most senior partner, Edwin Smith. The article was not in a Pittsburgh newspaper and had not mentioned Miss Montgomery's place of employment, and they agreed that most of the firm's clients would never know she worked there. But if she contacted Andrew Carnegie, the firm's largest client would know the firm had fired the young woman he found so captivating. They decided that Miss Montgomery would not be terminated, at least not immediately. Reed would meet with her again and explain the conditions of her continued employment. She was again escorted to his office.

"Miss Montgomery, because of your years of valued service to the firm, we have reconsidered our decision and decided to give you a second chance."

"Thank you very much, Mr. Reed. I love my job here."

"But let me be clear. There will be no third chance. We don't want to see your name in the papers again, especially the Pittsburgh papers."

"I don't want to see it either, I assure you."

"We have learned that Professor Brooks is now in custody in London and will be extradited to Pennsylvania to stand trial in Uniontown. So long as you are in our employ, you cannot see him again. Do you understand that?"

"Yes, sir."

"You can't go visit him at the jail. Or in prison, if he's convicted."

"I understand."

"I doubt there will be a trial. The case appears to be open and shut. I expect he'll plead guilty. But if there is a trial, you cannot attend. And if you get asked to testify, you are to let me know immediately. If you get a subpoena, or if the prosecutor or defense attorney tries to contact you, tell my assistant you need to speak to me, but don't tell her why. We will do what we can to get you excused from the trial so you won't have to appear."

"Thank you very much, Mr. Reed. Testifying is the last thing I ever want to do. This is all my fault. Professor Brooks spent all this money on me, and now he's under arrest because I told the sheriff where he was."

"You did the right thing telling the sheriff the truth, Miss Montgomery, and this is not all your fault. Professor Brooks is a married man in his forties and an elected public official. He took the tuition payments without permission and spent them on himself."

"And on me, Mr. Reed."

"But that was his choice. You should not have become involved with a married man, but his problems are his fault, not yours. Now, if you'll excuse me, you and I both need to get back to work."

CHAPTER TEN

UNIONTOWN

❦

1905–1906

BROOKS WAS SORRY

But Court Said It Saw No Mitigating Circumstances in Evidence.

NEARLY THREE YEARS IN PEN

The voyage home on the *Teutonic* was uneventful other than fog and heavy seas when the ship was a day out of Queenstown. Harry got seasick, and Mart found him on the upper deck, bent over, holding the rail, and retching into the sea.

"You look like you're a little under the weather, Harry."

"I suppose you think I'm getting my just deserts."

"That had not occurred to me, but now that you mention it, I suppose I do."

Harry turned his face to the side, looked at Mart, and managed a smile. "I suppose I do too."

Mart decided there was no need to handcuff Harry or keep a close watch on him because there was no way for him to escape. He could still have leaped off the ship to his death, but that would still have been fine with Mart, though it would ensure he would never see his $475.

The ship arrived in New York on Wednesday, August 23. After stopping at the police station, the three men boarded the *Duquesne Limited* for the trip across Pennsylvania. The same train had been in a horrifying accident less than two years earlier, just two days before Christmas. On its eastbound run, the *Limited* derailed when it hit a load of railroad ties that had fallen from a freight train. The passengers in the Pullman and dining cars in the back were uninjured, but those in the crowded smoking car immediately behind the locomotive were not as fortunate. The smoking car was gouged open by the steam dome on top of the boiler, the dome cracked, and the passengers in the car were cooked alive. Sixty-five died.

In the hope that Harry would consent to an interview, a reporter from the *Connellsville Courier* had come east and boarded the westbound *Limited*. But Harry had nothing to say. He disclosed only that he had not yet made any arrangements and refused to make any other statement of any kind. With no information from Harry to share with the paper's readers, the reporter could only describe him. He wrote that Harry had grown a full beard and looked worn and haggard. Though he appeared calm, the strain of the last few weeks had taken its toll. He gazed out the window in moody silence.

Mart and Detective McBeth, whom the reporter described as looking fine, were more accommodating. They said the trip had done them good, but they were glad to be back in America. They discussed their time in England, including the fifteen-day delay to give Harry an opportunity to appeal his extradition, and they described the trip home, including the rough seas and Harry's illness. When they stopped in New York, Harry had communicated with friends in Uniontown and expected one of his brothers to meet him with a bail bond when they got to the jail. Exactly how much money Harry had embezzled was still unknown.

Few people were present when the train pulled into the *Baltimore &* *Ohio* station in Uniontown early Friday morning. Even close friends had difficulty recognizing Harry because of his beard and ragged appearance. He walked up Gallatin Street to the jail with Mart and Detective McBeth on either side. The two officers had traveled more than 7,000 miles to bring him back to face justice for his crimes. Harry offered no information other than to say there are two sides to every story. He was disappointed that neither of his brothers appeared to post bond, and he remained in the general cell with the other prisoners.

————◄o►————

Three weeks after their return to Uniontown, Mart came to the door of Harry's cell with an envelope in his hand.

"I've got something for you."

"What is it?" Harry thought he recognized the handwriting.

"It's a letter from your mignon. One of my responsibilities as sheriff is to read all incoming and outgoing correspondence to make sure it's alright for the recipient to see it. I see no problem with your seeing this. I must say that Miss Montgomery has some admirable qualities." Mart left, and Harry sat down on his bunk to read the letter.

My Dearest Harry,

I am terribly sorry for the harm I've caused you. You're in jail all because of me. I let you spend all that money on me, then I told the sheriff where you were. I never would have done it if I had ever dreamed that he would follow you across the Atlantic and bring you back. He said I would be prosecuted if I didn't tell him. I thought I could tell him and stay out of trouble and you would still get away. He told me you were seeing other women. I should have known it wasn't true. I'm so sorry. I never would have told him.

At least for now, I cannot come visit you and, unless I'm required to testify, cannot come to your trial. The firm was going to fire me but decided to let me stay when I reminded Mr. Reed that Mr. Carnegie had offered to help me. But Mr. Reed said I could not see you under any circumstances or I would lose my job. This is the best job I've ever had, and I don't know if I could find another one after what was in the papers.

Harry, I miss you terribly. I miss the walks we took together. I miss your arms around me. I miss everything. You made me happier than I've ever been. I am praying for three things - that I won't be called to testify at your trial, that you won't be sent to prison, and that the day will come when we can be together again. No matter what happens, I will love you always.

Bess

Harry folded the letter, put it in his pocket, lay down, and cried.

————◆————

The imposing Fayette County Courthouse in Uniontown was built in 1892 at a cost of a quarter of a million dollars. The sandstone Romanesque structure resembled a castle and included a massive clock tower nearly 200 feet tall. In its early years, prisoners sentenced to death were hanged from it. Courthouse Number One, where Harry would be tried, was a magnificent room with an ornate fresco ceiling, beautiful stained-glass windows behind the bench, and dark mahogany paneling. On the wall were oil portraits of the Marquis de Lafayette, the Revolutionary War hero for whom the county was named.

Judge E. H. Reppert of the Court of Common Pleas impaneled a jury on December 6, 1905, and the trial began. The district attorney called seven witnesses. He began with Mrs. Schneider, who testified about the number of delinquent accounts, her dealings with Harry, and his disappearance after she spoke to him about the problem. She attempted to testify about what she learned from the bank tellers, but the judge sustained the hearsay objection raised by Harry's attorney W. C. McKean. The cross-examination was limited to getting her to agree that the conduct in question was completely out of character for the Professor Brooks she knew and that he had always conducted himself with honesty and propriety in the past.

Next up was school board president Mark Shepard, who described how he learned about the missing money and what he did to investigate the matter before turning it over to the authorities. He testified that the school board had determined that Harry had taken more than $2,000, and he detailed the harm the schools had suffered from a loss of such magnitude. A good teacher had to be laid off, and the budget for needed supplies was curtailed. The cross-examination was similar to that of Mrs. Schneider but included one additional point. Shepard conceded that Harry had signed a promissory note agreeing to pay back the full amount of the loss with interest.

The prosecutor then called two parents who'd paid Harry directly and the two tellers who'd cashed their checks for him. Harry's lawyer got the parents to admit that Harry had been honorable in all his previous dealings with them, but he did not challenge anything they said on direct examination. He chose not to cross-examine the tellers at all.

The final prosecution witness was Sheriff Kiefer. He spoke of his initial meeting with Rose. When the district attorney asked him what Rose had said about Harry's repeated trips to Pittsburgh and the purported conference in McKeesport the week he disappeared, Harry's attorney again raised a hearsay objection. The district attorney had anticipated the objection and responded that a statement is hearsay only when offered to prove that it's true. That's not why he was offering this testimony. On the contrary, he intended to prove that the story Harry told his wife was false. Judge Reppert overruled the objection, and Mart explained what Rose had told him and how he'd learned that Harry had not gone to McKeesport and was not preaching in Pittsburgh. He then testified about how the purchase of the dress led him to Washington and to the woman Harry had been seeing. Based on a commitment the prosecutor and Harry's attorney had made to Mr. Reed, Bess's name was not mentioned. Her role was relevant, but her name was not.

Without asking what Bess had told Mart to avoid another hearsay objection, the prosecutor then took Mart through the fact that Harry was traveling on the *Carpathia* under the name of H. B. Telfer, the involvement of the federal authorities and Scotland Yard, and his journey of more than 7,000 miles to bring Harry back to be tried for what he had done. Mart concluded his testimony by stating that Harry never denied taking the money in all the time they spent together on the trip home.

McKean's cross-examination was short and unsuccessful.

"Sheriff Kiefer, you and Professor Brooks discussed why he left the country and traveled under an assumed name, did you not?"

"We did."

"And he told you it was so he could get a job in England and pay back the money he'd borrowed from the schools, did he not?"

"Sure. He said that. We caught him. What else was he gonna say?"

Judge Reppert granted the motion to strike Mart's commentary and instructed the jurors to disregard it, but all twelve were smiling.

The prosecution rested without calling Bess. The DA had interviewed her in Mr. Reed's office and concluded that her testimony was not essential and the jury might view Harry with sympathy if they heard it. She would also support his claim that he intended to pay the money back, and she would testify that he told her that was his plan before he got caught. McKean had discussed calling her for the defense to buttress Harry's position on the point, but Harry would not allow it.

Harry's lawyer called three witnesses. Two prominent citizens vouched for Harry as a man of honor and a person of the highest integrity, but their testimony was of little use when they admitted on cross that they weren't denying that he took the money.

Harry was the final witness. His testimony was not a denial but a plea for sympathy. He blamed his misdeeds on family problems and intoxicants. He testified about the loss of three children, the effect on Rose and their marriage, his drinking habit, and his loneliness and search for happiness elsewhere. He said he greatly regretted that he'd taken the tuition payments but always intended to pay them back. He'd kept a detailed record so he would know precisely how much he owed and had voluntarily executed a promissory note in the full amount of what he had taken plus interest. He intended to honor his obligation, though he was unable to do so at present. His lawyer offered as exhibits the promissory note and Harry's record of the money he had taken.

The district attorney then cross-examined him.

"The tuition payments were for the purpose of paying the expenses to run the school, correct?"

"That's right."

"And to educate the children of Uniontown?"

"Correct."

"But you took them, did you not?"

"I took some of them, the ones I've admitted taking."

"And that money wasn't yours to take, was it?"

"It was not mine."

"And nobody gave you permission to take it, correct?"

"That's right, but I plan to pay it back."

"But you admit you had no right to take it, do you not?"

"I do. I'm terribly sorry, as I've said."

"And you had no right to spend it on your mistress, did you?"

"I had no right to spend it on anything."

"Professor, you heard Sheriff Kiefer's testimony. It's true that you fled on a Cunard liner to Liverpool, isn't it?"

"It's true that I took a Cunard liner. I don't know that I would call it fleeing. I was going to England to get a job to make enough money to pay back what I owed."

"Let's explore the question of whether you fled. You grew a beard to disguise yourself, did you not?"

"I grew a beard. It wasn't to disguise myself. I just didn't shave."

"I see. But you didn't tell anyone other than your mistress where you were going, did you?"

"That's true, I didn't."

"You didn't tell your wife here in Uniontown, did you? The woman you've been married to nearly twenty years, you didn't tell her, did you?"

"No, I did not tell her. I wrote her a letter and said I was leaving, but I didn't say where I was going."

"And you didn't buy your ticket on the *Carpathia* in your own name, did you?

"No, I used the name of a man who was in school with me in Kentucky years ago."

"H. B. Telfer, correct? You traveled under the name of H. B. Telfer, did you not?"

"That's the name I used."

"One final question, Professor Brooks, but before I ask it, I want to remind you that you're under oath. The reason you used an alias was to avoid detection, was it not?"

"I was afraid if I used my real name I would be apprehended before I had time to make enough money to pay back what I owed."

"Yes or no, Professor. You used an alias to avoid detection, did you not?"

"Yes, I did."

The prosecutor's closing argument was a brief summary of the facts as confirmed by Harry's own testimony. Professor Brooks admitted he took the money. He admitted he didn't have permission. He admitted he took a liner to Europe and didn't tell anyone other than his mistress where he was going. He admitted using an assumed name to escape detection. Based on his own testimony, he was guilty of embezzling and spending money that belonged to the schools, money that was sorely needed to educate the children of Uniontown.

McKean did not contest the facts but instead focused on Harry's good character. He'd made this one mistake, but he shouldn't be sent to prison. He should instead be allowed to resume the productive life he'd lived in the past so he could repay what he owed. That made more sense than putting him behind bars, where he couldn't work and couldn't repay his debt. It was also the right decision under the law. The proof showed that Harry always intended to pay the money back. If not, why would he have kept a record of what he borrowed? And because he intended to pay it back, he wasn't guilty of the crime of embezzlement.

After Judge Reppert instructed the jurors on the law, they retired to the jury room to deliberate. It didn't take long. After the foreman was selected, he asked the other jurors a question. "Professor Brooks seems like a good man, or at least like he used to be, but does anybody think he always planned to pay the money back?"

Several other jurors spoke up in turn.

"I don't. I might be willing to give him the benefit of the doubt if he hadn't fled the country."

"I agree. He used an assumed name. He grew a beard. He was trying to get away."

"Yep. And if he hadn't bought his lady friend a dress, he'd be over in Merry Old England right now living it up. Nobody would have ever known where he was, and he never would have paid back a penny."

"I agree, but what about the argument that we should let him stay out of prison so he can work and pay the money back?"

"The way I look at it, that should be up to the school board, not us. The schools are the victim. If they had wanted to keep him out of prison so he could work and pay them back, they would have cut a deal with him. But they decided to have him prosecuted and make him pay for his crimes. In my mind, he's definitely guilty. No question. I know we're supposed to disregard what the sheriff said about the professor claiming he was gonna pay it back only because he got caught, but I was already thinking that even before he said it."

"Me too. You don't use an alias and flee to a foreign country if you plan to pay your debts."

The foreman spoke again. "Does anybody disagree? A few of you haven't said anything. Does anybody have anything else they think we should talk about?" He looked around the room. "Alright then, let's take a vote. Professor Brooks is charged with one count of embezzling tuition payments from the schools. If you vote to convict him, raise your right hand."

All twelve jurors raised their hands. "Good. I'll tell Judge Reppert's clerk that we've reached a verdict."

Harry was in the courtroom when the judge and jury came in the next morning to announce the verdict. McKean didn't get there in time, so Harry sat in the gallery with the spectators. He showed no emotion when the guilty verdict was read. It was reported in the press that the jury needed only one vote.

Harry returned to jail to await his sentencing. The stream of visitors was now down to a trickle. He had told his friends before the trial that he couldn't talk about what happened; they just needed to wait for the trial to hear his side of the story. But then the trial came, they heard his side, and it was clear that he was guilty as charged.

Harry hoped that Triss would come see him when she was home for the holidays, but Christmas came and went, she didn't come, and he didn't hear from her. Who could blame her? Her father, the respected teacher and preacher who was supposed to be her role model, was now a convicted felon, sitting in jail and waiting to be sentenced. He had failed in his most important job: being a good father.

The sentencing was scheduled for Thursday morning, January 4, 1906. Before Judge Reppert announced his decision, Harry asked for an opportunity to speak. He addressed his remarks to the judge.

"Your Honor, when I say that I'm sorry, the word does not express my feeling. The mental anguish that I felt at times was more than I could bear. My ambitions were along another line, and I'm sorry beyond expression. It was never my intention to embezzle any money, and I had hoped to be able to meet all my obligations at some time. I shall consider all my obligations just as binding, whatever may be my lot."

Judge Reppert was not moved by Harry's apology. He declared that the evidence revealed no mitigating circumstances, and the situation Harry confronted sooner or later confronts all transgressors. The judge sentenced Harry to two years and ten months in the state penitentiary and fined him $400. The headline in the paper the next day was "BROOKS WAS SORRY."

Six weeks after the sentencing, Harry spent his twentieth wedding anniversary alone in his jail cell. Three weeks later, Rose filed a petition for divorce. Ten days after that, Harry was transferred from the Fayette County jail to Western Penitentiary on the banks of the Ohio River in Pittsburgh to serve out the rest of his sentence.

CHAPTER ELEVEN

APRIL 30, 1937

⟨⟨◎ ◎⟩⟩

TUPELO

The Hotel Tupelo was near the railway station on the east end of downtown. It was a favorite stopover for passengers on two railroads, the Frisco and the Gulf, Mobile, and Ohio. The hotel's restaurant, called the Blue Room, boasted of the finest dining in Northeast Mississippi. The room had high ceilings, ornate moldings, and brass chandeliers. There were gold-framed mirrors on the walls. The waiters wore white jackets and provided impeccable service.

Harry parked two blocks from the hotel and entered through the side entrance so no one would see him. He didn't know what he expected, but he knew what he deserved. He had arrived early so he could claim a table in the back corner, but Triss was already seated at the one he had in mind. He thought this was a good sign. The table would give them privacy, and it meant she wasn't planning to cause a scene, at least not yet. It was also good that she was already there. His back would be to the other diners, and they would be less likely to recognize him and speak. If one did, he would introduce his companion as Triss Soles, an old friend, and hope she went along. When their eyes met, he smiled, but she only nodded. He walked over and took the other seat.

"Good morning, Triss."

"Morning."

"I'm early, but you were even earlier."

"I couldn't sleep. I've already had two cups of coffee."

"Me too. I had two cups at home. I couldn't sleep either." There was a coffee pot on the table, and Harry poured a third cup for each of them. "We have a lot to talk about, but first I want to hear about you."

"I'm not here to talk about me."

"But I want to hear about you. You're my daughter, Triss. You're my oldest child."

"Now that Katherine's gone, I'm the oldest by twenty-five years."

Harry let the comment pass. "I haven't seen you in more than thirty years, and not a day goes by that I don't think about you. Your life was hard enough before I did what I did. We have time to talk about me, and I'll tell you everything you want to know, but please let me hear about you first."

"I'm fine. I have a good life."

"I'm glad to hear that. Please tell me all about it. I know you married Frank Soles not long after I left for Texas."

"And you didn't come to the wedding."

"I wasn't invited, and I was already gone."

"You could at least have come to see me before you left."

"I couldn't. It was prohibited."

"By whom? Who could stop you from seeing your own daughter?"

"The court. The divorce decree barred me from seeing or writing you or Katherine."

"Mama didn't tell me that. Nobody told me."

"I was advised that I would be arrested and held in contempt of court if I tried to see you."

"But nobody asked me what I wanted. I was nineteen when she filed for divorce and nearly twenty-two when you left."

"I wanted to talk to you, try to explain, but I was afraid I would wind up back in jail. So are you and Frank happy?"

"Yes. He's a fine man, and he's been quite successful. He's the lead lawyer and vice president of the Talon Company in Meadville, and he's in line to be the next chairman of the board. They invented zippers."

"Really? Please thank your husband for me. Zippers are a most useful and practical invention for an old man who has trouble with buttons."

"They are useful, and there's a great demand for them. We have a very comfortable life. We have a winter home in Palm Springs, and Frank has donated money to the YMCA to build a camp in Somerset County. He says there will be a lake named for me. Triss Lake."

"Outstanding! You always loved the water. What about children? Do you have any children?"

"Two. Dottie just turned seventeen. John will be fifteen this summer. I didn't have them until I was in my thirties. I thought I was old to be having children, but then I found out how old you were when you and your second wife had yours. Dottie is a year older than Margaret and Marjory."

"The twins were a big surprise. Two surprises really. The first was when Ethel told me she was expecting, the second when the doctor walked out holding up two fingers. But they're good girls, smart as a whip. They're cheerleaders. Tell me about Dottie and John."

"Dottie's a cheerleader too. They're good children too, both very bright and bound for college."

"That's no surprise. Their mother's very bright."

"Dottie's a musician, plays three instruments, and John's a fine athlete. Football, baseball, track and field."

"I'm so glad to hear it. You had so much to deal with. Losing Roswell, Grace, and George, our life after George died, having a father like me."

"You were a good father until the end."

"But I sure made up for it then, didn't I?"

"I have a question. What do they know? Your wife and children—what all do they know about your past?"

The waiter came over and asked if they were ready to order. Harry said they needed a few more minutes. Triss waited until the waiter was out of earshot and asked again. "What do they know?"

"Nothing. They don't know anything."

"Does your wife know you had five children with your first wife?"

"She doesn't even know I had a first wife."

"Then I guess she doesn't know what you did."

"Nobody does."

"How could you not tell her? You've been married to her for what, twenty-five years?"

"Twenty-seven. Not telling her what I did is another of my many sins, but I will say this: I kept my past a secret with the church's blessing."

"What do you mean?"

"When I got to Texas, the minister I reported to said that people wouldn't accept me if they knew the truth, that I would be of no use to God or His people. I was encouraged to keep my past to myself, so I did. I didn't tell Ethel. I didn't tell anybody."

"But she must have asked questions. Other people too. You had to tell them something."

"I didn't want anybody tracing me back to Pennsylvania, so I said I was from Kentucky, born and raised there. I was familiar with it from going to the university, so I figured it was a good choice. I said I was an only child, that I decided to leave home and move to Texas after my parents died."

"Daddy!"

Even under the circumstances, to hear her call him Daddy made him smile. "And I didn't just lie about where I was born, I also lied about when. Ethel thinks I'm sixty-one. Everybody else does too. And I can't say I committed that sin with the church's blessing."

"Sixty-one? Really?"

"It was wrong, but in a way, I'm glad I did it. If I'd told the truth about my age, the church would have made me retire by now. But I didn't, and they haven't. And I don't want to retire. I love preaching. I love teaching the people about the Bible and helping them find Jesus."

"But why did you lie about your age? I understand why you lied about what you did, but why lie about your age?"

"I didn't plan to; it just happened. Ethel and I were having dinner one night soon after we met. I thought she was in her late twenties, maybe thirty, but I hadn't asked and wasn't planning to. It was a subject I wanted to avoid. But then she brought it up, and I couldn't avoid it. She put down her fork, looked right at me, and said, 'I'm twenty-three years old, Harry. How old are you?' I wasn't ready for that, but I had to say something. She'd said twenty-three, so I said thirty-three. I'd been alone for years. I was very interested in her, and I figured telling her the truth would be the end of our relationship."

"Daddy! And she believed you?"

"She gave me a strange look. I said I'd always looked old for my age, and she didn't say anything else about it. I guess she wanted to believe me."

"But Daddy, you were born in 1862. That makes you seventy-five. You lied by fourteen years."

"I know how old I am, and I feel it. Sometimes I've had a hard time keeping up with the new age I gave myself. When the twins were born, I told the woman who was taking down the information for the birth certificates that I was forty-six. Based on the new birthdate I'd given myself, I was only forty-five. When Ethel asked me about the mistake on the certificates, I blamed the person who typed them."

"And what were you really? Fifty-nine?"

"You always were better at math than I was." They were both smiling now.

"You really are a scoundrel, aren't you? Your wife thought you were a thirty-three-year-old childless man from Kentucky. It's no wonder she knows nothing about all the rest."

The waiter approached again, and Harry again said they weren't ready. Then he turned serious. "As for all the rest, I believe it would ruin our marriage if Ethel found out, and I'm afraid it would ruin her life if other people did. I would probably lose my job, and she would lose the pension she'll receive after I'm gone. You're right that I'm a scoundrel. What I did to you and Rose and Katherine was shameful. But I know that God has forgiven me, and I'm asking you to forgive me too."

Triss leaned back in her seat. "But why should I forgive you, Daddy? After what you did? After you left us to fend for ourselves?"

Harry hesitated and took a sip of coffee. "Triss, I committed grievous sins, terrible sins. I did things I never could have imagined doing. It was like I was another man. There is no excuse for what I did, but you know how things were after George died. The last years in McKeesport were terrible. I thought things would get better when we moved to Uniontown, but nothing changed. I was miserable and lonely. I'm sure Rose was too. Poor woman lost three children in seven years. It was hard on me, but it was harder on her. That's no excuse, but it's the truth."

"I've thought about that a lot. It was terrible, that's for sure. I got out of the house whenever I could and was thrilled when you and Mama sent me to school in Philadelphia. I'm grateful Frank and I haven't gone through anything like it. But Daddy, think about what you did."

"I think about it every day. I'm ashamed every day. I always will be. Every man who gets to be as old as I am has regrets. I'm sure I have more than most. But since I came to the South, and even before then when I was in prison, I've tried to make amends. I've tried to help people, and I want to keep trying. But if the members of my church found out about me, I wouldn't be able to keep trying."

"Are you sure?"

"I've thought about it for thirty years, Triss. Christianity teaches that even the worst of sins may be forgiven, that there is grace and redemption for all who repent. But preachers are held to a high standard, and rightly so. If everyone found out about me, I would almost certainly be removed from my position. But even if the church allowed me to stay on, I don't think I could be effective. The members of the church might forgive me, but they would no longer respect me. And I don't believe they would listen to me."

"Maybe you're right, but where does that leave me? You want me to leave Tupelo the day after I arrived so you can keep your secret?"

"Of course not. It's wonderful to see you. I can't tell you how wonderful. I haven't seen you in more than thirty years, more than half your life and nearly half of mine. I don't want to lose you again. And to know that you're doing well is a great relief to me."

"But if I stay, how will you explain who I am? Who will you say I am? Your niece? Your cousin?"

"You already told Margaret that you're my daughter."

"I guess I did say that, didn't I?"

"And it's true. You are my daughter. And so I will say that you're my daughter."

"But how would that work, Daddy? I'm fifty years old. They think you're sixty-one."

"Well, you can't be fifty, that's for sure. How would you like to be forty-two?"

"Forty-two? You think people would believe that?"

"I'll say looking old for our age runs in the family."

"I don't know. Nobody even knows you had a child."

"I lay awake most of the night thinking about what I could say that would allow me to acknowledge that you're my daughter without exposing my past. I decided it might work to say I ran off with your mother and we got married when I was eighteen and she was sixteen. We were too young, and it was a mistake. She moved back home with her parents and filed for divorce, but by then she was pregnant. Not long after you were born, they moved away and took you with them. To keep me from finding them, they didn't tell anybody where they were going. Not too long after that, I left town and tried to put it all behind me. I never told anybody. Maybe I could say something else, but that's what I came up with at two this morning. What do you think?"

"You're good at this, aren't you?"

"It's sad to say, but I've had practice."

"I don't know, Daddy. You're talking about telling your wife and children one more lie. I don't think I want to be a part of it. You always taught me to tell the truth."

"I know I did, but I'm begging you, Triss. I'm an old man. My life is almost over. I'm not worried about me. I know that God has forgiven me, but it would be awful for Ethel and the children to find out what I did, especially since I never told them. And I don't know what would become of Ethel if the church turned me out, how she would support herself. She's your age. She could live thirty more years. I understand why you want people to know, but I wouldn't be the only one you'd be hurting."

"I don't know. After Katherine died, I asked Frank to hire a detective to find you. I was planning to tell the whole world what you did, to shout it from the mountaintop. When you left Pennsylvania without a word, I thought there was no way I could ever forgive you. Mama didn't want me to visit you when you were in the jail and in prison, but I kept waiting to hear from you. I thought you would write, but you never did, and I just got madder and madder. But I didn't know about the divorce decree. And I understand why you got involved with another woman. Poor Mama was in such a dark hole. I need some time to think."

"Take all the time you need."

She checked her watch. "Can you meet me back here at three o'clock? I'll let you know then."

"I'll be here."

Harry stood up and waited for Triss to stand, but she spoke instead. "Aren't you forgetting something?"

"Am I? What?"

"Can we order breakfast? I'm starving."

Harry smiled and sat back down.

They spent the meal talking about their children, her two and his second set of five. Dottie had the potential to be a concert pianist. If she fell short, it wouldn't be for lack of training or trying. John had dreams of playing shortstop in the big leagues–Arky Vaughan, the Pirates' star shortstop, was his hero–but he would probably wind up at Talon. Harry's two oldest, Elizabeth and Edwin, were grown and had left home. Elizabeth had married the son of a wealthy planter from the Mississippi Delta. She'd met him when Harry was the preacher at the First Methodist Church in Clarksdale. They had a young son named Andy. Edwin had a good sales position in Memphis. Danny, whose given name was Jannette, was about to graduate from high school. And then there were the twins, Margaret and Marjory. They were a blessing to an old man, Harry said, and were identical in every way. The only difference was that Margaret could wiggle her ears but Marjory couldn't. Sometimes even Harry had a hard time telling them apart. Those who couldn't just called each of them "Twin." They were smart, funny, and popular and were bound for great things. Harry hoped to live long enough to see what they would accomplish.

Triss summed up their conversation: "It sounds as if life has improved for both of us since 1905."

As they were finishing, Harry checked his pocket watch, said he had to get to a meeting, and asked the waiter for the check. When it came, Triss grabbed it before he could. He protested, but she had a ready answer: "There's more money in zippers than preaching the Gospel, Daddy."

They both stood up, and she came around the table, hugged him, and asked, "So, where are we from?"

"What?"

"Where in Kentucky are we from? We'll need to have our story straight."

"So you'll do it? Really?"

"I'm not saying it's right, because it's not, but sometimes you have to choose the lesser of two evils, and sometimes telling the truth is worse than telling a lie. I realize telling the truth would be worse now. So where are we from?"

"I don't know. I haven't gotten that far yet. I just always said I grew up on a farm in Kentucky."

"And what was my mother's name?"

"I don't know that either. I'll think of something between now and three o'clock."

———◄◦►———

When Harry returned to the Blue Room at three, Triss was already there, wearing the same clothes and sitting in the same chair at the same table.

"So you've been sitting here drinking coffee all day?"

"Not at all. I took a hike. I walked up Green Street and came back down Church Street. What the tornado did was terrible, Daddy."

"You should have seen it right after the storm. I conducted as many funerals in a week as I preach sermons in a year."

"I'm sorry you had to deal with that."

"Don't feel sorry for me. Nobody in our family was hurt. Many others suffered terrible losses. But good came out of it. The city pulled together. We're rebuilding. People have turned to God."

"They're fortunate to have you here."

"I don't know about that, but I'm glad I was here to do what I could. Have you had lunch?"

"I had an egg salad sandwich at the drugstore on Main Street. What's the name of it?"

"TKE. Thomas Kincannon Elkin."

"I sat at the soda counter and met a nice man sitting two stools down from me. He heard my accent when I ordered and asked where I was from."

"What did you tell him?"

"I told him the truth. McKeesport. I didn't tell him where I was born because you haven't told me yet."

"We'll get to that."

"He asked what had brought me here from Pennsylvania. I said to visit family, but before he could ask me who, I changed the subject to the tornado. I told him I'd just gone for a walk north of downtown and the destruction was horrifying. He said the tornado hit Tupelo on his birthday and was the worst birthday present ever."

"Did he tell you who he was?"

"Cliff something. I don't remember his last name. He said he was a banker."

"That's Cliff Eason. He and his wife Margaret are members of the church. Fine people. Their son Paul is in the twins' class. You haven't changed your mind about our plan, I hope."

"No. I figure you've probably suffered enough, and there's no point in making anybody else suffer. They didn't do anything wrong."

"Not a thing, and they would definitely suffer."

"I thought I wanted to tell your wife, but she's been with you longer than I was. Surely she knows who you are even if she doesn't know what you did thirty years ago. So, where are we from? Where was I born?"

"Courtney, Kentucky. Ever heard of it?"

"I don't think so."

"That's because it doesn't exist."

"Daddy!"

"In case somebody gets curious and starts asking around, I figure it's better to make up a place than to have a real one. The people in a real place might know I never lived there."

"So where is this Courtney, Kentucky? Is it nice?"

"Very nice. Just outside Lexington. Beautiful rolling hills and forests. Looks like western Pennsylvania."

"But what if somebody asks around and finds out there is no Courtney, Kentucky?"

"It was just a tiny place. Who knows what happened to it after we left? I've been gone thirty-five years, and you've been gone even longer than that. Maybe the families who lived there moved away. Maybe it was taken in by Lexington."

"You enjoy this, don't you?"

"Maybe a little, but I didn't just start inventing places today. There were no trees and no birds when I was in Western Pen. No sunshine. Even when they let us go out in the yard, the smoke from the factories along the river blocked out the sun. I would go back to my cell, lie on my bunk, and make up places I wanted to go when I got out. One of them was a place in the countryside outside Lexington. I never gave it a name until today."

Triss was smiling. "Then Courtney it is. Courtney, Kentucky. What about my mother's name? What shall we call her? We'll need to have the same answer if anybody asks."

"I don't know. I picked the place; you pick the name."

"Let's say Rose. We'll both remember that."

"You sure?"

"Why not?"

"No reason. I feel terrible about how her life turned out. We were very happy at the beginning, but then Roswell died, then Grace and George. After George, she never got better. And then I did what I did, and now she's gone too."

"I know. I was there. Let's give my Kentucky mother a different name then. What about Sara?"

"Sara's fine with me."

"What else do I need to know before you announce that I'm your daughter?"

"Your current life, I guess, but I don't know why we need to change any of that. Your children aren't too old to have a forty-two-year-old mother, and it's not like anybody's going to contact Frank and ask him your age."

"No, and he's too busy to take a call even if somebody tried. What else?"

"If anybody asks, let's say Sara's maiden name was Johnson. Her parents were Milton and Eliza."

"I need to be taking notes."

"I think it will be fine. I told Ethel I was thirty-three right after we met, and she hasn't said a word about my age since. I don't think she'll ask you any hard questions. She may ask me some, but not you. But you'll need to be careful with the girls. Danny questions everything, and the twins are brilliant. But I'll tell them our story, you'll come meet them, and it will all be fine. I'll have to mend some fences, but I think the girls will be excited to have a big sister they didn't know they had. That's what I'm counting on anyway."

"I'm counting on it too."

"It really is wonderful to see you, Triss."

"It's great to see you too, Daddy."

"I never stopped loving you."

"I didn't know it, but I guess I never stopped loving you either."

"Thank you. I don't deserve it, but it's wonderful to hear you say that. By the way, you said Frank hired a detective to find me. If you don't mind, I'd like to hear how he did it."

"He thought it would be hard, but then he found your name in a newspaper article. It was about a speech President Roosevelt made here, and it said a Methodist preacher named Henry Felgar Brooks gave the invocation. I couldn't believe it."

"That's funny. After I agreed to give the prayer, I started worrying. What if my name is mentioned in the papers and somebody in Uniontown sees it and decides to expose me? I thought about telling the mayor I couldn't do it." Harry smiled. "Now I'm glad I didn't."

"When the private eye showed me the article, I thought you'd sure come a long way. Not many men go from prison to the pulpit."

"God has been very good to me."

"The article said thousands of people were there. I wonder if any of them knew what you did."

"I wondered the same thing when I stood up to pray, but I'm sure none of them did. It's like I've lived two separate lives, the first one never touching the second."

"Until your long-lost daughter showed up yesterday."

"I was the one who was lost, not you. But now I am found."

CHAPTER TWELVE

1908

<o ⊙>

PITTSBURGH

Harry's best friend was another Methodist preacher named Harry. Other than the prisoners who lived alongside Harry and the guards who watched over him, the other Harry was now his only friend.

The two men had met in McKeesport sixteen years earlier, shortly after Harry was hired to be the new school superintendent. Harry was only thirty but already had an excellent reputation as a teacher and administrator.

In addition to his duties as superintendent, Harry taught several classes, including a Bible class to the high school students. The first term was devoted to the Old Testament, the second to the New. It was his favorite class, in large part because of the quality of his students. In the 1890s, most American teens went to work on farms or in factories by the time they turned fourteen. Only one in ten went on to high school. Most who did, including Harry's students, were bright and motivated.

One day in the middle of his first term, after the students had taken their seats in his classroom, Harry gathered his notes from his desk and stepped to the lectern. Before beginning his lecture, he scanned the classroom to ensure that everyone was present. All his students were there, but there was a visitor as well. Seated against the back wall was a man of about forty Harry had never seen before. Harry nodded to the intruder and asked, "May I help you?"

The man stood and smiled. "My apologies, Professor Brooks. I'm Harrison Matheny. I should have said something when I came in, but you were focused on your preparation, and I didn't want to interrupt you. I was wondering, do you mind if I stay and listen to your lecture? If you prefer that I leave the class to you and your students, I will certainly understand, but I would like to stay if you'll let me."

"I don't mind at all. Everyone is welcome to hear the Word of the Lord." Matheny nodded and sat back down.

The lesson of the day was from the book of Job. The visitor did not speak again, but not for lack of interest. He leaned forward in his seat, listening intently and taking notes. When the class ended, he waited until the students were gone, then stood, walked to the front of the classroom, and offered his hand. "My name is Harrison, but everyone calls me Harry."

"I'm Henry Brooks, but everyone calls me Harry too. You're the Methodist preacher, aren't you?"

"Guilty as charged."

"I thought so. To what do I owe the honor of your presence today? From what I've heard, I should be in your sanctuary listening to you, and yet here you are in my classroom listening to me."

"I have an ulterior motive. My daughter Evelyn is in your class."

"When I saw her last name, I wondered if she was the preacher's daughter."

"I came to see if you were filling her head with nonsense." He smiled when he said it, though Harry wondered if there was some truth in the confession.

"I trust you see that I'm not."

"I wasn't worried. Evelyn loves your class. She says you know the Bible better than I do. You know how teenagers are, so I came to see for myself. She didn't exaggerate."

"I'm certain that I don't know the Bible better than you do, Reverend, but it's not for lack of trying. I have spent many hours studying the Word and many more reading the volumes that have been written about it."

"It shows. I learned some new things about Job today that had never occurred to me."

"I learn something new every time I read Scripture, Reverend Matheny."

"Please call me Harry."

"Then you will have to call me Harry too."

"I'm afraid that will be confusing."

"Then what shall we do?"

"You be Harry, and I'll be Harrison. I haven't been called Harrison since my parents called me that when I misbehaved, but I'll get used to it."

"If you prefer, you can be Harry, and I'll be Henry."

"No, Harrison will be fine. It will remind me to behave. I have a request for you, Professor Brooks–I mean Harry. I learned some things from you today that I believe will be of value to my congregation, and I would like to learn more. With your permission, I'd like to come back to your class when I can. I won't be able to come to every class, but I'd like to come when I don't have another commitment."

"Reverend Matheny–I mean Harrison"–both men smiled–"I will grant your request on one condition."

"I thought everyone was welcome to hear the Word of the Lord, and yet now you're imposing a condition. What is it?"

"That you speak as well as listen–that if you have something to add, or if you believe I am in error in my interpretation of Scripture, that you speak up and say so."

"I don't know about that. This is your class. I will be here only with your permission. I don't want to disagree with you in front of your students."

"I disagree with you about disagreeing with me. I believe it's healthy for young minds to learn that not every Christian, not even every preacher, finds the same meaning in a passage from the Bible. I can give them the

Baptist perspective, and you can give them the Methodist. The Baptist will be correct, of course." Harry smiled again.

"So you won't be John the Baptist; you'll be Harry the Baptist."

"I am Harry the Baptist, and you're Harrison the Methodist. Do you accept my condition?"

"I do."

"Excellent. Will I see you on Thursday?"

"I'll be here." They shook hands again.

The arrangement was a great success. The two debated the meaning of Scripture before class and during it. They often continued after the students had left. Their capacity for speaking and listening and their respect for each other were such that each came around to the other's position on several occasions. When the class ended, they still disagreed but had swapped sides. The students found the classes fascinating and learned the fine art of disagreeing without being disagreeable.

The two men were both preachers named Harry but otherwise could not have been more different. Harrison was tall, thin, and fair, Harry short, thick, and dark. Their hairstyles reflected their personalities. Harrison had a shock of blond hair that seemed to have a mind of its own. One day it was parted on the right side, the next on the left. On the third, there was no part at all. Harry's hair was invariable. Every one of the dark hairs on his head was plastered down in its appointed place every day. Harrison was always smiling as if he'd just heard a joke or was about to tell one. Harry was serious at best, severe at worst, and was slow to smile or laugh.

And yet now Harry had found someone who made him do both. The two men soon became close friends. They began meeting for lunch every Friday, then added Monday, then Wednesday as well. They went to the same diner on Main Street and sat in the same seats at the same table. Their talks expanded from Scripture to their work, then to their families and personal lives. When Grace died in 1893, Harrison was the first to arrive at the Brooks home. When George died four years later, Harrison was there again. And when Rose moved to another bedroom and the Brooks home became a place of constant sorrow, Harrison spent many long hours with his friend who had lost three children and now seemed to have lost his wife too. He advised Harry to be patient and try to understand the suffering of a woman who watched three of her children die.

Harry and Rose had both been German Baptists all their lives, and he had preached in many Baptist churches since he was called into the ministry. He loved the church. But after George died, Rose stopped going to church, and Harry's experience with Alice Pendergast at the funeral left a bitter taste in his mouth. He began going to the Methodist church to hear Harrison preach, and he took Triss with him.

Harrison gave Harry the writings and sermons of John Wesley and encouraged him to study them. There was much about Methodist doctrine that Harry liked. It seemed less rigid and judgmental than the conservative German Baptist Church, more willing to forgive and slower to condemn. There seemed to be a greater appeal to reason and more of a willingness to explore different interpretations of Scripture.

After a year of study and attending Sunday services, Harry decided to become a Methodist. Harrison was overjoyed, and the two men became even closer. When Harrison was out of town or ill, Harry preached in his stead. On other occasions, Harry filled in when Harrison's only excuse was that he was tired of talking and just wanted to sit and listen. Harry was also requested to serve as a guest minister at other Methodist churches in and around McKeesport.

When Harry was approached about running for school superintendent in Uniontown, Harrison encouraged him to throw his hat into the ring. Harrison would miss the man who had become his best friend over the last decade, but he thought it would be good for Harry and Rose to leave the home where two of their children had died, that a new start might lift the veil of sadness. He also believed that Harry, Rose, and their daughters would benefit from being nearer to their extended families.

After Harry won the election and the family moved the thirty-five miles south to Uniontown, he and Harrison remained close. They wrote letters to each other constantly–if one took more than a week to respond, the other would send a second letter demanding two in return–and they regularly took the train to see each other. Rose's depression did not improve, but Harrison continued to counsel love and patience. He reminded Harry that the loss of children is often harder on the mother than the father.

When Harry disappeared in the summer of 1905 and his crimes were uncovered, many of his friends abandoned him. Some remained loyal until he was convicted but then stopped coming to see him. The one friend who always stood by him was Harrison. He understood the loneliness and despair that had led to Harry's sins. Harrison came to court in Uniontown for Harry's trial in December 1905 and his sentencing the following month. When Harry expressed remorse for his conduct, Harrison nodded along. He knew that Harry meant it because he knew Harry.

At the end of the sentencing, Harrison asked the guards if the two men could have a moment alone. He faced Harry, put a hand on each of his shoulders, and said, "Look at me." Harrison waited for Harry to raise his eyes, then continued. "You have sinned, but you have repented, and God has forgiven you. God loves you, and I love you too. You still have much to give, Harry, and God has a plan for you. Never forget that." Harry nodded but said nothing. The two men hugged for the very first time, and Harry was led from the courtroom to his cell.

Once a week, every week, while Harry was in Western Penitentiary, Harrison took the short train ride from McKeesport into the city, then walked from the train station to the prison. For nearly three years, he was the only one who came. On his first visit, he was sitting on a bench grinning when Harry was brought into the room for visitors. Before standing up to greet Harry, he spoke.

"Harry, I was reading Ecclesiastes yesterday, preparing my Sunday sermon, and I thought about you."

"Thank you for coming, Harrison. What made you think of me? I'm almost afraid to ask."

"Well, Ecclesiastes 7:20, as you know, says there is not a just man on Earth who sinneth not. And when I read that, I said to myself, 'We all know that's true–it's right there in the Bible–so why did Harry have to go and prove it so dramatically? Why'd he have to sinneth so much that reporters put him on the front page?'"

The sound of Harry's own laugh sounded foreign to him. He remembered the last time he'd heard it. It was the last night he'd spent with Bess before he caught the train to New York and then the ship bound for Liverpool. She insisted on calling him Mr. Telfer—said he needed to get used to it—and slapped his hand when he responded to Harry or Mr. Brooks.

"I sure gave the reporters something to write about, didn't I? Newspapers from one side of the state to the other, from Pittsburgh to Philadelphia. I got more press for my sins than any preacher ever gets for doing good. Few people outside McKeesport have ever heard of you, but I'm practically famous."

"Infamous, more like it." Both men laughed, but then Harrison stood and put his hand on Harry's arm. "Harry, I've made a vow. I'm going to come see you every week. You made a bad mistake, but you're a good man, and God still has a plan for you. I don't know what it is, but I know He has a plan. When I come, we can talk about whatever you want to talk about. If you want to talk about what you did, we can, but we don't have to. That's up to you."

"I think you understand why I did what I did, Harrison. It was a terrible sin. It's like I was a different man from the one I thought I was. But I had been so sad and lonely for so long, and then suddenly I was happier than I'd ever been. I didn't plan it; it just happened. During those months, I couldn't think of anything but Bess. I didn't think of how wrong it was to take the school's money or how I would ever pay it back. I thought only about Bess and how much I wanted to be with her. I would have robbed a bank at gunpoint to see her. I'm ashamed of what I did, but I understand it. I wish you could meet her, Harrison. She's a wonderful, caring woman. She's nothing like they made her out to be in the papers."

"I'm sure you wouldn't have fallen in love with her if she was like they made her out to be. But you need to let her go, Harry. That's the past. You need to think about the future, about where you're headed, not where you've been."

"I'm not sure she's the past, Harrison. We love each other. We want to be together. Three years is a long time for her to wait, but maybe she will."

The time that Harry served in Western Penitentiary was not hard time compared to what inmates endured in most prisons. Western Pen, known as The Wall because of the barricade forty feet high surrounding it, was the first correctional facility in the world with electric lights, running water, steam heat, and a toilet in every cell. In terms of amenities, it was more comfortable than many homes. And Harry was not required to work. As a result of the Muehlbronner Act, which was adopted by the Pennsylvania legislature with the support of unions opposed to competition from cheap goods made by convicts, inmates were allowed to do little productive work. Harry wished he had been required to work. He could have learned a trade that he could put to use after his release, and he would have had less time to dwell on his sins and all the pain he had caused. He sat for hours alone in his cell, reading the Bible, praying, and waiting for Harrison's next visit. He missed Bess terribly, but he also missed being outside on God's green earth. There were no trees in the prison yard. He did not see or hear a single bird from the day he walked in through the front gate of the prison until the day he walked out.

Harrison kept his vow and came every week. After Harry received the divorce decree prohibiting him from ever seeing his daughters again, Harrison was there. After Harry got the letter from his brothers disowning him and instructing him to stay away from the family when he was released, Harrison was there again. And Harrison was also there after Harry got the worst news of all. It was a letter from Bess, which he sat on his bunk and read—just as he had when he got the letter from her when he was in the Fayette County jail. He took a deep breath and began.

Dearest Harry,

I have dreaded writing you this letter, but I can't put it off any longer. I must tell you that I am engaged to be married. My fiancé is a young partner in the firm named John Finch. He is a fine, honorable young man. I told him all about you and admitted that I still love you. He said that's alright,

that he still loves his wife too. She died two years ago. But he loves me too,
and I love him, and I promised that I would never leave him or betray him.

He has two young children, Harry, a little boy named Robert who's five
and a beautiful daughter who's three. Her name is Elizabeth like mine, but
she goes by Betsy. We will marry in a month, and I will leave the firm and
stay home with the children. They need a mother, and I will get to be their
mother. I never told you this because it wasn't possible for me to have
children, but I've always dreamed of being a mother. I've wanted it more
than anything.

I'm sorry for all the pain I've caused you, Harry. The times we were
together were the happiest times of my life, and yet you are in a prison cell
because of me. I pray that you will find happiness after you are released.
Love always,
Bess

When Harry shared each piece of bad news, including Bess's engagement, Harrison responded with the same message: God has a plan for you. He encouraged Harry to start a Bible study for the other inmates, and Harry did so. He talked to Harry about what he might do after he was released. He convinced Harry that he must not give up, that his life was not over, that he could still be of use to God and His people.

In July 1908, when Harry passed the thirtieth month of his confinement and would be free in only four more, Harrison brought a cake his wife had baked to mark the occasion. Harry rarely showed emotion, but he cried when he saw the cake.

"Harrison Matheny, you saved my life."

"No, God saved your life."

The two men hugged for the second time.

"I have remembered what you said to me in the courtroom at the sentencing. You said that I have much to give. I don't know how much I have, but whatever it is, I want to give it."

"You have a great deal to give. How do you want to give it? Have you decided what you want to do?"

"I have. Even if a school would have me, I don't want to go back to teaching. I want to spread the Word of God. Do you think there's anything I could do to be of service to the church? I don't mean as a preacher with a church of my own. I know that's not possible after what I did, but do you think there's anything?"

"I have no authority, but I will inquire and make my opinion known. But don't count on my being able to carry the day. You have something of a blemish on your record, you know."

Harry looked down at his prison uniform. "I'm well aware."

A week later, the guard again came to Harry's cell and again said he had a visitor. Harry walked down the hall, anxious to see Harrison, hoping for good news. When he walked into the room for visitors, he stopped short. For more than two years, he'd met in this room with no one but Harrison Matheny. Now he had another visitor for the very first time. The man stood, unsmiling, twirling his hat in his hands before him. He did not offer his hand.

"You are Henry F. Brooks, I understand."

"I am."

"And a former school administrator."

"That too. I was the superintendent of the Uniontown schools. I was discharged by the school board, and rightly so."

"I am Reverend Harold P. Chisholm, Mr. Brooks. I am here on behalf of the bishop. He received a request from one of the preachers in the conference, and I'm here to evaluate it. I have some questions."

"I will do my best to answer them."

"I have studied your case file in detail, and I understand the gravity of your offenses. I need to make sure that you understand as well. You have committed grievous sins and brought shame on yourself and pain and hardship to your family. Are you aware of that?"

"Painfully so. It's the greatest regret of my life."

"Have you repented of your sins?"

"Every day, Reverend."

"Do you believe God has forgiven you?"

"I know He has."

"I understand you hold a Bible study here for other prisoners. Tell me about it."

"I started a few months after I got here. Reverend Matheny encouraged me. At first, it was one night a week with just a few inmates. But word spread, and now it's two nights a week with more than a hundred. I meet with half of them on Tuesday and the other half on Thursday. We've finished the Old Testament and two-thirds of the New. I'm going to start meeting with each group two nights a week so we can get to the end of the book of Revelation before my release. We have Sunday services too."

"That's admirable. Do you believe you have brought any of these inmates to God, Mr. Brooks? Have they repented of their sins? Have they found Jesus?"

"I can't take the credit, Reverend, but I believe many of them have found Jesus. Some guards too. They heard about the studies and began coming. Would you like to speak to some of them? Or come to one of our Bible studies? I'm sure it could be arranged."

"I don't think that will be necessary. Tell me this: I understand you seek a position in the church and that you want to spread the Word of God. What sort of position do you want?"

"I will accept any position the church offers me."

"Any? What about location? The bishop questions whether you could be effective in Pennsylvania or the surrounding states. You are somewhat notorious here, as I'm sure you know."

"The location doesn't matter to me, Reverend. If I can serve God, I will go wherever the church sends me."

"That's surprising. I was told that you've lived in Pennsylvania all your life."

"Reverend, this has been hard for me to accept, very hard, but other than my friend Reverend Matheny, there is nothing left for me in Pennsylvania. My wife has divorced me, I am barred from seeing my daughters, my brothers have disowned me, and the woman I love has married another man. I blame none of them–I brought it all on myself–but there is nothing left for me here. If the church has a use for me, I will go wherever I'm sent and make a new life there."

"I understand that you preached in Reverend Matheny's church in McKeesport, and he has vouched for the fact that you're quite a biblical scholar. I have no reason to doubt him, but the bishop wants me to satisfy myself that you are. Please tell me what Ecclesiastes chapter seven verse twenty says and what it means to you."

Harry smiled. "The verse says that no man, not even a just man, is without sin. Since I've been in prison, I've read the verse many times because it gives me great comfort. As you said, I committed grievous sins, sins for which I've paid a terrible but just price. But that verse tells me that I'm not alone, that all men are sinners. And I know that God is with me and that He has forgiven me. I want to serve God, Reverend Chisholm. I want to spread the Gospel. Please give me a chance. I just want a chance."

The reverend smiled for the first time and stuck out his hand. "I appreciate your determination, Mr. Brooks. I will report our conversation to the bishop. The decision will be up to him and the elders. We will let you know."

Harrison came the following day.

"So, how did it go?"

"As well as can be expected, I think. It was obvious that Reverend Chisholm didn't want to be here. Like me before I walked through that gate, I don't think he'd ever been in a prison or seen a man wearing one of these." Harry patted his uniform. "But I believe he knew I was sincere."

"It's up to the bishop and the elders now. I hope they have something for you. I did what I could."

"Thank you, Harrison. I know you're taking a chance standing up for me, asking the church to trust a convict who did what I did."

"I'm not taking a chance, Harry. I have faith in you."

Harrison did not come the next week—it was the very first time he'd missed—but he sent word that he was meeting with the bishop. The following Tuesday, the guard came and got Harry again. Harrison looked glum when Harry walked into the visitors' room.

"I have news. It's bad, but I guess it could be worse. There's a position for you, but it's not much of one."

"Tell me about it."

"It's serving as a missionary in Texas to Mexicans. It's for the rest of your life, and it's without pay." He'd decided to tell Harry all the bad news at once.

"I accept. When do I leave?"

"You have to finish serving your sentence first, remember? But you would be able to leave as soon as you're released."

"Wonderful. I'm ready. It's too cold in Pennsylvania for an old man anyway."

"But how will you live? You have no money."

"God will provide."

"But you don't speak Spanish."

"I will learn."

"Harry, are you sure you want to do this?"

"Harrison, let me tell you something. I may seem like the same man you knew before, but I'm not. Before I wound up in here, I was more intellectual than spiritual in my feelings about God and the Bible. I was more of a theologian than a Christian. I enjoyed our debates about the Bible and thinking about what it meant, and it was a pleasure to put together a good sermon and see the people's faces when I delivered it. I was a good performer, but I was not a righteous man. Even righteous men sin, but they don't do what I did."

"So what changed you?"

"I believe I needed to lose everything before I could change. But after I lost everything, when I was alone in my cell, I asked God to forgive me, truly asked Him, for the very first time. And when I did, I knew for the very first time that I was saved. I felt God's presence and knew that He was with me. I also saw God's presence in the lives of other prisoners, other men who'd lost everything. I saw what He did for them. And I want to spend the rest of my life helping other people find Jesus and be saved by God's mercy. I don't care if it's convicts in Pennsylvania, Mexicans in Texas, or Eskimos in Alaska. Just tell me where, and I'll go."

Harrison grinned and shook his head. "Alright then. I'll report to the bishop that you've accepted, and we'll make arrangements for your travel. Here is one piece of good news about the position. When you get to Texas, you're to report to Dr. Edwin Mouzon at Southwestern University in Georgetown. The bishop assures me that Reverend Mouzon is a fine man, a Godly man, and destined for great things in the Methodist Church. He was born and raised in South Carolina but moved to Texas years ago. He's just been appointed to head the school of divinity at Southwestern and is to oversee your mission."

"And teach me Spanish, I hope. I'll be leaving soon, Harrison. Will I see you again?"

"Of course. I'll still come every week and will see you to the train when the time comes."

"You saved my life, you know."

"God saved your life, Harry. He has a plan for you."

———◦———

On December 1, 1908, the Tuesday after Thanksgiving, the two Methodist preachers named Harry stood together on the platform at Union Station in Pittsburgh. Harry was about to board the train to Texas to start his new life there.

"Write to me when you get settled, Harry. I'll write you a letter before you get there, but I won't know where to send it until I get one from you. Then I'll send you two, the one I've already written and a response to yours."

"I'll do better than that. I'll probably write you at least once before I get there. Maybe more. It's a long way from Pennsylvania to Texas. I hear the people down there have a funny accent."

"Down there, you'll be the one with the funny accent."

"Harrison, I can never repay you for everything you've done for me and everything you've meant to me the last three years. You were always there. You and God. Nobody else. I see God's hand in what you've done for me. The two of you saved my life."

"I am grateful that God brought us together. How long has it been since we met, fifteen years?"

"Sixteen. It's been sixteen years since you showed up in my classroom. I've lost two children since then, betrayed my wife, and become a thief. And yet, through it all, you never gave up on me. I've never had a better friend. Nobody has." The two men hugged each other for the third and final time, and Harry boarded the train.

Two days after Harry's departure, a brief article about his mission in Texas ran in the *Jeannette Dispatch* of Jeannette, Pennsylvania, a town of 8,000 in Westmoreland County. Under the headline "H. F. Brooks to Be a Missionary," the article stated:

> Having served a term in the penitentiary for embezzling school funds in Uniontown, former Superintendent H. F. Brooks will become a missionary. Brooks has been given an opening in Texas. It is understood that he will serve the balance of his life as a missionary without pay. He will work among the many Mexicans living within the borders of the Lone Star State. When the shortage of funds was discovered a few years ago, no one was more surprised than the intimate friends of Brooks. He was regarded as a model school man, possessing an exemplary character. He left this country and sought refuge in England but was brought back and tried and sentenced in Fayette County.

Harry mailed two letters to Harrison when he got off the train in Georgetown, one describing the scenery he was passing through, the other his excitement about his mission in Texas and his gratitude to Harrison for making it possible. He soon received two letters in return. For the next twenty years, until Harrison died in McKeesport, the preachers named Harry maintained a lively correspondence. But after they parted ways at the train station in 1908, the two friends never saw each other again.

CHAPTER THIRTEEN

1908

)

GEORGETOWN

Harry stared up at the imposing façade of the Administration Building that stood at the entrance to Southwestern University. The building reminded him of the courthouse where he was tried and convicted exactly three years earlier. Georgetown and Uniontown were 1400 miles apart, but the two buildings had been constructed within a decade of each other and looked just alike. Both featured gray stone and magnificent windows, three full stories and part of a fourth. Both had huge towers rising from the same side. But the tower here was different from the one in Uniontown. There were no clocks on this one, and no prisoners had ever been hanged from it. Harry said a short prayer asking God to make his experience in this building better than in the other one, opened the front door, and walked in. The receptionist directed him to Dr. Mouzon's office. Seconds after Harry knocked on the door, a smiling man opened it and stuck out his hand.

"Reverend Brooks, I've been expecting you. Come in. Have a seat."

"It's a pleasure to meet you, Dr. Mouzon. I've been looking forward to this day since the day I was offered the position. I'm Harry Brooks, but I don't know that I qualify as a reverend any longer."

"That's not what I hear. I hear you've been a fine reverend at Western Penitentiary. I've heard and read all about you. You've led a fascinating life, Reverend Brooks."

"I suppose that's one word for it. Please call me Harry."

"Only if you call me Edwin."

"That may be a challenge. You're Dr. Mouzon, the head of the school of theology."

"I'm younger than you are, Harry, and you've overcome greater challenges than calling me Edwin. I'm confident that you can overcome this one."

"I'll do my best. I want you to know how grateful I am that you're willing to give me this opportunity. After what I did, I was afraid the church would have no further use for me."

"Let me tell you something I always try to keep in mind, Harry. It's human nature to judge other people, and I believe one of the hardest things for a Christian, and the church too for that matter, is to be as forgiving as God is. All men are sinners, including you and me, but all men who repent are forgiven by God and receive the gift of His grace. I understand that you have repented."

"I have. More times than I can count."

"That means God has forgiven you and given you another chance. And the way I look at it, the church should be willing to give you another chance too. It's a sin for a man to waste his talents, and I believe it's a sin for the church to waste the talents of a man who wants to serve the Lord."

"I don't know how talented I am, but I know I want to spend the rest of my life serving the Lord."

"I've been told that you're very talented, and we plan to use your talents to the fullest. We are glad to have you here."

"I'm very glad to be here. When do I start? What will I do?"

"I'm not sure of all the details–you and I will work them out as we go along–but I've decided on a few things we'll ask you to do. You don't speak Spanish, do you?"

"Not a word. I'd never seen a Mexican until I saw one in the train station here today, and I'm not even sure he was a Mexican."

"I figured there weren't many Spanish speakers in Pennsylvania, so I've arranged a tutor. You will spend three hours with him every morning but Sunday."

"Excellent. What else?"

"The faculty of the theology school meets for lunch every day to discuss our classes and share ideas for the school. We're brand new, and there aren't many of us. I want you to join us and give us the benefit of your thoughts from your career as an educator. I have told them we will have a new man with us who will be serving as a missionary to the Mexicans. I haven't told them about your past."

"Why not?"

"Because I'm afraid some of them might not be as forgiving as God is, and I see nothing to be gained from finding out. In the evenings, we've arranged for you to conduct Bible studies for the Mexicans who work in the fields around town. Your tutor will attend and serve as your interpreter until you're comfortable without him."

"I know that I'm not to be paid. Do you know where I might find a small room in town where I could do some work in my spare time in exchange for room and board?"

"That won't be necessary. You will have a room on campus and will take your meals in the cafeteria when you're not eating with the faculty or with one of our families."

"I told my friend Harrison that God would provide."

"Your friend Reverend Matheny is not shy about you, Harry. He sent me a ten-page letter of introduction. He told me you're a gifted preacher and an exceptional biblical scholar, that the two of you spent many hours debating Scripture. He said he learned more about the Bible from you than from anyone else, even his professors in seminary."

"That's very kind of him. He's a wonderful man, the best friend a man could have. He saved my life when I was in prison. I don't know how much he learned from me, but I learned a great deal from him. He's the reason I'm a Methodist."

"He didn't take credit, but he told me you were a German Baptist when he met you. He said your becoming a Methodist was a sign of your growing wisdom and maturity."

"That sounds just like him."

"I'm glad you mentioned him because that reminds me that there's something else I want you to do, at least if you're willing. This is entirely selfish on my part, but I want to take Reverend Matheny's place in your debates about Scripture. I want to set aside an hour for us to meet every afternoon. I want to learn from you just as he did."

"But you're the dean of the school of theology, Edwin. You have a doctorate. How could you learn anything from me?"

"There is always more to learn about God's Word, Harry. It's a foolish man who thinks he already knows all there is to know. And thank you for calling me Edwin."

Harry smiled, remembering the day Harrison showed up in his class-room in McKeesport. "I guess you're right. I learn new things from Scripture all the time. I'll be honored to meet with you. I'm sure I'll learn more than you will."

"Excellent. Let's meet here at three o'clock. Bring your Bible."

"I'll be here. Is there anything else you have in store for me? I want to do everything I can. My father died before I turned ten and has been gone almost forty years, but I still remember something he used to say. He would work in the fields from dawn to dusk, then come inside, plop down in his chair, and declare that he'd worked from can till can't. That's what I want to do, Edwin. I want to serve the Lord from can till can't."

Edwin smiled. "Alright then, we'll put our heads together and think of more things you can do. Maybe there's a class you'd like to take, and we may need you to teach one. You can start off as a substitute."

"That would be wonderful. I've been a substitute preacher many times. That's what led to my troubles, as you may know. I fell in love with a woman I met when I was preaching at a church in Pittsburgh."

"That reminds me of something else, some advice I want to give you. A lot of men who've had troubles in the East come to Texas to start over. You're not the first, and you won't be the last. But that doesn't change what I said about Christians and forgiveness. Some people might accept you even if they knew where you spent the last three years, but I'm afraid that many wouldn't."

"What are you saying?"

"I'm saying that sometimes you have to choose between the lesser of two evils, between two things that are both wrong. Like the choice of what you tell the people here. You could tell them everything–about the woman from Pittsburgh, the money you took, the time you spent in prison. That may seem like the right thing to do, but I'm afraid it would make you far less useful to God and His people. The other choice is not to tell anybody. Hiding what you did might seem wrong, but what is the lesser of two evils? To keep your past to yourself if it means you'll be more useful to God? Or disclose it, risk rejection by the people you want to serve, and have your talent go to waste?"

"I've wondered about that. Would people trust a man and listen to him if they knew he was a thief and an adulterer?"

"Or even that he had been."

"So you think I should keep it to myself? I'm ashamed of what I did, but I would be ashamed to hide it too. But what good is making a public confession if it keeps me from leading people to God?"

"Exactly. It's up to you, but Reverend Matheny says you're a gifted preacher and have a great deal to offer God's people, and I don't think God would want you to do something that would cause them to reject what you have to offer. You don't have to lie, but you don't have to tell anybody either."

"I'll think about it."

"Good. My next class is about to start. My assistant will take you to your room and show you where to meet us for lunch."

"Thank you, Edwin. I already like it here."

"I like it here too."

CHAPTER FOURTEEN

1909–1910

⋘⚬⚬⋙

CARLTON

Harry got his wish to work. During his time in Georgetown, he worked from can till can't. His days were filled with activities: Spanish lessons, meetings with the faculty, debates with Edwin about Scripture, classes at Southwestern that he took and taught, and Bible studies with the Mexicans who lived in and around town. He was busy from the time he got out of bed in the morning until he got back in at night.

After five months, Harry no longer needed an interpreter to lead the Bible studies, and he began thinking about what he should do in the coming years. By the end of May, he had decided he could be more useful if he left Georgetown to spread God's Word in other parts of Texas. Here, he told Edwin, he was surrounded by Christians who already knew the Bible. He felt like he was preaching to the choir. He wanted to go where the need was, where he could do the most good for the most people. He asked Edwin to allow him to become a circuit rider.

Methodist circuit riders had a long and glorious history in Texas. At great personal risk, they spread God's Word on the frontier, traveling to settlements where there weren't enough people or money for a full-time pastor. Being a circuit rider was a hardship for a family man, and preachers willing to take on the role were hard to come by. But Harry no longer had a family, so he volunteered. He could teach Bible studies in English and Spanish during the week and preach on Sundays.

Edwin was reluctant to grant Harry's request. He pointed out that being a circuit rider was hard and dangerous. In the early years, fewer than half the preachers who rode the circuit lived to see their thirty-fifth birthdays. It was a job for a young man, and Harry was now forty-seven. But Harry had researched the issue before he made the request. Life for circuit riders in Texas was not as difficult as it had been in decades past. They no longer traveled alone on horseback but now rode trains and occasionally a stagecoach. Nor was it as dangerous. The Comanches had been defeated, and the risk of being tortured or murdered for invading their lands was all but gone. A circuit rider still traveled from town to town, stayed with strangers, and depended on their kindness, but Harry did not regard that as a hardship. He welcomed the opportunity to meet new people and believed he could make a much greater difference on the circuit than he ever could on campus or in Georgetown. Edwin smiled as Harry made his pitch, then gave his blessing. "Alright, my friend, go forth and spread the Lord's Word."

Harry received his first circuit assignment the last week of June. He would travel to four communities in four weeks, then return to Georgetown and report to Edwin before beginning his next round of churches. Harry's first stop was in Carlton, a small town surrounded by cotton farms a hundred miles northwest of Georgetown. To get there, he took the two-year-old Stephenville North and South Texas Railway, which had spurred the town's recent growth. He arrived on Thursday, the first of July. Three days later, on Independence Day at the Carlton Methodist Church, Harry would deliver his first Sunday sermon as a Texas circuit rider.

A man met Harry at the church and took him by wagon to a farm just over the Erath County line. A large farmhouse and barn stood in the middle of a cotton field. The plants were already three feet tall. Henry and Mary Land were staunch Methodists and had offered to host Harry during his stay in Carlton. When he arrived, Henry was still in the fields, but Mary heard the wagon pull up and came out to the porch to greet their guest. Once they were inside, she introduced him to their five youngest children, their son Grady and his four little sisters, including twins Hattie and Carrie. Mary, who said they also had four grown daughters, was busy preparing a special dinner to celebrate the ninth birthday of their youngest, Irene. One of their older daughters, Ethel, was expected to arrive at the farm shortly. She lived in Ft. Worth, where she worked for a judge, but was coming home for her baby sister's birthday. She planned to stay for the weekend to celebrate the Fourth of July.

Harry felt at home right away. The girls were charming; they made him miss the daughters he hadn't seen in four years. Like Harry and Rose, the Lands had a daughter named Grace. She was twelve, a year older than his daughter Katherine, who was growing up without him. Irene was thrilled to be the center of attention and to have a special visitor for her birthday. She asked Harry if that was why he had come, and he said of course. When dinner was almost ready, Mary turned to Irene.

"You better go get your daddy. Tell him he's going to miss your birthday dinner if he doesn't come in and wash up."

"Yes, ma'am." She looked up at Harry. "Come with me, Reverend Brooks." She held out her hand, Harry took it, and they walked out into the heat.

They found Henry in the barn working on a plow. Harry stuck out his hand, but the older man hesitated. "I'm awfully dirty, Reverend."

"My hands have been dirty before, Mr. Land. They will wash just fine." They shook hands, Henry showed him around the barn, then they walked back to the house.

Ethel had arrived while they were gone. Irene saw her, squealed, and ran to hug her. Ethel picked her up and spun her in a circle. The two men smiled and waited. When Ethel put her sister down, Henry spoke.

"I would hug you too, but I would ruin your dress. I will have my hug after I clean up. Ethel, this is Reverend Harry Brooks. He is staying with us for a few days and will be preaching at the church on Sunday."

"It's a pleasure to meet you, Miss Land. You have a wonderful family."

"Thank you. We are fortunate to have each other. To have a family like ours is a gift from God."

"Truly it is." Harry forced a smile. He was thinking about the family he had left behind.

Mary directed Harry to sit between Ethel and Irene on one side of the dinner table, and Henry asked their guest to say the blessing. Harry prayed that his time in Carlton and with the Land family would be beneficial, and he thanked God for the food they were about to eat and for the Lands' generosity in hosting him. When he said he was grateful that he could be with the Lands to celebrate Irene's ninth birthday, he thought of Roswell, Grace, and George, none of whom lived to see their ninth birthdays. He also thought of Katherine, who turned nine while he was in prison.

Ethel was a lovely young lady, tall with dark hair and penetrating eyes. She told Harry about going to business school in Tyler and her job with the judge in Ft. Worth. The judge had told her that the fine points of the law sometimes get in the way of logic and common sense, and he made a practice of asking her opinion about the cases before him. He didn't always agree with her, but he always asked and always listened.

Harry by now had mastered the story he'd invented about his past. He grew up as an only child on a farm outside Lexington, Kentucky, and started out working as a traveling salesman and a schoolteacher. But he soon realized his calling in life was to preach the Gospel. After his parents died, he decided to come to Texas, which was growing and had a great need for preachers.

After that, his story changed to the truth. Since his arrival in December, he had studied Scripture with Dr. Mouzon, the head of the new school of theology at Southwestern University. He had also learned Spanish so he could share the Word of God with Mexicans. Just weeks ago, he had volunteered to become a preacher on the circuit. Carlton was his very first assignment.

Mary brought the birthday cake from the kitchen, Irene blew out the candles, and Mary cut the cake into ten pieces. Everyone but Irene ate one. Because it was her birthday, she was permitted to have two. After Mary and Ethel washed and dried the dishes and put them away, Henry announced that he needed to turn in.

"Reverend Brooks, we are delighted to have you with us. I would stay up and visit, but I can't work from can till can't if I'm still lying in the bed when the sun comes up. Grady, I will need you tomorrow. You need to get to bed too."

Harry stood and shook Henry's hand. "Thank you for having me, Mr. Land. It's been a lovely evening. My daddy was also a farmer, and he also said he worked from can till can't. I will work with you tomorrow. A Bible study has been scheduled at the church tomorrow evening, but I have nothing before then."

"Thank you very much. That's very kind. I'll be grateful for the help, but you don't need to keep a farmer's hours while you're here. Stay up as long as you want."

Mary soon told Grace and Irene that it was time for them to get ready for bed. Not long after, the twins followed. Mary and Ethel sat in the living room with Harry, but Mary didn't last long. She didn't want to fall asleep in front of their special guest, she said, and wished them goodnight and headed to the bedroom. Harry and Ethel stayed up talking for another hour. It was easy and comfortable. He was reminded of a conversation from his past and smiled when he realized when it was. It was more than four years ago, the first time he had lunch with Bess.

Harry worked alongside Henry and Grady most of the next day and remembered why he'd vowed never to be a farmer. Henry was used to the hard work. He was more than sixty years old but never needed a break. They took one when Harry needed to. Henry offered to let Harry take the family's carriage into town for the Bible study. When he was cleaned up and ready, Ethel approached him.

"Reverend Brooks, if it's alright with you, I would like to ride into town with you and attend."

Harry looked at Mary, then back at Ethel. "If your mother doesn't need you here, I would enjoy the company. Everyone is welcome to hear the Word of the Lord."

Mary had been watching the two of them and saw how they looked at each other. "That's fine, Reverend, but I could use some peace and quiet around here for a change. Ethel, you may go if you take one of the twins with you."

Carrie was the first to speak up. "May we both go? Please."

"Sure. That will give me more peace and more quiet."

There was no quiet on the rides to and from town. The twins hardly let Harry or Ethel get a word in edgewise. They would have to wait until after the girls went to bed to talk to each other again.

Harry's Bible lesson was from the twenty-third Psalm, written by King David ten centuries before Christ was born. Harry spoke not only of the meaning of the psalm but also of the beauty and cadence of the language. The words would be beautiful even if they weren't God's Words, he said. What we should take from the psalm, Harry submitted, is not that believers will never suffer loss or pain. Of course they will. But the psalm teaches us that God is always with us, that through all the trials and tribulations of life, His goodness and mercy will follow us. And the twenty-third chapter concludes with the best news of all, the best news there has ever been. After this life is over, we will have another one. It will be in the House of the Lord, and it will last forever.

Ethel thought it was the most wonderful Bible lesson she had ever heard. She had thought the judge was the smartest man she had ever known, but now he was reduced to second place. She sat in silence on the ride home while the twins talked to Harry, and she waited to tell him what she thought until after everyone else was in bed. He blushed when she told him.

"Thank you, Miss Land. That's very gratifying. I want my words to be meaningful to those who hear them." He smiled. "And here's a confession. Preachers have egos too."

"Please call me Ethel. Women also have egos, and being called Miss Land makes me feel like an old maid."

Harry laughed out loud.

"What's so funny?"

"Nothing. It's just that another young woman I once knew said the exact same thing. She was not an old maid, and neither are you."

"Thank you for that."

"You're very welcome, Ethel."

The two spent little time together the next day. Harry again worked in the fields with Henry and Grady and again took the carriage into town for a Bible study. But this one would be in Spanish. When Ethel talked to Harry during lunch, she had noticed that Mary was watching them and smiling. Asking to tag along for a Bible lesson when she wouldn't understand a word Harry was saying would surely lead to some pointed questions. But she was still up when Harry returned to the farm, and the two again talked before going to bed, this time for two hours. Ethel wanted to know what it was like to learn a foreign language, if Harry could think in Spanish or if he had to translate everything to English in his brain. He said he wasn't sure and would have to think about it. In English.

The next morning, the Lands needed both the carriage and the wagon to get everyone to town for church. It hadn't taken Harry long to get ready for today's sermon. One benefit of moving to Texas was that he could use old sermons he'd preached in Pennsylvania without worrying that someone would complain that he was repeating himself. It was a benefit he would take with him for the next thirty years as he moved from church to church in Texas, Louisiana, and Mississippi.

For his Independence Day sermon in the small white church in Carlton, Harry had decided to give the same sermon he'd given on his first Sunday in the far grander Calvary Methodist Church in Pittsburgh. He would preach from the book of Job, but this time he would not talk about what the story had meant to him after the loss of three children. Nor would he tell the congregation of the comfort he'd felt when he read the book while lying on his bunk in his prison cell. But even without using his own suffering to make the point, the lesson was still valuable. To keep from getting distracted, Harry reminded himself not to look in Ethel's direction. He started the sermon the same way he had the day he met Bess.

"Genesis is the first book of the Bible. Most of us have known that since we were children. But what most people don't know is that other books were written before Genesis was. Many students of the history of the Bible believe that the first of God's Words that were written down for His people were the Words in the book of Job.

"Like my father and like most of you, Job was a farmer. He was a righteous man, a man who was faithful to God. He was also wealthy and prosperous, but then he lost everything. He lost his wife, his children, his servants, and his livestock. He lost his health. But through it all, he kept his faith in God. And in the end, God restored to him everything that had been taken away.

"Some biblical scholars believe that God gave us his Word in the book of Job 1700 years before Christ was born. That is more than 3,600 years ago. In the thirty-eighth chapter of Job, God identified three constella-tions of stars that can be found in the night sky—Orion, Pleiades, and Arcturus.

"I grew up in the East. Wherever I went, there were trees blocking the sky. I miss the trees and the birds that live in them, but I love the wide-open sky here in Texas. I love the sunrises and the sunsets and the night sky, with nothing blocking the stars from horizon to horizon. The Milky Way paints a bright swath across the heavens. God's creation is magnifi-cent indeed.

"The Lands, my gracious hosts this week, have fed me well and treated me like a king. Last night, after all of them were asleep and the house was quiet, I walked outside, looked up into the night sky, and picked out the three constellations God spoke of in Job, constellations written down in His Word more than a hundred generations ago. If you walk outside tonight, you can see them too. The stars, like the lessons from the book of Job, are eternal."

After the benediction, Ethel walked to the front of the church.

"That was a wonderful sermon, Reverend Brooks. Truly wonderful. Thank you."

"You're welcome, Miss Land."

"It's Ethel, remember?"

"Not in the church, Miss Land."

She smiled. "I'll see you outside, where I can be Ethel."

Mary and the other wives had prepared dinner on the grounds. The congregants huddled in the thin slice of shade on the north side of the church to eat. Harry couldn't remember ever being this hot in Pennsylvania. It was one thing to sweat through a pair of overalls while helping Henry on the farm, but now Harry was sweating through his best suit.

After the meal was over, the five younger children said goodbye to Harry and Ethel and headed back to the farm in the wagon, with Grady holding the reins. The four adults climbed into the carriage for the short ride to the train station. Harry was headed west to Santa Anna, his next stop on the circuit, and Ethel was going north to Ft. Worth to return to work. The judge had a trial starting the next day, and he wanted her there first thing. All four climbed down from the carriage to say goodbye. Henry spoke first.

"Reverend Brooks, I thank you for your hard work on the farm and for your fine sermon today. You have been a blessing to our family and to Carlton. Thank you for coming."

"You're very kind, Mr. Land, but I'm the one who's been blessed this week. I've been living by myself in a room at the university for more than six months. It's been a joy to spend time with a big, happy family."

"I hope you will come back to see us. I don't know if you'll be assigned to come back, but please stay with us if you are."

Mary put her hand on Harry's arm. "Henry, I have a feeling we'll be seeing the reverend again, whether he's assigned to come back or not. I may be wrong, but I think he'll want to come see us again when everybody's home." She smiled at Ethel.

Harry and Ethel talked about the book of Job and his sermon during the half hour before she had to board her train. When he sensed that time was running short, he checked his watch.

"Ethel, I've enjoyed getting to know you. I truly have. May I write you in Ft. Worth? I would like to if it's alright."

"Certainly. May I write you in Georgetown?"

"I would be honored. Here's my pen. Please write your address for me. When I write you, I'll include my address so you can respond."

She looked up from her writing and smiled. "Will I see you again, Reverend Brooks? Or will we just be friends who write letters?"

"Please call me Harry. If I'm going to call you Ethel, you can't very well call me Reverend Brooks. As for seeing me again, you will unless you refuse."

"I won't refuse. Here's my train now. I need to go."

Harry carried her bag to the steps. As she climbed aboard, she looked back over her shoulder and smiled. "I bet you're a good writer, Harry. Write me a good letter. Write me a letter about trees. I grew up in Mississippi, you know. I miss the trees too."

"I will do my best."

On the ride to Santa Anna, Harry wrote two letters, first a long one to Ethel and then a much shorter one to Harrison. It took several tries before he was satisfied with the first one. He wanted to appear both interesting and interested, but he did not want to seem forward. When he thought he'd struck the right balance, he signed and folded the letter, sealed it in an envelope, and put it in his suitcase. He mailed it on Monday morning from Santa Anna. When Ethel opened it three days later in Ft. Worth, this is what she read.

Dear Ethel,

You asked me for a letter about trees. I have never written a letter about trees, but I promised you that I would do my best.

My favorite tree in the East was a white oak that stood by itself on a hill not far from the farm where I grew up. It was two miles away, and I would take a path through the woods to see it. I went as often as I could, at least once in every season of every year. It was a magnificent tree. There was no other tree near it, and it had room to spread its arms wide. It was nearly a hundred feet tall and broader than that. It provided homes for countless birds and squirrels. They raised their families there every spring. Deer ate the acorns that fell from its limbs.

The shaggy white trunk and long limbs of the tree were the same the year round, but the leaves were always changing. They started out tiny and light green in the spring, then became larger and darker as summer came on. When the weather got cold again, they turned crimson and then fell. New leaves appeared when spring came again. In that one tree, I could see the changing of the seasons and the miracle of God's plan.

My love for birds and my love for trees are bound together. When I was a boy, I set out to learn the calls of all the birds that lived in the trees around our farm. I would rise before dawn, go to the woods, lie still, and listen. I would focus on one bird each morning and memorize its call. Then, when the sun came up, I would spot the bird and make a note in my journal. The journal got lost somewhere along the way, but I still know the calls. Perhaps we can go for a walk in the woods someday. You can test me. You'll see.

The doctrine of natural revelation is the belief that the beauty found in nature proves that God exists. For anyone with eyes to see and ears to hear, how could it not be so? How could there be a beautiful sunset without God? Or a magnificent oak tree? Or the song of a bird? How could nature be so magnificent if God had not created it? The answer to me is clear. God created this beautiful world for us. For that, I am grateful to Him.

So, there is your letter about trees. I will look forward to receiving a letter from you. More than that, I will look forward to the time when I can see you again.

Sincerely yours,

Harry

The train was almost to Santa Anna when Harry finished the letter to Ethel, but he had time to dash off a short note to Harrison. He wrote that he'd met a very special woman. She was smart and pretty and a Methodist. As the train pulled into the station, he signed it.

—————◄o►—————

Once a month for the rest of the year, Harry returned to Carlton. He always stayed with the Lands, and Ethel always came home from Ft. Worth to see him and hear him preach. Harry also arranged to preach at a church in Cleburne, only thirty miles from Ft. Worth, so he could take the train into the city to spend time with Ethel. In November, he asked Henry for her hand in marriage. Henry consented, Ethel accepted his proposal, and they arranged to be married at the First Methodist Church in Carlton in February. Edwin Mouzon would conduct the ceremony. On the day of the wedding, February 17, 1910, he and Harry boarded the train in Georgetown dressed in their finest suits.

"This is an exciting day, Harry. Thank you for asking me to perform the ceremony. It's an honor."

"It's an honor for Ethel and me to have you marry us, Edwin. I don't think I've ever told you this but, come tomorrow, it will be exactly twenty-four years since I married Rose. It seems like a lifetime. For that matter, it seems like a lifetime since I left Pennsylvania, but it's been just over a year."

"I would say things have gone better for you here than they did there."

"That's not saying much."

"What does Ethel know, Harry? Does she know you were in prison?"

"No."

"What about your children? Does she know about them?"

"No. I haven't mentioned them."

"Does she even know you were married?"

"Not that either. I hated not to tell her, but I figured I should tell everybody the same story. If I told Ethel the truth, she might tell other people. Then everyone would find out, and I didn't want that to happen for the reasons we've discussed. Or she'd have to lie and tell the same story I've been telling since I got to Texas, and I didn't want her to have to do that either."

"So she thinks you grew up in Kentucky?"

"That's right."

"And that you were an only child?"

"That too. And she doesn't know how old I am either. She thinks I'm thirty-four."

"What? You told her you were thirty-four?"

"I actually said thirty-three. I've had a birthday since then."

"What on earth? I said it might be bad if people found out what you did, but I didn't tell you to lie about your age."

"I know, and I didn't mean to. It just happened."

"How does something like that just happen, Harry?"

"We were at dinner in Ft. Worth, and out of the blue, she told me she was twenty-three and asked me how old I was. I thought she was older than that. Maybe I just hoped she was. Anyway, my first thought was that she wouldn't see me again if she knew how old I was. I had to say something, so I said thirty-three."

"You're what? Forty-five?"

"Forty-eight."

"That means you're more than twice as old as the woman you're marrying."

"Not more than twice. At least not since last month. She turned twenty-four on the eighteenth. Her birthday is less than three weeks after mine."

"So exactly twice as old then."

"I know it was wrong, but once I'd said it, I couldn't figure out how to take it back. At least not without losing her."

"You need to tell her, Harry. This isn't like hiding what you did in Pennsylvania. That's over and done with. This is hiding your age from the woman who's planning to spend the rest of her life with you, and not by just a year or two either."

"I know I should tell her. You think I should tell her before the wedding or after?"

"I understand your predicament, but I think she has the right to know the man she's marrying is twice her age and fourteen years older than she thinks he is."

Harry stared out the window but didn't respond. After several minutes, he took a deep breath and turned toward Edwin. "Here's what's wrong with me, Edwin, at least one of the things. I talk myself into believing that my sins aren't nearly as bad as they are. I convinced myself it wasn't so bad to see another woman because Rose was depressed and withdrawn and I was lonely. I convinced myself it wasn't so bad to take the school's money because I was just borrowing it and would pay it back. And then I convinced myself that not telling Ethel the truth about my age was not so bad either."

"She might agree that it's not, Harry, but then again, she might not."

Harry stared out the window again. Ethel would be the first of Henry and Mary's nine children to marry. The whole family would be waiting for them at the church, even the three sisters he had still not met. If Harry told Ethel the truth when they got to the church, she might call off the whole thing. But if he said nothing, she wouldn't know she was marrying an old man until it was too late. He and Edwin sat in silence for the rest of the trip. The only sound came from the wheels on the tracks. It reminded Harry of his trip with Mart Kiefer from New York to Uniontown more than four years before.

Ethel looked radiant in her floor-length wedding dress. Hattie and Carrie had been in charge of meals at the farm the last two weeks to give Mary time to make the dress and add beads to the neckline and sleeves. Henry shook Harry's hand, then Edwin's. Mary hugged them both. Florence, Katherine, and Josephine, the three sisters who had come home for the wedding, stood in line to meet the handsome preacher who was joining the family.

When Henry said they should get started, Harry leaned over to Ethel and asked to speak to her, and they walked out the front door of the church. Everyone inside waited and wondered. Harry's thoughts were racing. What was the lesser of two evils now? He held Ethel's hands and looked at her.

"Before we get married, there's something I need to tell you. I want you to know that I love you very much. You've made me very happy." He hesitated, looked away, then looked back at her and smiled. "Now let's go inside and get married."

Edwin had to leave right after the ceremony to get back to the station and catch the late train. Harry walked him out and thanked him again.

"You didn't tell her, did you?"

"I was going to, but I just couldn't. I couldn't do it to her, and I couldn't do it to her family."

"Or to yourself."

"You're right. I couldn't do it to myself either. But telling her right before the wedding didn't seem right. It seemed cruel."

"It would have been much better to tell her before now, that's for sure. But you need to tell her. It's fourteen years, Harry."

"I know. I will. I'll find the right time."

CHAPTER FIFTEEN

1911–1925

(@ @)

TEXAS, LOUISIANA, MISSISSIPPI

The city of Amarillo could not have existed before 1875 because the Texas Panhandle was in the center of Comancheria, the huge territory in the Southwest that was dominated by the Comanche Indians. At its peak, the tribe had no more than 20,000 members, but Comancheria covered an expanse of more than 250,000 square miles and parts of what are now five states, not only Texas but also Oklahoma, Kansas, Colorado, and New Mexico. The Comanches were the fiercest of the Plains tribes and did not permit white settlers on their lands. Because of Comanche attacks, the western edge of the frontier in Texas had receded to the east in the middle of the nineteenth century as settlers retreated toward Louisiana seeking safety. After the Civil War, the government decided to put a stop to the attacks. After a lengthy military campaign led by Colonel Ranald Mackenzie, the last band of the Comanches finally surrendered at Fort Sill, Oklahoma in 1875. The enormous region that had been off-limits was now open for settlement, development, and business.

Amarillo, which is Spanish for yellow and was likely named for the color of the soil in the creek that ran nearby, was established in 1887 at the intersection of two new railroads that crisscrossed the Panhandle. The Atchison, Topeka & Santa Fe ran from northeast to southwest, the Fort Worth & Denver City from southeast to northwest. Promoters recognized that the railroad crossing was an ideal location for a new cattle market and bought 600 acres from the State of Texas for two dollars an acre. In the space of only a few years, Amarillo became the largest cattle shipping market in the entire world. Fifty thousand head of cattle often stood on the outskirts of town waiting to be loaded onto railroad cars. The discovery of natural gas in 1918 and oil two years later contributed to the growth of the economy. The town's population grew by a factor of more than thirty from 1890 to 1920, from fewer than 500 residents to more than 15,000.

Harry gave up riding the circuit not long after he and Ethel married, but in the years that followed, the couple didn't live in any one place for long. The practice of the Methodist Church was to transfer preachers often, and Harry was chosen to serve as the minister of Methodist churches in six different towns in Texas during the first decade of their marriage.

Harry had married Rose a month before her twenty-fourth birthday and Ethel a month after hers. The weddings to the two twenty-four-year-olds were twenty-four years apart. Like Harry and Rose nearly a quarter-century earlier, he and Ethel started a family immediately. Their daughter Elizabeth was born on February 8, 1911, nine days before their first anniversary. Her birthplace was Santa Anna, where Harry had preached on the circuit the week after he met Ethel. The Methodist church there was his first to serve as a full-time pastor.

Harry was then transferred to Cleburne, where their second child and only son, Edwin Mouzon Brooks, was born in November 1912. By then, the man for whom the baby was named was serving as the dean of the Perkins School of Theology at Southern Methodist University in Dallas. Edwin had also been elected bishop of the Methodist Episcopal Church, South, a position he held until his death twenty-five years later.

Harry next became the pastor at Mulkey Memorial Church in Ft. Worth. Then the family moved to Mineral Wells, fifty miles west of Ft.

Worth, where Harry served as the minister of the First Methodist Church. Their third child was born there in August 1918. They named her Henrie Jannette, but everyone called her Danny.

At the end of 1918, Harry was transferred to the growing Northwest Texas Conference and assigned to the Methodist church in Vernon, just south of the Oklahoma border and the midway point between Ft. Worth and Amarillo. Less than two years later, Harry was transferred yet again, this time to the First Methodist Church in Amarillo. By New Year's Day 1921, the day Harry turned fifty-nine, Ethel was expecting their fourth child. She was due in March.

Then came the surprise. Ethel went into labor on March 16. After several hours, the doctor walked out of the bedroom holding up two fingers. There was not only a fourth child but a fifth one as well. They were Harry's ninth and tenth. He and Ethel named the twins Margaret and Marjory. They were running low on names by then and didn't bother to give either twin a middle name.

In the past ten years, Ethel had packed up their belongings and moved five times and given birth to five children in four towns. And now she was 400 miles from her family and in her least favorite of town of all. Her practice was to suffer in silence, but she made an exception one night after she and Harry were in bed.

"I don't like it here, Harry."

"It's not my favorite place either, but we have to go where the church sends us."

"I know, but it's so dry and dusty. The wind blows all the time. It smells like a cow pasture."

"But there are good people here, and they need a preacher. We won't be here long. We never are."

"You remember when you wrote me the letter about your favorite tree?"

"Of course. The magnificent white oak. I miss that tree."

"We haven't seen a tree like that since you wrote the letter, Harry. We were going to walk in the woods, remember? I was going to test you on bird calls. We can't do that here. I miss spending time in the woods."

"Me too."

"Isn't there some way we can move? Maybe to East Texas? Or back to Mississippi? It's full of trees."

"I would have to change conferences again to do that."

"Can you try? I don't want us to live the rest of our lives in West Texas. I want the children to grow up with trees. I climbed trees when I was young. I want them to climb trees too."

"I'll ask, but we'll have to do what the church says."

Harry did ask, his request was granted, and in 1922 he became the pastor of the First Methodist Church in Shreveport, Louisiana. Nearly two years after that, he was transferred to Capitol Street Methodist Church in Jackson, Mississippi. Ethel, who was thirty-seven, had returned to her home state for the first time since leaving it more than twenty years before. Harry, who was sixty-one but claimed to be forty-seven, had never set foot in Mississippi.

All the churches Harry pastored had grown significantly under his leadership, but the church on Capitol Street exceeded all expectations. In Harry's first two years there, 500 new members joined, bringing the total membership to nearly 2300. The church had two choirs, an eighteen-piece orchestra, and a splendid Boy Scout troop. The congregation taxed the capacity of the church at every service, and Sunday School was so popular that classes had to meet in the parsonage. After reviewing the state of the church, the author of an article in the April 17, 1925, issue of the *Christian Advocate* concluded that "the activities of the Church are a veritable beehive of religious industries."

———◄○►———

Edwin Mouzon and his wife Mary also left Texas and returned to the East in the early 1920s. They lived in Nashville during Harry and Ethel's years in Jackson. In addition to his duties as bishop, Edwin spoke frequently on issues of interest to the church, served on the board of trustees of Nashville's Scarritt College, and headed a group seeking the reunification of the Methodist Episcopal Church and the Methodist Episcopal Church, South, which had split over the issue of slavery before the Civil War. He was a very busy man, and Harry rarely heard from him, but the handwriting on the envelope that arrived in Jackson in June 1925 was unmistakable. Harry opened it and read the letter inside.

Dear Harry,

I miss our debates and good times together. I trust that you and Ethel and your fine family are doing well. It's hard to believe it's been fifteen years since the two of you were married. I remember the day well.

My duties keep me busy, but I still manage to keep up with you, and it brings me great joy to see your passion for serving God and His people. I understand that you are now a Doctor of Divinity. Congratulations, but don't expect me to call you Dr. Brooks the next time I see you. You're Harry, I'm Edwin, and so it will always be. I expect that you knew more about Scripture than your instructors at Asbury, just as you know more than I do.

Now that I've buttered you up, I have a request. As you may know, the Congress of the American Prison Association will be held in Jackson in November. The church has been offered the opportunity to appoint a delegate to participate in the Congress, and I would like to appoint you. With your background, I know you would offer a unique perspective on how prisons can be improved to help achieve the goal of rehabilitating the incarcerated so that they can return to society as responsible, law-abiding citizens, preferably Christian citizens.

Please let me know if you will take on this important role for the church. Capitol Street Church is growing by leaps and bounds, as I knew it would with you in the pulpit, and I'm certain that your obligations to the church take nearly all your time. But if you can make room in your busy

schedule to grant my request, I believe you will make an invaluable contribution to this worthy cause.

Please let me know at your earliest convenience.
Your friend in Christ,
Edwin

P.S. If you still haven't told her, it's not too late.

Harry winced when he read the last line. He was now sixty-three years
old, but Ethel, their children, and the rest of the world thought he was
forty-nine. What would happen if he told Ethel? What if she told others?
What effect would it have on the faith of the 2300 members of his church
if they found out their minister was a liar? And what if they found out he
was also an adulterer and a thief, or at least that he had been? What was
the lesser of two evils?

The next day, Harry sent Edwin a long letter in which he reported on
all the good news at Capitol Street Church, thanked Edwin for his fine
work as bishop and on the reunification project, and said that he would
be honored to serve as a delegate to the Congress of the American Prison
Association. Harry did not believe in coincidences, he wrote, and he saw
God's hand in placing him and the Congress of the prison organization in
the same place at the same time. He did not mention Ethel and did not
confess that he had still not told her.

Harry was asked to give the invocation when the Congress opened
on Saturday, November 7. He prayed that the week would be a success
and that God would bless the efforts of the delegates and their leaders.
He asked for God's help in achieving the goal of rehabilitation for those
who have committed crimes. Rehabilitation is possible for all men who
are behind bars, just as redemption is possible for all Christians who have
fallen short. No man is without sin, but no man is beyond salvation either.
Harry asked God to give the Congress the wisdom to adopt principles and
policies that would save as many men as possible.

Harry was tempted to cite his time in prison to advocate for his views during the Congress because he knew how effective the use of personal experience could be. It was why he had used the deaths of his three children in the sermon he preached from the book of Job on his first Sunday at Calvary Methodist Church. But he wouldn't cite his experience at Western Pen this week. If he were ever going to disclose the troubles from his past, Ethel would have to be the first to know. But he would not be reluctant to express his opinions about prisons to the other delegates. That was not his way. He had three points to make, and he made them over and over during the week-long Congress.

The first was the value of work and the evil of idleness. As the Bible says in the sixteenth chapter of Proverbs, idle hands are the devil's workshop. Keeping prisoners locked in their cells might make the task of prison officials and guards easier, but it makes the goal of rehabilitation much harder to achieve. Prisoners should be required to work. They should learn a trade and develop a work ethic. It shouldn't be slave labor. They should be paid a fair wage from the fruits of their labors. They should be able to use the money to support their families or save it for the day when they will be released. Men who are released from prison with neither money nor skills are likely to return to a life of crime. Those who've learned a trade and have a few dollars to help them get started are much more likely to stay on the right side of the law.

Harry's second point was the need for religious instruction and worship. Millions of men, both in prison and out, have been saved by turning to God. There should be Bible studies and Sunday services conducted by trained pastors committed to helping the prisoners. Hymns should be included. "I once was lost but now am found, was blind but now I see." How many men who've lost their way have found comfort in these words? Many of the men in America's prisons are lost. They are blind but, with God's grace, they can see.

Harry's third point was that prisoners should get plenty of time in the prison yard and plenty of sunshine. If at all possible, there should be trees in prison yards. And prison cells should have views of the outside with trees the inmates can see. With trees come birds and the songs they sing. Lying on a bunk in a prison cell all day, day after day, separated from God's green earth, will destroy a man's soul. But the sights and sounds of nature are a balm for the soul. God wants us to save souls, and there's a practical benefit to society that comes from doing so. A man whose soul has been saved will not wind up back in prison. The people's taxes won't have to be spent a second time to provide him room and board and guard him.

Two corrections experts, a former warden and an accountant who had studied prison finances, questioned the basis for Harry's beliefs. He obviously had strong feelings, and he expressed them eloquently, but he was a preacher. What did he know about prison life and running a prison? Had he ever been inside a prison? Had he ever seen a prison with trees? Or even heard of one?

Harry had thought this might happen and was prepared for it. He said he had a friend named Telfer back in Kentucky who was down on his luck, robbed a store, and got caught and sent away to the state pen. When he returned to his hometown after his three-year sentence, his biggest complaints were that he wasn't able to work and was stuck in his cell with no sunlight and no contact with nature. The only thing that saved him, he said, was the Bible study led by another prisoner. Harry was almost always ashamed when he told a lie, but he wasn't ashamed of this one.

The Congress ended on November 14. Whether Harry's contribution during the week would make a difference was now in God's hands, but he had said his piece. As the last item of business before the benediction, the president of the Association announced the date and location of next year's Congress. It would be held the third week of October in Pittsburgh. When Harry heard the news, he wondered if he should attend. He could give the other delegates a tour of Western Pen and look up his old friends there, men who were still incarcerated and guards who had come to his Bible studies. He decided against it.

CHAPTER SIXTEEN

APRIL 30–MAY 1, 1937

《❧ ❧》

TUPELO

Harry decided to break the news to Ethel about Triss after they were in bed on Friday night.

"There's something I need to tell you. It's something I should have told you a long time ago."

She rolled over on her side and faced him. "What is it?"

He lay on his back, staring at the ceiling. "I was married before and had a child. It was a long time ago, long before I met you."

Ethel stiffened. She propped herself up on an elbow. "What? You had a wife and a child?" She slapped him hard on the arm. He looked over at her briefly, then returned his gaze to the ceiling. She had never struck him before.

"I was married less than a year. My ex-wife is dead. I found out this morning. My daughter's in Tupelo. She came looking for me."

"She's here now? Where? When were you married?"

"She's staying at the Hotel Tupelo. The girl and I were young. I'd just turned eighteen. She was sixteen. We thought we were in love and went to the justice of the peace."

"Who was this girl? How could you hide this from me?"

"Her name was Sara Johnson. I should have told you, but it was something I tried to put behind me. I didn't want to think about it, much less talk about it."

"But I'm your wife. Don't you think I deserved to know that I'm not your first wife?"

"You did, and I should have told you. I'm sorry. It was just something I never wanted to think about again."

"Why not? What happened?"

"My parents were already dead. I was too young to get married, and Sara was even younger. Not long after the wedding, she decided she wanted to move back home and live with her parents. She didn't want to be with me anymore. She moved home and filed for divorce a week later. She didn't know it yet, but by then, she was pregnant. By the time the baby was born, we were no longer married."

"Did you ever see the baby?"

"I would go by their farm to see her. Sara named her Tressa for her grandmother and called her Triss. But Sara didn't want me around, and neither did her parents. Then one day I went, and they were gone. The furniture too. They'd sold the farm and all the equipment."

"Where'd they go?"

"I found out this morning that they went to Pennsylvania, but I didn't know then. I asked everybody in town. Nobody knew. I'm sure they didn't want me to find out."

"So you gave up?"

"I had no idea where to look or what to do."

"I don't think I could ever give up. I can't believe you've never told me any of this. It wouldn't have mattered. I still would have married you. It's not like you committed some crime."

Harry rubbed his eyes. "I know, but I never wanted to think about it again. I wanted to pretend it never happened."

"But now your daughter's here. How old is she, Harry?"

"I was nineteen when she was born, so that would make her forty-two."

"Goodness. I'm only nine years older than she is."

"I guess that's right." The difference in age was actually eleven months.

"How long has she been here?"

"She showed up at the parsonage yesterday. Margaret answered the door, and Triss introduced herself and said she was looking for her father. I talked to her for a few minutes on the porch and then met her for breakfast at the Hotel Tupelo today. I told Margaret not to say anything to anybody until I sorted things out. I haven't told her anything else."

"So did she always know you were her father? How did she find you?"

"The Johnsons moved to McKeesport, outside Pittsburgh. Triss says she didn't know she was born in Kentucky or that I was her father until two years ago. Sara remarried when Triss was still little. Sara and her new husband didn't tell Triss he wasn't her real father."

"How'd she find out?"

"Triss's stepfather died five years ago. A few years later, Sara got sick. When the doctor told her she might not make it, she sent for Triss and told her the whole story and where her birth certificate was hidden. Triss said her mother felt bad about all of it–lying and leaving Kentucky without a word. After Sara died, Triss decided she wanted to find me."

"I can't believe you've never told me a word of this."

"I know. I should have. It was wrong. I'm sorry."

"So that's how she found out you were her father, but how did she find out you were in Tupelo?"

"Her husband's a man named Soles. He's an executive at Talon, the company that makes zippers. After her mother died, Triss asked him to hire a private detective. The man didn't have much to go on and thought it was a long shot, but then he found a newspaper article about the president's visit to Tupelo. My name was mentioned, and it matched the name on Triss's birth certificate."

"I don't know what to think about all this, Harry. What does she want? What do you want?"

"I'm not sure about her. Definitely not money. Her husband's very successful. She wouldn't even let me pay for breakfast. But I know what I want. I want to recognize and treat her as my daughter. She is my daughter, and she's Edwin and the girls' sister. She's your step-daughter too."

"She's old to be their sister. How much older than the twins?"

"Let's see. She was born in '95, they were born in '21, so twenty-six years."

"I can't believe you have a daughter who's almost my age. You started having children when you were young and kept having them until you were old."

Harry closed his eyes again. Ethel had no idea how old. "This is what I'd like to do if it's alright with you. Tomorrow's Saturday. I'd like to tell Danny and the twins at breakfast. Then I'll need to call Elizabeth and Edwin. If everything goes well, I'd like to invite Triss to dinner tomorrow night."

"I don't know, Harry. I don't know what to think, and I sure don't know what the girls will think. You know Danny and her temper. She's eighteen years old, and you're about to tell her that I'm not your first wife and she has a sister you've never told her about."

"I'm sure she'll be angry. Probably the twins too. They should be. All of you should, you most of all. It's just that it happened so long ago. I haven't seen Triss in more than forty years. I was sure I'd never see her again, and I didn't see any reason to tell you."

"Well, you were wrong."

"I know, but what's done is done, and none of this is Triss's fault. She was just a baby."

"I know it's not her fault. You can tell the girls at breakfast. They need to know. But let's just take it one step at a time from there."

"Thank you."

Ethel rolled over with her back to him and pulled the quilt up. "I can't believe you've never told me, Harry. I can't believe it. I know it happened a long time ago, but it's wrong. You had another wife, and you never told me." She lay still, her mind racing, then rolled back over and faced him. "What else have you not told me? Is there anything else? If there is, you need to tell me now."

Harry kept his eyes fixed on the ceiling. "No. Nothing else."

She rolled away from him again. "I sure hope not."

"I'm sorry, truly sorry. Can you forgive me?"

Seconds passed, and Harry tried again. "Can you?"

She reached up and turned off the lamp. "I'm going to sleep now."

———◄○►———

In the morning, Ethel didn't speak to Harry or look at him. She cooked breakfast in silence while he sipped his coffee and read the *Daily Journal*. When the girls came to the table, they could see that something was wrong, but they didn't ask. When Harry was finished eating, he put his napkin on his plate and cleared his throat.

"There's something I need to tell the three of you. It's something I should have told you and your mother a long time ago. Long before she and I met, when I was still in Kentucky, I got married. I was eighteen. I was the same age you are now, Danny."

The girls all looked at Ethel. She was looking down, a blank look on her face. Harry continued.

"My wife was only sixteen, and before long she decided she didn't want to be married. She moved back in with her parents and filed for divorce, but then she found out she was expecting. Not long after the baby was born, she and her parents moved away and took the baby with them. I didn't know where they went and had no way to find them." Harry paused and took a breath. The girls were looking at him, then at Ethel, then back at him. "I was sure I would never see the baby again, but now she's found me. Margaret, that was the woman who came on Thursday. I had no idea what had become of her, or even if she was still alive."

Danny was the first to speak, as Harry expected. She was the oldest of the three and the most direct. She was not sympathetic, as he also expected.

"So this woman's our half-sister. You were married before, we have a sister, and you never told us."

"I'm sorry. I should have told you, but it happened so long ago. I was sure I would never see her again."

"And you never told Mama you were married before either. Mama, did he ever tell you?"

Ethel answered without raising her eyes. "Not before last night."

"I should have told her. I've apologized. I was your age. I was a teen-ager."

Marjory interjected. "What's her name? Tell us about her."

"Her name is Tressa Soles. She goes by Triss. She's lived nearly all her life in Pennsylvania. She's married and has two children, a girl and a boy. They're both right at your age. I think her daughter's a year older and her son's a year younger."

Then it was Margaret's turn. "If she's our sister, that makes them our niece and nephew. That means Marjory and I have a niece who's older than we are."

Harry was relieved to talk about Triss's children. "That's right. Her name is Dottie. His is John."

Danny spoke again. "So what do we do now? We have this sister in town we didn't know we had. What do we do?"

"That will be up to you and your mother. She's my daughter, and I plan to treat her as my daughter. She's your sister, and I would like for you to get to know her, but that's up to you. She doesn't have any other broth-ers or sisters. Other than her children, we're her only blood kin."

Margaret leaned across the table and put her hand on Ethel's arm. "Mama, what do you think?"

Ethel looked up at the girls but avoided looking at Harry. "I'm not sure what I think. Your father should have told me a long time ago. He should have told y'all too. I think he knows that. To find out that he had another wife he never told me about was quite a shock. And a child. But not telling me is his fault, not hers, and what he did doesn't change the fact that she's his daughter and your sister. So I'm prepared to welcome her into our home and treat her as I would any other member of the family."

Harry was even more relieved. "Thank you, Ethel, that's very kind. Girls, what do you say?"

Marjory had more questions. "How old is she, Daddy? When did you last see her? What was it like to see her again?"

"She's forty-two. She was three months old the last time I saw her. As for what it was like to see her again, it seems like a miracle. Her mother took her away, and I had no idea where. I never in a million years thought I would ever see her again. If your mother agrees, I would like to invite her to join us here for dinner tonight. Is that alright with you girls?" The twins nodded, but Danny said she needed to go to the high school to continue preparing for graduation.

Ethel spoke up. "Danny, you've been at that school every night this week. I think they can do without you one night so you can meet your sister."

Harry reached over, patted Ethel's arm, then stood. "Thank you. Thank all of you. I'm sorry for not telling you sooner. I'm going to call Edwin and Elizabeth and tell them, and I need to finish preparing tomorrow's sermon. Then I'm going to walk down to the Hotel Tupelo and have lunch with Triss and invite her to dinner."

The calls went fine. Elizabeth's toddler, Andy, was into everything. She was shocked but had neither the time nor the energy to interrogate Harry. Edwin was neither curious nor angry. He understood Harry's reason for not telling anyone before now and said he probably would have done the same thing.

After reviewing the notes for his sermon and making a few changes, Harry prepared another document. It was a list of the things he'd told Ethel that Triss would need to know before she came to dinner. Before leaving, he stopped by the kitchen and apologized to Ethel again. She was polishing the silver and didn't look up.

———◄○►———

It was the first day of May, and the weather was perfect. Harry walked east on the sidewalk along Main Street, tipping his fedora and speaking to everyone he passed. He detected the scent of lemon in the air from magnolia blossoms. It was the first time this year Harry had noticed it. Most of the trees this far east of the parsonage had survived the tornado. Last night and this morning had gone better than he'd expected and much better than he deserved. Ethel had every right to be angry, but they had a stable marriage. If nothing else came to light, she would get beyond this. She was a good woman.

Triss was not in her usual spot in the Blue Room but instead was waiting outside on the sidewalk. "Can we walk up to the drugstore? It's a beautiful day, and I want another one of those egg salad sandwiches."

"It is a beautiful day. We can do that as long as you let me pay this time."

"So how did it go? I've been worried."

"Better than I deserved. You are cordially invited to join us for dinner tonight at the parsonage. Ethel said she will treat you like any other member of the family."

"That's very kind of her. She's not angry?"

"She is, but not at you and not as much as I would be."

"Any surprises?"

"Not really. I have a list of things we need to go over at lunch. There are a few things I told Ethel last night that you and I haven't discussed."

"What about your daughters?"

"Danny was mad, which I expected, but she won't stay mad if Ethel doesn't. And they all realize that none of this is your fault. I think they're looking forward to meeting their sister with the funny accent who's more than twice their age."

"I would be more than twice their age even if I was really forty-two."

TKE had high ceilings and tile floors. The soda counter was in the back along the west wall. Triss didn't sit at the counter this time. Instead, she and Harry chose one of the tables. After they ordered, Harry pulled out the list and handed it to her. She studied it.

"'Didn't know born in Kentucky'? What does that mean?"

"You didn't know you were born in Kentucky until Sara told you two years ago."

Triss covered her mouth to keep from laughing. "I didn't know I was born in Kentucky until yesterday. It says 'stepfather as father.' What's that about?"

"Sara remarried when you were still a baby. She and her husband didn't tell you he wasn't your real father. You grew up thinking he was."

"How did I find out the truth? The truth–it's funny to call it that."

"Sara admitted it on her deathbed two years ago and told you where your birth certificate was hidden. She felt bad about lying to you and not telling me where they went."

A man who had been seated at the counter approached their table. It was the banker who had spoken to Triss the day before.

"Ma'am, it appears that my favorite lunch spot has already become your favorite as well. It's nice to see you again. Is Dr. Brooks one of the relatives you've come to Tupelo to see? It's nice to see you too, Reverend."

Before Triss could speak, Harry stood up and extended his hand. "Since I know both of you and you don't know each other, let me introduce you. Triss, this is Cliff Eason. He's an officer at the People's Bank on Main Street and a devoted member of our church. He and his family can be found in the same pew every Sunday morning. Cliff, this is Triss Soles of McKeesport, Pennsylvania. Her husband is an executive at Talon, the company that makes zippers."

Cliff shook Triss's hand, and Harry continued. "Cliff, Triss is my daughter."

Cliff's smile disappeared as he looked from Triss to Harry. "Your daughter?"

"Yes, my daughter. It's a long story. Could you please do me a favor and not tell anyone before tomorrow? I want the members of the church to find out about Triss from me. I plan to introduce her to the congregation at the eleven o'clock service."

"Introduce me to the congregation? That's news to me."

"You're my daughter. The members of my church need to know about you. They need to meet you."

"I'm not sure I'm ready for an introduction. We'll need to talk about that."

Cliff decided it was time to leave them alone to sort things out. "Mrs. Soles, it's a pleasure to meet you. I apologize for acting startled."

"No apology is necessary, Mr. Eason. It would have been odd if you weren't startled."

"Thank you. And Reverend, I will not mention this to anyone before church tomorrow. The Easons will be in our regular pew. Mrs. Soles, your father is a fine preacher and a fine man. I don't know what Tupelo would have done without him after the tornado. I hope you will join us for the service. If he introduces you, I expect the congregation will be startled too, but I'm sure they will make you feel welcome."

"Thank you, Mr. Eason. It's nice to meet you."

"I appreciate your keeping this under wraps, Cliff. I'll see you tomorrow. I hope Triss and I will both see you."

Cliff left, Harry sat back down, and he and Triss went over the remaining items on his list.

CHAPTER SEVENTEEN

NOVEMBER 18, 1934

◖◗

TUPELO

In the decade after his time at Capitol Street Methodist in Jackson, Harry served as the pastor of three more Methodist churches in Mississippi, all leading churches in the north half of the state. By 1933, the year of his third transfer, Harry and Ethel had been married twenty-three years and lived in eleven cities in three states, moving to a new church nearly every other year. It's a wonder they bothered to unpack. Their children learned how to make new friends in a hurry and grew accustomed to leaving them behind.

Harry's first church after Capitol Street Methodist was in Clarksdale, a farm town in the fertile Mississippi Delta no more than fifteen miles from the nearest bend in the Mississippi River. The city was the birthplace of the Delta Blues, which were put on records for the first time while the Brooks family lived there. After several years, they moved across the state to Starkville, the home of Mississippi State University, the state's first land-grant college. Three years later, Harry was transferred again, this time to Tupelo. In all three cities, he served as the senior minister of the First Methodist Church. At the time, the full name of the Methodist Church in the South was still the Methodist Episcopal Church, South.

The early 1920s in America were a healthy, peaceful respite from the carnage of the Great War and the Spanish Flu, but Harry's first ten years in North Mississippi were hard for both the state and the country. The time began with a devastating flood, was followed by the Great Depression, and ended with a devastating tornado.

Harry, Ethel, and their children arrived in Clarksdale the autumn before the Great Flood that came in the spring of 1927. The swollen Mississippi broke levees on both sides of the river in April and inundated 27,000 square miles, an area more than half as large as the entire State of Mississippi. Sections of Mississippi, Arkansas, and Louisiana were flooded, more than 700,000 were left homeless, and an estimated 500 drowned, perhaps far more. But the levees along the river above Clarksdale held, and the town was not damaged. Harry led a service at the Methodist church giving thanks that the town had been spared and encouraging residents to be generous to those downriver who had not been as fortunate. He encouraged other ministers in town to deliver the same message.

Two and a half years later, the stock market crashed, losing a fourth of its value in just one week. The slide continued, and the Great Depression followed. Millions of Americans were thrown out of work. Families were hungry and desperate. The nation's unemployment rate peaked at twenty-five percent in 1933, the year the Brooks family moved to Tupelo.

With the country reeling, America was ready for a change. In the 1932 election, Democrat Franklin Roosevelt defeated Republican incumbent Herbert Hoover in a landslide, winning the popular vote by nearly eighteen percent and the electoral college 472 to 59. FDR received ninety-six percent of the vote in Mississippi, second only to his ninety-eight percent in South Carolina. Four years later, his percentages in the two states were even higher.

Even before his inauguration, Roosevelt and his advisors began devising the program that came to be known as the New Deal. The plan to put Americans back to work involved an unprecedented increase in the size and scope of the federal government and the creation of many new federal programs, which came to be known as the alphabet agencies. One of them was the Tennessee Valley Authority, the TVA.

The Tennessee Valley, historically one of the poorest regions in the country, was ravaged by the Depression. Average annual family income was less than $700. Some scraped by on less than a hundred dollars a year. Poor agricultural practices and erosion had damaged much of the land and made it unsuitable for farming. Thirty percent of the residents had been stricken with malaria.

The statute creating the TVA was passed by Congress in May 1933, just two months after Roosevelt's inauguration. The principal sponsors were Congressmen George Norris, a Republican from Nebraska, and John Rankin, a Democrat from Northeast Mississippi. The new agency had several principal goals. Foremost among them was to bring electricity to the areas of the region that did not yet have it. Only ten percent of rural families in America had electricity in 1930. Only two percent of those in Mississippi did. The TVA ultimately provided power to nearly all of Tennessee as well as parts of Mississippi, Alabama, Georgia, North Carolina, Virginia, and Kentucky. The second goal was to provide jobs for those who were out of work. Thousands were employed by the TVA in the construction of hydroelectric dams and related facilities throughout the South. A third goal was to restore the damaged land by improving farming practices, including the use of fertilizer and crop rotation.

Wilson Dam, on the Tennessee River near Muscle Shoals, Alabama, was older than the TVA but became one of its principal assets. The Army Corps of Engineers began construction of the dam in 1918. The original purpose, driven by World War I, was to provide electricity for two nitrate plants on the river that would make explosives. The dam and its system of locks would also make it easier for large vessels to navigate the treacherous section of the river above the dam. Construction was completed in 1924, but the war was ancient history by then, interest in the dam had waned, and the electricity it generated was put to only limited use in the years that followed. In 1933, however, the TVA acquired the dam and made it a cornerstone of the agency's plan to provide electricity to the rural South.

Tupelo, on the tip of Appalachia eighty-five miles southwest of Muscle Shoals, was recruited to become the first customer for electricity generated by the TVA. The agency and the city signed a contract in late 1933. Just after midnight on February 7, 1934, less than nine months after the TVA was created, power generated by the turbines at Wilson Dam lit up the town. In the ensuing months, consumption of electricity by residential customers in Tupelo more than doubled.

President Roosevelt and his wife Eleanor planned a trip to the South in the fall of 1934. They would travel by train, touring Wilson Dam, then continue to Tupelo, where they would be honored with a parade, and the president would give a speech celebrating Tupelo for becoming the First TVA City. The Roosevelts would then head back east to their Little White House in Warm Springs, Georgia.

Two weeks before the Roosevelts' visit to Tupelo, a man knocked on the door of Harry's office in the church. Harry welcomed him in. "Mayor Nanney, what a pleasure. You must be busy with preparations."

"It's an exciting time, Reverend Brooks."

"What can I do for you? How can I help?"

"I was hoping you would ask me that. I have a request for you. I hope you will consider it an honor to fulfill it. White House officials want the minister of one of the city's churches to give the invocation before President Roosevelt speaks. I have met with the Board of Aldermen, and you are our choice."

"That is quite an honor, Mayor, and quite a surprise. There are many ministers in Tupelo who've been here far longer than I have."

"I know that, but just between the two of us, none of them can speak as well as you can. No president has ever come to Tupelo, and we want to put our best foot forward. We want you to represent the city. May I tell the Board that you will give the invocation?"

"Of course, Your Honor. I'm a minister and a Methodist, but I'm a Democrat too. And the TVA has been wonderful for Tupelo. Mrs. Brooks and I celebrated by getting her a Singer sewing machine. It will be both an honor and a pleasure to give the invocation."

"Wonderful. We'll let you know the details before the time comes." He stood up and smiled. "I will give you the same instructions I was given. The president will be on a tight schedule, so you'll need to keep it short. Don't start blessing all the birds that you love so much."

They shook hands. "The birds will be disappointed, but I won't mention them. You have my word."

Harry was excited at first, but then he began to worry. Would there be some sort of background check? What if officials found out about his past? Even if they didn't, would his name be mentioned in the eastern papers? It had been more than a quarter of a century, but did people in Uniontown still hold a grudge? Mart Kiefer maybe? Or members of the school board? What would they think if they learned that Harry had been allowed to share a stage with the President of the United States? Would they try to expose him? Harry worried for a while and considered making up some excuse to back out, but then he decided the risk was slight. As with all things, he entrusted the matter to God.

The president's brief visit was scheduled for Sunday morning, November 18. Those in attendance included not just the 7,000 citizens of Tupelo, but at least ten times that many who'd come into town from miles around. Roosevelt was the voice of hope. Many thousands of Mississippians wanted to catch a glimpse of him and hear his speech. Estimates of the number of people in Tupelo on the day of the speech were 75,000 or more. The city runneth over.

Before dawn, people were lined up six deep along the parade route downtown. Flags and bunting decorated homes and businesses. A huge portrait of the president decorated the wall of Reed's Department Store on the corner of Main and Spring Streets. Every inch of Robins Field, the high school football field where FDR would speak, was packed with people. The front yards of the homes in the surrounding neighborhood were covered as well. Harry and other dignitaries sat on the stage that had been built alongside Church Street School just southeast of Robins Field and awaited the president's arrival. Secret Service agents had come to Tupelo to inspect the parade route five days earlier, but they evidently had not looked into Harry's past.

The engine pulling the Roosevelts' Pullman car arrived at the Tupelo train station at eight a.m., and the president was helped down with a ramp to get into his specially equipped car. The motorcade first drove five miles to the outskirts of town to see a Homestead project, a federal housing program that Mrs. Roosevelt had championed. They visited a family living in one of the new homes, then returned to the city for the parade, which was led by eight policemen on motorcycles, 500 members of the Mississippi National Guard, and 1,000 Boy Scouts. The route went through a black neighborhood, where the band from George Washington Carver High School played "America" as the procession passed. The parade ended at Church Street School, where FDR was helped from his car and then onto the stage. He shook hands with those who were waiting there, including Harry.

Harry had watched as the people gathered, but when he rose to give the invocation, he was struck by just how enormous the crowd was. There were thousands upon thousands of faces looking up at him, waiting for him to speak. It was far more people than he'd ever seen in any one place in his nearly seventy-three years. He asked those present to bow their heads.

Harry first prayed for the president and first lady. He asked the Lord to watch over them and keep them safe and healthy. He then asked God to bless Mr. Roosevelt's efforts to help all those across America who were suffering. He prayed that God would give the president and every other every public official, both those behind him on the stage and elsewhere, the wisdom to make the right decisions in these difficult times. He expressed gratitude for the wonderful people of Tupelo, asked God to bless them, then closed his short prayer by turning to the reason for the president's visit. "Lord, I thank You every day for all you have given us and for all our many blessings. But today, I want to thank you for a special blessing You have given us. I know that all of us gathered here agree with me when I say, thank God for the TVA." The huge crowd had been silent while Harry prayed, but cheers drowned out his amen.

After Harry returned to his seat, Mayor Nanney spoke briefly, followed by Representative Rankin and Senator Pat Harrison from the Mississippi Gulf Coast. The senator had known the president for many years and introduced him. FDR was then helped from his wheelchair to the lectern, where he spoke without a script.

The president began his speech by saying "I shall not make a speech to you today." The reason, he continued, was that he and the people were assembled more as neighbors than anything else. He compared what he saw on people's faces on this trip to what he had seen when he came to the South during the 1932 campaign. What he saw then brought tears to his eyes, but now he could see hope and determination. He knew that all was well and the country was coming back. He said he planned to take the story of Tupelo and the TVA to the rest of the country, that what was being done here would be copied in every state. He closed with these words: "The responsibility for success lies very largely with you, and the eyes of the nation are upon you. I, for one, am confident that you are going to give to the nation an example which will be a benefit not only to yourselves, but to the whole one hundred and thirty millions of Americans in every part of the land."

Even with frequent interruptions for cheers and applause, Roosevelt's speech lasted no more than ten minutes. He was the last to speak and was then helped down from the platform. A line of Boy Scouts kept the crowd back so the president and first lady could make their way to their vehicle. Some of the Scouts, including Billy Booth and Paul Eason, were members of Troop 12, which was sponsored by the Chapman Men's Bible Class at the First Methodist Church. Billy wound up last in line, pressed up against the president's car. When FDR struggled to get in, Billy supported him by the elbow and helped him up. After the president was seated, he turned, thanked Billy, and patted him on the head.

The Roosevelts returned to the train station, boarded their Pullman car, and were gone by ten o'clock. They had been in Tupelo no more than two hours, but Mayor Nanney had gotten his wish. The city had made a good impression. According to a member of the White House staff traveling with the Roosevelts, the president had experienced larger and more colorful receptions than this one, but for respectful admiration and considerate hospitality, Tupelo had surpassed them all.

After the crowd had cleared, Harry found the twins waiting for him on the sidewalk in front of the school. They were thirteen, but they still walked arm in arm with him, one on either side. They headed south along Church Street toward the parsonage, where they would stop briefly before going next door to church for the Sunday morning service. Both girls said that Harry had done a fine job, as had the handsome president. The girls were amazed that so many people were there. They had never seen anywhere near that many. Harry said he was far older than they were, but he'd never seen that many either.

Harry felt a twinge of guilt because his daughters had no idea how much older he was. In just six weeks, four days after Christmas, the family would celebrate his fifty-ninth birthday. As always, he would play along, but it wouldn't really be his birthday, and he wouldn't really be fifty-nine. His real birthday would be three days later, on New Year's Day, when he would turn seventy-three. But only he knew that.

And there was something else that only Harry knew. When he'd stood at the lectern and looked out on all the people in the enormous crowd, his first thought was that nobody in the multitude knew that the preacher standing before them was a convicted felon. Then his mind had turned to those sitting behind him. He was on the stage with a host of powerful elected officials–a governor, two senators, a handful of congressmen, even the President of the United States–and none of them knew either. Not the Secret Service agents, not anybody. There were many thousands of people there–who could say how many?–and not one of them knew. Only Harry knew. He was the only one.

———◄○►———

The following summer, President Roosevelt requested America's ministers to give their opinions about the country's recovery from the Depression. Harry was one of those who responded. In his letter to the president, Harry raised a concern about another of the alphabet agencies, the WPA.

The Works Program meets a general need, but there is a pretty general criticism of it that it applies only to those who have been on relief rolls. There are hundreds and thousands of people who have not asked the government for one penny of help. Some of them have nothing scarcely to live upon. Others have but little, but out of their self-respect and regard for the government of our nation, they have not asked for anything. These are in need. I personally feel that they ought to be included in the Works Program.

Harry knew a thing or two about the importance of maintaining self-respect in the face of hardship. Whether his letter found its way to President Roosevelt and whether he read it are unknown.

CHAPTER EIGHTEEN

1935

《❦ ❧》

WILMORE

Harry settled in for the long train ride to Kentucky. He was one of a handful of ministers who'd been invited to serve as the faculty at a four-day conference at the Asbury Theological Seminary, where he'd received his Doctor of Divinity degree a dozen years earlier. The seminary was in Wilmore, thirty miles southwest of Lexington. Harry was excited but nervous too.

The title of the conference was "Crafting the Sermon: How to Bring People to God." The speakers would be five Protestant pastors from different denominations, all with excellent reputations for the quality of their sermons, both the message and the delivery. Harry had been chosen to represent the Methodist Church. Those in attendance would include not only seminary students but also preachers seeking to learn from other preachers with more experience and greater skill.

Harry had even more experience than the sponsors of the conference knew. They were aware of his quarter-century of preaching in Methodist churches in Texas, Louisiana, and Mississippi, but they knew nothing about the first half of his life when he'd preached in Baptist and Methodist churches in Pennsylvania and then led services during his time at Western Pen. By the time of the conference, Harry had been preaching in pulpits for more than forty years, and he was very good at it. Relying on nothing more than a few notes typed or written on an envelope, he could keep a congregation's full attention for half an hour or more, even with Sunday dinner waiting. Mayor Nanney was right; Harry was the best speaker of all the ministers in Tupelo.

Harry was excited about the conference because he would get to listen to the other members of the faculty. He wanted to hear what they had to say about how they approached the task of preparing a sermon. He might be seventy-three years old, but he believed a person is never too old to learn, that there is always room for improvement. That was why he had gone back to school and become Dr. Brooks after turning sixty. It sure wasn't for the title.

But Harry was nervous too because, in all his years in the ministry, he'd never been called on to teach someone else how to preach. He wasn't sure he could do it. He wasn't even sure he could explain how *he* did it. It was second nature by now. It was like riding a bicycle. He just did it.

To help prepare for the conference, he had brought along a file folder full of his sermons. He didn't have transcripts or detailed outlines, just the envelopes covered with his notes. He often used church stationery, and he had envelopes from the church in Mineral Wells, the Polk Street Methodist Church in Amarillo, Capitol Street Church in Jackson, and the First Methodist Churches in Clarksdale and Starkville. The envelopes spanned more than twenty years of sermons. On some, he couldn't read the words in his own handwriting. On others, he could read them but couldn't remember what he meant. But it was a long train ride and, by the time he got to Wilmore, surely he would have something to say about Crafting the Sermon. And when the train pulled into the station, he had a subject he could talk about each of the four days of the conference.

The topic Harry chose for the first day was finding inspiration for sermons in the world around us. He provided three examples from his own experience. The first was a sermon he'd preached about the danger of moral and spiritual drift, which was inspired by a day he'd spent in a boat on the Ohio River. He sat in the boat, resting on the oars, and paid no attention to his surroundings. He was surprised to find that he was soon half a mile downriver, carried by the current, just drifting along. Regaining the lost distance was hard work, and it gave Harry a new appreciation for what happens when people let themselves drift. Moral and spiritual drift is similar. It requires no conscious thought or decision. The ease constitutes the peril. The moment a person ceases to progress, he begins to drift. He soon finds himself a long way from God.

The other two examples were from observations Harry made while out walking. He liked to go for long walks in the towns where he preached. Along the way, he would work out the upcoming Sunday sermon in his head, and he often found inspiration for future sermons as well. Once, while walking in Amarillo, he came to the crossing of the tracks of the two great railroads, the Atchison, Topeka & Santa Fe and the Fort Worth & Denver City. It was this crossing that, in a few short years, had turned a blank spot on the map in the middle of Comanche territory into the largest cattle shipping market in the world. The crossing made him think of highways, of the paths throughout the world connecting distant points. History is filled with them–the Jerusalem, Damascus, and Jericho Roads, the Appian Way. Highways are not only for people. The fish of the sea, the birds of the air, and the cattle of the field all follow a path to reach their destinations. The birds that fly south in the fall are not flying blind. They know where they're going. Christians know too. The path they are to take is spelled out in Scripture. In John 14:6, Jesus told his followers: "I am the way. No man cometh unto the Father but by me." But passage along the path to God is not free. The coin we must pay to get from earth to heaven is obedience to God and faith in Jesus Christ. But it is a democratic path, open to all who pay that coin.

Harry's third example was more recent. While walking on a spring day in Starkville, he had stopped on a bridge over a creek and looked downstream. Two young boys were wading, the water up to their knees. One had a net. He would swoop it under the surface along the bank, then lift it up, and both boys would peer down into the net to examine the catch. Sometimes it was a fish, sometimes a crawfish, sometimes a tadpole, sometimes all three. Neither boy noticed Harry. Their focus on God's creatures in the creek was absolute. How marvelous a boy is, Harry had thought, and how marvelous it is to be a boy. He'd returned to his study and prepared an entire sermon on what a boy is and what a boy needs. It was so well received that he preached it again soon after he moved to Tupelo. If, God willing, he lived long enough to become the preacher of another church, his new congregation would hear it too.

The subject of Harry's talk on the second day of the conference was the need to make sermons relevant to the lives of the congregants who hear them. It is not enough to explain what Scripture means in the abstract. An effective preacher should also explain how those sitting in the pews can apply the Scripture to their daily lives.

Harry tried to use the Bible to teach lessons that the members of the church could put to use. He cited verses from Genesis, Kings, and Proverbs to illustrate God's admonition to parents to raise their children to be righteous. Children need an example. What do they see when they look at their parents? Where are their parents leading them? God's plan is for a home in which the father and mother walk in the way of the Lord, with the children walking after them. People talk about the need to rid the world of harlots and libertines. The way to rid the world of them, Harry had said in his sermon, is to quit raising them.

In the fourth verse of the ninth chapter of John, Jesus said, "I must work the works of Him that sent me, while it is day: the night cometh, when no man can work." Harry had used this verse to preach on the obligation of all Christians to do the work of the Lord. Work is the most glorious privilege offered by God to man. Jesus was a teacher, but he was a worker too. He came saying, "I must work." The Christian should work as hard to provide spiritual food as the groceryman does to provide physical food. Harry borrowed a phrase from Lincoln's Gettysburg Address to drive home the point. Jesus gave the last full measure of devotion, dying on the cross to save us from our sins. Doing the work of the Lord is the least we can give in return.

In the midst of the Depression, Harry had preached a sermon pointing out that poverty in material wealth is often present alongside abundance in spiritual wealth, and the latter is what matters. Indeed, it is all that matters. He relied on the parable of the rich man in the twelfth chapter of Luke to emphasize that earthly riches are not what is of real value. They are not lasting. The rich man's granaries may have been full, but he could not fill his soul from them. The Christian should distinguish between material and spiritual needs. He should avoid covetousness and seek first the kingdom of God, as Jesus instructed in Matthew. He should turn toward the source of light and life.

Harry's topic for the third day was the use of literature and stories to make sermons interesting. If a sermon is not interesting, the congregants will not remember it. And if they don't remember it, they might just as well stay home on Sunday morning and read the newspaper.

The Bible was the principal text for all of Harry's sermons, but it was not the only one. In one of his sermons, the one about what boys need, he had cited *Tom Sawyer* and *Huckleberry Finn*, two classics by his favorite author. When he had preached on the subject of brotherhood, he'd quoted the final verse of "The House by the Side of the Road" by Sam Walter Voss.

Let me live in my house by the side of the road
Where the race of men go by
They are good, they are bad, they are weak, they are strong
Wise, foolish, so am I.
Then why should I sit in the scorner's seat
Or hurl the cynic's ban?
Let me live in my house by the side of the road
And be a friend to man.

In his sermon about a Christian's obligation to do the Lord's work, Harry had told the story of Edwin Markham's "How the Great Guest Came" and recited the final lines. In the poem, a cobbler dreams that the Lord will come to him the next day. The Lord does not come, but three others do. A beggar with bruised feet comes, and the cobbler gives him shoes; an old woman comes, and the cobbler gives her bread; a lost child comes, and the cobbler leads her home. The poem ends with these lines:

> *"Why is it, Lord, that your feet delay?*
> *Did you forget that this was the day?"*
> *Then soft in the silence a voice he heard.*
> *"Lift up your heart, for I have kept My word.*
> *Three times I came to your friendly door.*
> *Three times My shadow was on your floor.*
> *I was the beggar with the bruised feet.*
> *I was the woman you gave to eat.*
> *I was the child on the homeless street."*

Harry had followed the poem by reminding the congregation of the words of Jesus from the book of Matthew: "As oft as ye did it unto the least of these, ye did it unto me."

Harry also used stories about historical figures to make his points. He had begun his sermon about what boys need with a story about Benjamin Franklin. In his teens, Franklin had walked through the streets of Boston, penniless, wearing ragged clothes, and a girl had laughed at him. But Franklin had a genius for hard work, and he helped found a new nation. More than fifty years after being ridiculed on the streets, he secured military assistance for that new nation from King Louis XVI at the Palace of Versailles.

In the same sermon, Harry had said that boys love heroes who have accomplished great things. He cited Teddy Roosevelt, the youngest president but also a soldier and adventurer; Alvin York, the World War I hero who single-handedly killed and captured more than a hundred Germans on a single day; and Charles Lindbergh, the first person to make a solo flight across the Atlantic. Boys are also curious and inquisitive, Harry had said. They want to know the reason for things. They need companionship, direction, and sympathy. They need the opportunity for full development of the body, mind, and spirit. All of this is necessary, Harry told his congregation, because the future of the world depends on the American boy.

Harry saved his most difficult subject for the last day of the conference. It was how to preach on the subject of sin. When Harry preached about sin, he often discussed the other great religions of the world. He was a student of other religions and respected their followers. He had gone to school with a young Chinese boy who had a wonderful philosophy. The boy was not a Christian, but Harry rejected the notion that he was a heathen. But one of the things that sets Christianity apart from other religions is its teaching about sin. Christianity is the only religion in the world that provides a remedy for sin.

In a sermon Harry had preached twenty years earlier in Mineral Springs, he'd emphasized that the Bible always deals with man as a sinful being. Sin is like a serpent; it courses through the blood, corrupts the mind, perverts the conscience, and enfeebles the will. He told the members of the congregation that all people have felt the power of sin in their lives. Harry had certainly felt it in his.

But the Bible, he continued, provides a remedy for sin. God provides a remedy. That remedy is salvation, but it is not automatic. The sinner must meet God halfway. He must repent, honestly regret his sin, and seek forgiveness. And there must be expiation—satisfaction for the crime. The sinner must make the wrong right. But for those who do these things, there is God's grace and salvation. All of us are sinners, but we can enter the kingdom of heaven because God is willing to forgive us.

Harry could have used his own journey from sin to grace, which had begun years earlier, and explained how he righted his wrongs by serving nearly three years behind bars and seeking God's forgiveness. It would have made the sermon more interesting and more memorable. In fact, it would have made it unforgettable. But Harry continued to believe what

Edwin had told him on the day they met in Georgetown. If the people knew what he had done, they would not respect him. And they would not allow him to lead them.

When Harry wasn't speaking at the conference, he sat in the audience and listened to the other preachers. After the last session, he stopped by the drugstore on the walk back to the train station and bought a half dozen envelopes. Not stationery, just envelopes. On the ride back to Tupelo, he prepared outlines for six sermons he would preach based on what he'd learned.

CHAPTER NINETEEN

APRIL 5, 1936

⟪⊙ ⊚⟫

TUPELO

*"One minute, Tupelo, the country's first TVA city, was peaceful;
the next there were dead and dying on every hand."*
George McGuire, *Tupelo Daily News*, April 6, 1936

It was Palm Sunday, the fifth day of April in 1936. The weather was unusually hot and humid for early April. The air felt heavy; a gusting wind came from the south.

Just two weeks earlier, Harry had marked the thirtieth anniversary of the day he began his sentence at Western Penitentiary. On the day he walked into the front gate, he started counting down the thousand days until he would walk out and be a free man again. On the anniversary, he thanked God for all his many blessings during the last three decades of his life, including the blessings that came from the years he spent behind bars.

One of his greatest blessings in the years since then was the honor of serving as the minister of the First Methodist Church in Tupelo. The Palm Sunday morning service, which began the Holy Week that would end with Easter and the celebration of the Resurrection, was wonderful. The

207

choir sang beautifully, and many of the congregants complimented Harry on his sermon as they filed out of the church.

After Sunday dinner, Harry walked around the parsonage to inspect the new roof. The workers had finished installing it just before dark the day before. After satisfying himself that they had done a fine job, Harry climbed the front porch steps and went inside for his customary Sunday afternoon nap. He would then prepare for the Sunday evening service and all the other activities scheduled for Holy Week.

In their home on Highland Circle less than a mile northwest of the parsonage, the Easons were preparing to go for their Sunday afternoon drive. The children wanted to stay home and play in the neighborhood with their friends, but that would have to wait. This was a weekly ritual. Doris, the youngest, sat in the middle of the front seat between parents Cliff and Margaret. Paul, the oldest at fourteen, sat in the back with the two other girls, Myra and Puddie. They drove north on Highway 45 to see the new construction at the homesteads. It was Cliff's thirty-eighth birthday. Margaret would prepare a special dinner to celebrate when they got home.

After the evening service, Harry returned to the parsonage, where he met with the head of the Sunday school, the choir director, and the organist to prepare for the coming week. Just before nine o'clock, the wind picked up, and Harry walked out onto the front porch to check the weather. The sky in the west was black with streaks of lightning. In the southwest, it was bright with fire. The Sunday School superintendent and choir director had already left, but the organist was still there. She hurried out to her car so she could get home before the worst hit. But then came the noise, a deafening roar. A tree fell across the driveway and blocked the organist's escape. When she tried to pull back up to the house, another tree fell in front of her. Neither hit her car. She got out and ran into the house as a third tree crashed through the new roof. They were on the edge of the storm, not directly in its path, but still the trees came down. Harry called for everyone–Ethel, Danny, the twins, and the organist–to join him in the central east room. They huddled together as the house shook.

The tornado traveled fast, lifting huge objects from the ground and sending them twirling into the sky. Houses were shattered like bits of kindling. Wreckage and debris flew everywhere. The funnel cut a path through the residential section of Tupelo, going just northwest of the parsonage and just southeast of Highland Circle. The houses that were hit directly collapsed into splinters and were blown away. In one block of Madison Street, twenty-eight homes and an apartment building were wiped off the face of the Earth in a matter of seconds. Not a single building remained. The tornado continued to the northeast and decimated the neighborhood surrounding Gum Pond where many of the town's black residents lived. It then rose into the air and left the city behind.

The storm took no more than three minutes to pass through Tupelo, but it left a staggering toll in its wake. More than 200 residents were killed, likely close to 300. A thousand were injured, and far more than that were left homeless. The tornado is still the fourth deadliest in the nation's history. No tornado since has killed nearly as many. It was classified as an F5, with winds of 260 to 320 miles an hour.

As soon as the roar of the storm faded, screams could be heard. Efforts to gather the dead and dying and help the injured began immediately. Rescue parties spent the rest of the night searching through the debris in the driving rain that came after the tornado. A woman cried in anguish as a heavy beam was lifted from the broken body of her dead three-year-old son. A man screamed deliriously as fellow citizens lifted a wall and chunks of mortar from his wife's lifeless body. She was crushed beyond recognition, every bone in her body broken. A man's next-door neighbor died in his arms.

Another man spent the night searching his neighborhood for his family. He had let his wife and four children out at their house after returning from church and was parking the car in the garage when the tornado hit. The home was blown to bits, but the garage was spared. He called and called but couldn't find any of them. All five were found the next day, all dead. A woman picked her way out of the debris and found a neighbor lying in the driveway next to her house. The neighbor cried out, "I'm killed." She died from her injuries two days later. A teenage boy was able to climb from the ruins of his home but, when he surveyed the scene, was completely disoriented. There was nothing left standing that he could use to find his bearings—no house, no trees, no vehicle, no discernible walkway or street, no light, no nothing.

The tornado struck shortly after the Easons finished Cliff's birthday dinner. After the worst was over, Cliff and Paul went out to survey the damage. They walked to the south entrance of Highland Circle, then turned east on Jackson Street in the direction of the roaring sound they had heard. When lightning lit up the sky, they saw that Church Street School was no longer standing. Most of it was gone, the rest reduced to rubble. They continued downtown to the hospital next to the First Methodist Church to see what they could do to help. A woman who was strapped to a door to stabilize her broken back screamed in pain as she was carried up a flight of stairs. A local doctor, Dixon Kirk, walked straight to the hospital after the storm passed and didn't leave again for seventy-two hours. He treated the injured for three straight days and nights—with his wife bringing him meals—before he returned home for a bath and a nap.

The roof was blown off the hospital, much of the building was damaged, and makeshift facilities to treat the injured were set up in other buildings during the night. One was in the annex next to the First Methodist Church. Harry, Ethel, and their daughters took care of some of the injured in the parsonage as well. Dead bodies were laid out on pews in the sanctuary. Injured residents were also treated in the Lee County Courthouse and the Lyric Theater. Surgery was performed on the stage in the theater. Doctors and nurses made do with what they had. Instruments that were used to amputate crushed limbs were sterilized by heating them in the popcorn machine.

The first to die in Tupelo were Jim and Jennie Burrough and all eleven of their children. They lived on the western edge of town, the direction from which the storm came. The tornado demolished their home in an instant, killing all thirteen of them and scattering their bodies over a 300-yard radius. No trace of their house remained. The next morning, the ground where it had stood looked like it had been swept with a broom. The thirteen members of the family were buried in a single grave that was seven feet wide and thirty-five feet long and was dug by hand by Jim's co-workers at the Tupelo Cotton Mill. Three trucks were needed to transport the bodies to the cemetery. Only twelve caskets were available, so the Burroughs' two youngest daughters were buried together in one. Jim's mother kissed each casket before it was lowered into the ground.

The scope of the utter devastation did not come into view until the sun rose on Monday morning. Newspapermen from other cities arrived and began reporting on what they found. A writer for the *Memphis Press-Scimitar* described what he observed on his walk into town.

> Only by imagining everything mopped off the map–a scene of 100 per cent destruction–can you imagine how this area looks today. Timber, timber is everywhere. It's scattered in lengths from one to ten feet for miles. Hardly anything is standing. Bricks, stone, and concrete fell before the wind's onslaught. We came by plane and landed in a field three miles out–near a dead cow. Walking that three miles I passed many victims, some dead and many injured. Prying into a house I found two little boys, apparently twins, about five years old. They were clasped in each other's arms in death. It had been a brick house. Another place I pulled a gray-haired woman out from under debris. Six Negroes were lying dead beside a creek.

A reporter from Columbus, Mississippi, recorded similar observations.

> It is useless to attempt to describe the terrible disaster. It beggars description. We stood in the midst of the devastated area. It is a sight of desolation and ruin, the like of which this earth has never seen before. Not even the destructive fire of the great armies of the World War on the Western front could

have caused destruction as complete as that which occurred at Tupelo. To view the scene, one wonders how a single soul escaped death. It was a miracle.

In the days that followed, survivors shared stories attesting to the power of the storm. Two families who were riding in their cars were lifted to the treetops, spun around, then lowered to the ground, right side up. In one of them, no one was hurt, and the only harm to the car was a broken window. The other landing was not as soft. The car was demolished, but only the driver was injured, and he had only a broken arm. The city's 50,000-gallon water tank, weighing many tons, was found six miles from where the tornado had uprooted it. A missing car was discovered in the middle of a field a thousand feet from the nearest road. The winds carried a kitchen cabinet thirty miles, then lowered it gently to the ground, undamaged. Canceled checks and other papers were found as far away as Nashville, 200 miles to the northeast. A family Bible was blown away and landed in Corinth, fifty miles away, without a scratch on it. The couple who found the Bible drove it back to Tupelo and returned it to its rightful owner.

Stories about miracles involving small children spread in the days after the storm. A small child was blown over Gum Pond and was found on the railroad tracks. A white family was surprised when they discovered a small black child in an upstairs bedroom. She had been blown through an open window from her home several blocks away. A six-month-old who was carried away from his home by the wind was caught in mid-air by a man on the next street. A man who had buried his wife earlier that day found a three-month-old dangling from a tree limb. All four of the children escaped unharmed.

Animals also managed against all odds to survive. After the storm, chickens that had lost every feather wandered the streets. Cattle lost their horns. A cow was shorn of every hair on her body but continued to produce milk. A woman saved herself and her canary by climbing into her icebox seconds before her apartment was destroyed. She climbed out and walked barefoot to her brother's home. He was surprised when he came to the door and found her in a soaking-wet nightgown holding the bird. But not all the animals in town were so fortunate. A trench seven feet wide, eight feet deep, and 150 feet long served as a mass grave for hundreds of dead ones.

Even before the shock wore off, efforts to rebuild began. Though the country was in the middle of the worst depression of the twentieth century, generous contributions of money and all manner of goods came pouring in. The American Legion, Red Cross, and countless volunteers performed heroically. Presbyterian minister Sam Howie set up a kitchen that served three meals a day to nearly 4,000 survivors and rescue workers. Employees of the Works Progress Administration and Civilian Conservation Corps took the lead in clearing the streets and hauling away mountains of debris. Architects and engineers volunteered their time to plan new buildings to replace the ones that had been blown away. The Red Cross considered building barracks to house the homeless, but the Frisco Railroad in St. Louis volunteered more than a hundred boxcars. Additional tracks were laid to accommodate them, and Box Car cities, segregated by race, were established in the city. Volunteers planned programs and entertainment for the children living in them. Less than a week after the tornado, an editorial in the *Tupelo Journal* was optimistic. "We face the future confident that vision, planning, and courageous toil on our part will again make Tupelo a prosperous, a beautiful, and an increasingly progressive city."

Harry's focus in the days following the storm, with Ethel's assistance, was on consoling the city's grief-stricken residents, Methodists as well as others. Hundreds of Tupelo's citizens had lost family members. Many more had lost everything else. Ten members of the First Methodist Church were killed, 150 were injured, and more than 200 of the members' homes were severely damaged or destroyed. Harry met and prayed with church members late into the night, encouraging them to turn to God.

Harry spent the daylight hours conducting funerals. Services were scheduled every hour, on the hour, beginning the day after the storm and continuing until all the bodies were in the ground. Harry's services were needed not only for the members of the First Methodist Church but for many others as well. All told, he conducted funerals for more than sixty victims of the tornado.

The sheer number reminded him of the family story that had been passed down about all the burials at sea on the voyage that had brought his great grandfather Joseph Brooks to America. In the services for the storm victims, Harry recited the same verses from the books of Ecclesiastes and John that had been read when the victims of typhoid fever were cast into the sea nearly a century and a half before. He made a point to spend time with the family before each funeral so he could say something meaningful about the person lying in the coffin. He presumed they all were Christians, even those he didn't know, and he shared the Bible's promise of everlasting life with their families.

◄○►

When all the funerals were over and the town's cemeteries were littered with fresh graves, Harry drafted an essay about the tornado and its aftermath that he shared with the other Methodist churches in Mississippi. In the essay, which he entitled "A BEAUTIFUL CITY DEVASTATED," he wrote:

> Two weeks ago, Tupelo, a beautiful little city, with her great oak trees, her beautiful lawns, shrubbery, and flowers springing into bloom, was resting quietly on the plains of Northeast Mississippi. Her people by the hundreds had given themselves to the celebration of Palm Sunday, commemorating the triumphant entry of our Lord into the City of Jerusalem.
>
> The church services had been dismissed, the people generally had returned home and were quietly reading or having converse about their home altars, some had retired, others were driving in their cars. This pastor had had a meeting with his choir leader and organist, arranging and talking over the

music for Holy Week and Easter Sunday morning, also a meeting with Mr. W. L. Elkin, the General Superintendent of his Church School, planning a week of instruction for a class of Church School children who were to be received into the membership of the church on Easter Sunday morning. He had just gone to the porch, he looked to the west and the sky was sky was black with clouds, and the southwest was aflame with fire, fast coming this way. For a few moments there was a deathless stillness, then a roar of wind that sounded like the rumble of a thousand freight trains running on tracks irregularly constructed. The electric lights went out, inside the house a fearful expectancy possessed our minds and hearts. Mrs. Brooks and the children joined me in the central east room. The house shook like a large cake of jello suddenly turned on a plate, a crash broke upon the house, a huge oak had fallen on the roof. When we emerged from the house, the rain began to come in torrents, the lawns all around us were full of trees fallen, some of them had stood for years, shingles, boards, porch chairs, bricks, porch pillars, everything lay in the streets and lawns everywhere.

We hurried across the street to a seeming place of safety. There were no lights anywhere, the sky was black with clouds. Soon we began to hear the cries for help. Trees and debris filled the streets to the west and north, men came carrying on improvised cots the wounded, others came leading their maimed, still others carrying them on their shoulders, others carrying children and babies in their arms to the hospital, and when the rain began to pour through the roof, then the march turned toward the annex of the First Methodist Church, when that was filled then to the dry spots in the parsonage, and then to the courthouse and the Lyric Theatre. The city hall became a morgue where the dead lay for identification.

Truckloads of the wounded were brought from all parts of the city, fighting their way through yards and over wreckage to the improvised hospitals. Other trucks came from the east side of the bottoms, from the Auburn community, and out toward Mantachie. Everywhere they were pleading, "O, get me a doctor, get us a doctor." Nurses at the hospital were helpless because of the danger of their building. Doctors from seemingly everywhere with their kits and nurses began to work. From Memphis, New Albany, Corinth, Guntown, Saltillo, Pontotoc, Houston, Okolona, Aberdeen, and Amory they came. They came by air, by automobile, and finally by train. First aid men and women preceded the doctors and nurses, giving aid to those they could and turning the more seriously injured over to the doctors. Bandages, adhesive tape, and medicines were hurried here by air and later by train. Never in my life have I seen more heroic work done than by these doctors and nurses.

Near midnight, men and women dressed in white suits with a cross of red on their sleeves were seen emerging from buses, cars, air ships, and hurried, special commissioned trains. All over the city everywhere, the cry went up, "Thank God the Red Cross has come." They brought bags and kits bulging with supplies, and all night long and for two or three days these noble servants of the suffering and injured humanity went everywhere, dressing wounds, quieting the nervous, and relieving pain.

It was an awful night, a few fires broke out, rescue bands formed and went through the stricken area, uncovering men, women, and children pinioned under the wreckage of houses and homes. The cry of fathers for their families, of mothers for their children, and children for their mothers and fathers was heart rending. Some children were so badly disfigured that several claimed them, babies were found in the streets and picked up by strange but sympathetic men and carried to the improvised hospitals. All night long, people were being taken out from under the ruins, some dead, others badly injured. As fast as they could be given treatment, they were taken by trains and trucks and ambulances to the hospitals of Memphis, New Albany, Pontotoc, Houston, Okolona, Amory, Meridian, and Booneville where some may have passed away and whose bodies were returned here or back to some "old home place" for burial, others convalesced rapidly and have returned home, still others remain in these hospitals for treatment. No one not seeing the spectacle can believe its story, even those of us who were here cannot fully believe it. The people were dazed and shocked, we knew not the extent of the awful storm. When day broke in the east and the sun began his climb over the hills, the scene before us was horrifying. A section of the city, beginning on Willis Heights and extending clear across the city at least one-half mile in width and some places more, was swept to the ground.

The shrill sound of the ambulances as they carried the wounded and later the dead, and the awful days of the burial of the dead, going from one funeral to another, one hour allotted for each, beginning at nine o'clock and continuing every hour in the day: these things I cannot dismiss. It has written its story on my heart and on the heart of every pastor in this city. Our Brethren in the ministry from all over this section came to our help, comforting the wounded and the dying, burying the dead, and consoling the sorrowing. One family of thirteen was buried in the same grave. Husband and wife were buried together; mother, father, with a child in their arms now rest in peace together in the same grave.

I must not close without commending the noble Red Cross for their splendid work under the leadership of Mr. Wilson; the great, faithful work of regulating traffic, dispersing the pilferers, guarding the people and interests of the city was under the regulation and command of General O'Keefe, Major Birdsong and the noble National Guard of our state; both officers and men conducted themselves as gentlemen. Their rule was firm but tender with sympathy and regard for all the people. They were gentlemen and soldiers. No nobler body of men can be found anywhere than the American Legion–the soldiers of the World War. They stood at the street crossings, they established their kitchens, their supply rooms of food and clothing. They fed the hungry, they clothed the naked, they supplied the needy, they proceeded to bring comfort and good cheer to those in need. May God bless these noble men of the World War.

Some readers may be wondering, how are the people coming back? Never have I seen a people more heroic than these. Noble sons and daughters of the city beautiful. Husbands and wives separated for years have been brought together, enemies have met and joined in friendship, men estranged from God and their churches have re-dedicated themselves. This last Sunday we met for worship in theaters, the courthouse, and the churches not destroyed. The people came by the hundreds, yea by the thousands, and filled every house with anxious worshipers. The people's hearts and minds are turned to God. The wonder is that thousands were not killed. It was a grateful people that met and thanked God for His protecting care. They felt "His everlasting arms underneath them."

Now we know that people are kind, from everywhere came money, clothing, food, medicines, and not in small amounts but in big boxes, loaded on trucks, trains, by rail, express, parcel post, every conceivable way. The whole country opened their pantries, store houses, wardrobes and chests and sent them this way. They were not all discarded things, but new things–comforters, blankets, quilts, pillows, and bed linens, towels, and cooking utensils. The good housewives of the South know how to choose, and they exercised their knowledge. The city is coming back. The Insurance Companies with their adjusters are here, most of them have been and are very considerate. Architects and builders are here, plans are being drawn, construction work is already going on. The T.V.A. has large crews of men at work stretching wires and preparing for the introduction of low-priced electricity into the homes, shops, and stores. Mayor Nanney and his noble Board of City Aldermen are directing and planning for a more beautiful city than the one blown away. Landscape men and all classes of men to make homes beautiful and comfortable are at work. Yes, Tupelo is coming back, and in our coming back, we hope and pray that we will come with a holier regard for God, for His Sabbath, for His Church, for our homes and the character of our citizenship.

Some beautiful lessons of devotion and faith are coming out from under the wreckage of homes. In one place the house was blown over and into a completely wrecked state, the mother was under the ruins but was able to extricate herself. She was much bruised and bleeding, but she began a search for her children. She found them all but her eight- or ten-month-old baby. She sought it everywhere but could not find it, when suddenly she heard the howl of the family bulldog, a faithful guardian and playfellow of the children. When she found him under the debris, he was bruised and bleeding and underneath him lay her baby, its clothes covered with the blood of the faithful, heroic dog but not one scratch of injury on the baby. Both mother and dog have been treated for their injuries and are recovering.

On Palm Sunday the teacher of the Beginners Class of the Church School told the children the story of the storm on the Sea of Galilee, when Jesus was asleep in the hinder part of the boat, and how the frightened Disciples came to Jesus and said, "Master, carest thou not that we perish?" and how Jesus rose and rebuked the wind and said unto the stormy sea, "Peace, be still." And the wind ceased, and there was a great calm. Early that same evening the family of one of our homes was discussing storms and little Martha McGaughy told the story of Jesus and the storm. When the real storm came an hour later, the child walked the floor, crying out, "Jesus, get awake and say peace, be still, come, Jesus, say it." After the storm was over, and deathless stillness filled the home, Martha said, "Daddy, didn't I tell you Jesus would come and say peace, be still, and Daddy, Jesus has come."

Some critics may say, in fact several have received letters already saying, that it was a curse sent upon the people of Tupelo for their wickedness. There is wickedness here as there is in many other places, but there are hundreds of devout Christian people here, good, strong Christian men and women who have stood for Christianity, and we would say to all critics to go to your Bibles and find the 13th chapter of St. Luke 1-5, and St. John 9:1-3. In these Scriptures you will find our explanation.

◄◦►

The rebuilding of the city took years, but carpenters, gardeners, and other craftsmen stayed on the job until new homes and new trees stood where the old ones had been. But even when the physical damage to the city could no longer be seen, emotional and psychological scars remained. Many residents remained terrified of storms for the rest of their lives. Some passed the fear down to their children and grandchildren. One survivor wandered aimlessly through the streets of downtown for many years. Whenever he heard thunder, even in the distance, he would take off running and screaming.

But despite it all–the death and destruction, the terrible injuries, the lasting grief, and fear–good things came from the storm. The tornado had much the same effect on Tupelo that prison had on Harry. Both the city and the man suffered terrible losses–Tupelo lost nearly 300 good citizens, and many survivors lost everything; Harry lost his family, his freedom, and his career–but both came through the harrowing experiences stronger, closer to God, and resolved to build a better future.

More than two years after the fateful night when the tornado struck, Nell Boggan Reed, who chaired the local chapter of the American Red Cross, gave a positive report on the state of the city. "Here we are," she wrote, "with the exception of a few missing trees and a few people I hope are in heaven, a newer and better Tupelo."

In the decades after Mrs. Reed made her pronouncement, the city thrived. During a time when many small towns across America shrunk and some disappeared altogether, Tupelo's population grew from just over 7,000 to nearly 40,000. On five separate occasions, four more than any other city in Mississippi, Tupelo was recognized as an All-American City by the National Civic League for its civic engagement, collaboration, and innovation. There are many reasons for Tupelo's success, including good leadership and good people, but the experience of suffering through the terrible storm together and then working together to rebuild the city is undoubtedly one of them.

CHAPTER TWENTY

MAY 1, 1937

⟨⊙⟩

TUPELO

When Harry returned to the Hotel Tupelo at six o'clock to pick Triss up for dinner, she was waiting outside on the sidewalk. He tried to get out to open the door for her, but she climbed in before he could.

"Is everything alright? Anything new I need to know?"

"Nothing new. I haven't talked to them since this morning. Ethel's been cooking, and I took the long way home after lunch and have been in my study since then. The girls have been out with friends, but they're home now. I don't think they know what to expect."

"Me either."

"This will be a new experience for all of us."

"Are you nervous?"

"A little. You?"

"Very. But I'm excited too. When I asked Frank to help me find you, I had no idea I would also find a brother and sisters too. I lost the four siblings I had, but now I have five more. How old were you when you left Pennsylvania anyway?"

"It was a month before my forty-seventh birthday."

"And yet you remarried and had five more children. Amazing."

"It amazes me too. You'll like the girls. Danny has a sharp tongue but a great sense of humor. The twins are sweet and fun. I wish Elizabeth and Edwin could be here."

"Any advice?"

"We just both need to be careful. Stick to talking about your children and Pennsylvania, and you'll be fine."

The sun was setting in the west when Harry and Triss reached the parsonage. They climbed the steps together that she had climbed alone two days earlier. When Harry opened the door for her, she walked in ahead of him and looked around. The home had ten-foot ceilings, large windows, and polished oak floors. It was furnished with formal furniture that had been well cared for by a half dozen ministers and their families in the decades since the home was built. To the left of the foyer was the dining room. To the right was the living room, where Ethel and the girls were waiting. Ethel and Danny were seated on the chintz sofa, the twins on the window seat. They all rose when Harry and Triss walked in. After Harry made introductions, Triss stepped forward to shake Ethel's hand. "Mrs. Brooks, it's a pleasure to meet you."

"It's a pleasure to meet you too, but please call me Ethel. Harry says I'm only nine years older than you are. That wouldn't be enough difference for you to call me Mrs. Brooks even if you weren't family."

"Alright then, Ethel it is. Daddy has told me good things about you."

"Thank you." Ethel cocked her head. Harry may have been Triss's father, but it seemed odd that she would call him Daddy when she'd never spoken to him until the day before.

After Triss shook hands with Danny, she turned to Margaret and offered her hand, but Margaret stepped toward her with both arms outstretched. "You're my sister, Mrs. Soles. I believe we should hug."

Triss spoke as they embraced. "I agree, but you're my sister too, and you can't very well call me Mrs. Soles no matter how old I am. Call me Triss, please."

"Alright, Triss. I'm Margaret. Marjory and I may look alike, but we're not. She's the bookworm. I'm the one all the boys like."

Marjory rolled her eyes. "The boys like me too, but unlike her, I find time for other things. Schoolwork, for example."

"My daughter Dottie finds time for other things too, but only because we make her. If it weren't for her music lessons and our staying on her about her grades, I'm afraid she'd be chasing boys all over McKeesport."

Marjory continued. "Dottie's your daughter, so she's our niece. Is she really a year older than we are?"

"She is. Daddy has two daughters who are younger than his grand-daughter."

Ethel looked in Harry's direction, then turned to Triss. "It's impressive that you're already calling him Daddy."

Triss hesitated before she spoke. It was no more than a second, but it was enough for Ethel to notice. "That's what he told me to call him. I'm trying to mind."

Harry broke in. "Maybe our teenage daughters will learn something from you about minding. Ethel, should we sit in here for a while, or is dinner ready?"

"It should be ready by now. Danny, please come help me put it on the table."

Harry and Ethel owned few personal belongings because they had lived in one furnished parsonage after another for all the years they'd been together. The furnishings in Tupelo were the nicest yet. In the dining room were a long mahogany table, matching buffet, and Queen Anne chairs. On the buffet was Harry's one prized possession, an antique clock a member of his congregation in Ft. Worth had given him years ago. Harry sat at one end of the table, Triss at the other, Ethel and the girls along the sides. Dinner was pot roast with potatoes, carrots, and gravy, Ethel's wonderful homemade bread, and chocolate chess pie for dessert. It was all delicious. Triss said it was a treat to have a wonderful home-cooked meal for a change.

Triss and the girls did most of the talking. Because Dottie and John were also in high school and because the twins, like Dottie, played the piano, there was plenty to talk about. Triss asked the girls if they had boyfriends and said she'd met a man, Cliff Eason, whose son was in the twins' class. Margaret said Paul was one of the cutest boys in the entire school, but he didn't seem to know it. He acted like he was afraid of girls. When the school had a dance, you couldn't pry him off the wall. Ethel said little but was thinking that Triss looked older than any forty-two. Ethel had always been suspicious of Harry's claim that he was born in 1875, but once they were married, she never brought it up. What was the point?

The talk turned to Danny and her upcoming graduation. She told Triss about the senior class boat trip the previous weekend on the Tombigbee River. One of the boys in the class fell overboard. He couldn't swim, and another boy had to jump in and save him. The officers of the class of 1937, with the principal's permission, had decided to add a third honor to the graduation ceremony. There would be not only a valedictorian and a salutatorian but a savatorian as well.

Triss was relaxed and enjoying the girls. She turned to Harry at the other end of the table. "Daddy, you remember that time we took a canoe out on the Monongahela and tipped over?"

She realized what she'd done as soon as the words were out. She could feel herself blush. Harry tried to undo the damage. "That must have been your stepfather because it sure wasn't me."

"What was I thinking? Of course it was." Triss took a sip of her iced tea and looked down.

Ethel and the girls looked at each other but said nothing. They had gone in an instant from participants to observers. It was as if the music had stopped and only Harry and Triss were still dancing. He broke the silence. "What did you say the name of the river was? Monongahela? Is it in Pennsylvania?"

Triss put down her glass. "That's right. It merges with the Allegheny in Pittsburgh to form the Ohio."

"I know the Ohio from my time in Kentucky–went boating on it–but I've never set foot in Pennsylvania. I've always wanted to tour the battle-field at Gettysburg and see where Pickett made his charge and Lincoln his speech." He appeared calm. He'd been telling people he was from Ken-tucky for thirty years.

"Western Pennsylvania is beautiful. You'll have to come sometime. All of you will." Triss looked from one side of the table to the other. She was trying to hold steady. "My sweet husband has donated money to the YMCA to build a camp. As I told your father, the lake at the camp will be called Triss Lake. You'll have to come see it."

Ethel noted the change. Now he was "your father." She pushed her chair back and stood. "It sounds nice. I've never been to the North. Mar-garet, I believe it's your turn to help me with the dishes."

Triss protested. "Please let me. I came to Tupelo uninvited, and you've welcomed me into your home and fed me a wonderful meal. The least I can do is help with the dishes."

"Thank you for the offer, Triss, but we can't have our guest doing the dishes. Margaret and I will clean up. It won't take us but a minute."

———◄○►———

Harry and Triss rode back to the hotel in silence. When he pulled up in front, she turned toward him.

"I'm so sorry, Daddy. I can't believe I said that."

"We all make mistakes. Look at some of the ones I've made."

"What are you going to do?"

"I don't know, maybe hide out in my study. But I'll have to come out at some point. I'll wait and see what Ethel says, I guess."

"I wonder what they're talking about right now."

"I'm afraid I know what they're talking about."

"I'm so sorry. Do you still want me to come to church tomorrow?"

"Let me see how it goes. I'll call you in the morning."

He walked her to the door, they hugged, then he returned to the car. When he got back to the parsonage, he turned off the ignition but stayed behind the wheel.

What should he do? What was the right thing to do? At this point, after hiding the truth for all these many years, it was too late to do the right thing. He could only do the least wrong thing. Whatever he did would hurt Ethel and might do more than that. He weighed the options. What was the lesser of the evils? As a Christian, what was he called to do?

One choice was to insist that the story he'd told Ethel and the girls was true and that Triss just wasn't thinking straight about the river trip. But Ethel was a smart woman. She'd seen Triss blush and would know he was lying. But what would she do about it? It might be like the lie he'd told her long ago about his age. She might just let it go. Triss would soon leave town, and life would return to normal. Maybe this was the best choice. It would sure be the easiest. But then Triss might come back, at least he hoped she would, and the questions would come up again. He should never have asked Triss to lie for him. After all he'd put her through, he never should have done that.

Could he tell Ethel part of the truth but not all of it? He could admit he was older than he'd claimed and that he'd raised Triss in Pennsylvania but leave it at that. He could say nothing about the worst of it–about Rose and his other children or Bess and his trouble with the law. But where would that leave him? Even if Ethel never found out about all the rest, she would know he'd lied about his age to get her to marry him and then lied about Triss this week. And how would he explain his claim that he'd spent all his life in Kentucky before he came to Texas? What possible motive could he have had for that? Then there was Triss. If pressed by Ethel or one of the girls, what would she say now that their story had started to fall apart?

The third option was the one he didn't want to think about. It would be the hardest and cause the most pain, but it was the one he believed was dictated by Scripture. It was to tell Ethel the whole truth, all of it, from beginning to end. The truth about his age and Rose and their four dead children; the truth about Bess, the tuition payments he spent, and the attempted escape to Liverpool; the truth about his trial and conviction and the time he served in Western Pen.

He thought of the sermon he'd prepared for the next morning and the admonition given by God to his people in the book of James: "Confess therefore your sins one to another, and pray for one another, that ye may be healed." The words were clear; he should confess his sins to Ethel. To heal himself, the Bible said he must tell her everything.

But wouldn't it be wrong to hurt Ethel to heal himself? He had carried the weight of guilt all these years. Confessing the truth might bring him relief, but what would it do to her? She would feel betrayed, no doubt, and she would never feel the same about the man to whom she had devoted her life. Harry had convinced Triss to go along with his lie because the truth would hurt others, Ethel most of all. Wasn't that still the case? Lying to her had been wrong, but telling her the truth might be even worse. And what would she do if he told her? Would she tell the children? Would word spread? If so, what would happen then? Was telling Ethel the whole truth really the lesser of two evils?

It was all Harry's fault. He'd chosen to hide what he'd done in the first half of his life, and there was no good way out now. He squeezed the steering wheel and thought back to 1905 and that fateful day in February, the day that Bess walked down the aisle and introduced herself. Their lunch that followed had started his life on the long path that had wound up here. There was the blissful time with Bess, the money he spent that wasn't his, then the ship bound for Liverpool and his three long years behind bars. After that came the long train ride to Georgetown, his time at Southwestern, then meeting Ethel in Carlton. Then there were the half dozen churches all over Texas, packing up and moving with babies every other year. They had come east fifteen years ago, first to Shreveport, then to the four churches in Mississippi. His journey that had begun on the northern end of Appalachia had ended on the southern.

Thirty-two years had passed since the day he met Bess. If she had walked out of the Calvary Methodist Church as soon as the service ended, he would likely still be in Pennsylvania. Later, if he had not bought Bess the dress at Carlisle's, he almost certainly would have made a clean escape to England. He would be speaking with a British accent now, not the drawl he'd acquired during his three decades in the South. And if he had told Ethel the truth about his age, she might not have married him, and he wouldn't be here now. But Harry couldn't undo anything he'd done in the past. He had taken Bess to lunch and courted her, he had bought her the dress, and he had lied to Ethel. And so here he was tonight, sitting behind the wheel of a parked car in Tupelo, Mississippi, wondering what to do.

It was true that Harry had been punished for the sins he'd committed in the first half of his life. But concealing those sins was a sin in itself, and his only punishment for that one had been the weight of the guilt he'd carried. There had been no reckoning, no expiation, no confession to his wife. And now he was outside the parsonage, dreading going inside. One thing was certain: Ethel would ask, and she would ask tonight. He knew her well enough to know that. And when she asked, he would have to answer. He squeezed the steering wheel again and wondered: What should his answer be? What should he say? After praying for the wisdom to answer wisely, he stepped out of the car and looked up, searching the night sky for Orion. When he found it, he took a deep breath and walked inside.

CHAPTER TWENTY-ONE

DECEMBER 1942

⟪⊙⟫

GREENWOOD

Harry and Ethel lived in Tupelo for five years, including the year and a half after Triss's surprise visit in the spring of 1937. It was their longest time in any one city in a marriage that lasted nearly thirty-three years. As was true of all of Harry's churches, the First Methodist Church in Tupelo prospered under his leadership. More than a hundred new members joined the church each year, over 600 altogether.

Harry and Ethel moved for the twelfth and final time in November 1938. He was promoted to the position of District Superintendent of the Greenwood District of the North Mississippi Methodist Conference, and he and Ethel moved back across the state to the Mississippi Delta, which they had left nearly a decade earlier. In his new position, Harry had administrative responsibility for nearly a hundred churches but, for the first time in nearly thirty years, did not have a church of his own. He missed being a full-time pastor with his own church, though he enjoyed the opportunity to work with the other preachers in the district to help them attract new members and improve their ministries. It was his last job.

A year after the move, the Methodist Episcopal Church and the Methodist Episcopal Church, South finally reunited. Slavery had caused the split nearly a century before, but the two churches did not resolve all their differences and come back together until three-quarters of a century after slavery was outlawed. The new, merged denomination was called simply the Methodist Church. Edwin Mouzon had worked for decades on the reunification project, but he died in 1937, two years before his dream was realized. Harry regretted that his dear friend was not alive to celebrate.

Harry turned eighty on New Year's Day 1942, less than a month after Pearl Harbor. An eightieth birthday should be a major event in a man's life, especially during a time when few men lived that long, but there was no celebration for Harry. Because of his longstanding claim that he was born in December 1875, his friends and family observed his sixty-sixth birthday three days before he turned eighty.

Harry was now an old man, much older than he let on, and his health began to deteriorate. He began suffering from abdominal pain in the summer and was diagnosed with stomach cancer. Nothing could be done and, by the first of November, he was no longer able to work. He spent the last month of his life at home in bed.

Triss had suffered a fatal heart attack two years earlier in the vacation home she and Frank owned in Palm Springs. When she died just before her fifty-fourth birthday, Harry achieved something no man should ever want to achieve. He outlived his first wife and all five of their children.

All of Harry and Ethel's children were now grown and gone, but they all came home to see Harry in his final days. Elizabeth came from the large farm outside Clarksdale where she lived with her husband and two sons. Edwin came from Memphis, Danny from her home near Greenwood, and Margaret and Marjory from Columbus, where they were in their senior year at Mississippi State College for Women. Harry died in his sleep early on the morning of December 12, 1942, with his family by his side. There were things about Harry's past his family didn't know, but he had been a good husband and father. They loved him dearly.

Harry's funeral was held at the First Methodist Church in Greenwood the following afternoon, Sunday, December 13. Friends and officials from the Methodist Church came from all over Mississippi to honor him. The services were conducted by Reverend W. R. Lott, the minister in Greenwood, who had come to know Harry during their time together as preachers in the North Mississippi Conference and to love him during their years together in Greenwood. Reverend Lott was assisted by J. M. Ward, another District Superintendent, and Dr. Clovis Chappell, a Harvard-educated theologian who wrote more than thirty books and was the pastor of Galloway Methodist Church in Jackson. Friends from churches Harry had served as pastor were the pallbearers, and the preachers in the Greenwood District served as honorary pallbearers. The sanctuary, decorated for Advent, was filled to overflowing. It was a beautiful, sunny day, and the doors and windows were opened wide so those outside on the sidewalks could see and hear.

Like the funerals for his father, grandfather, and great grandfather before him, Harry's funeral began with the singing of "Amazing Grace." And like Reverend Amos in 1863, Reverend Ward instructed the congregation to sing all the verses and sing them loud. It was now a family tradition. The three preachers had agreed with Ethel that Reverend Lott, who was closer to Harry than the other two were, should give the final and principal eulogy. After the reading of Scripture, including John 3:16, he walked to the lectern and smiled.

"Children of God, it is my distinct honor and great privilege to be with you today to celebrate the life of Dr. Henry Felgar Brooks, my friend Harry. To Mrs. Brooks, my friend Ethel, he was a devoted husband. To Elizabeth, Edwin, Danny, Margaret, and Marjory, he was a loving father. To the three little ones, Andy, Brooks, and Betty, he was a doting grandfather. To most of you, he was a preacher, one of the most gifted the Methodist Church has ever known. I could sit and listen to Harry Brooks preach the Gospel all day, every day. The church has lost a giant.

"But though I loved to hear Harry preach, he was much more than a preacher to me. He was my friend. And what a friend he was. Always wise, always encouraging, always there. I love the old hymn, 'What a Friend We Have in Jesus.' And what a friend I had in Harry. I thank God for Harry Brooks and for his friendship.

"Those of you who knew Harry well know that he was a man of strong convictions and that he was not shy about sharing them. Not long after coming to North Mississippi, he wrote an impassioned letter to the General Conference complaining that the church spent too much time and money on administration and not enough on evangelism. When he became District Superintendent and thus a member of the administration he'd complained about, I asked him if he'd changed his mind now that he was on the other side. 'Not a bit,' he said. 'I don't want to deal with finances and staffing. Give me a church. Let me bring souls to Jesus.' That was Harry. He loved to preach. He lived to preach.

"I saw Harry for the last time a week ago. He knew his time was short and was in a great deal of pain, but his spirits were high. Physically he was dying, but spiritually he was as strong as an ox. He knew where he was headed because he knew he'd been saved. His concerns were for his family, not for himself.

"Harry, you will not be surprised to learn, had some advice to give me about what I should say today. I was not surprised either. When he told me to take notes to make sure I got it right, I held up a pen and a pad. I told him I was a good Boy Scout. I was prepared. Harry loved the Boy Scouts. At the top of the first page, I wrote, 'Harry's Eulogy for Harry,' and below it I wrote what he asked me to tell you.

"He said I was to start with a familiar verse from the seventh chapter of Ecclesiastes: 'For there is not a just man on earth, who doeth good, and sinneth not.' Harry asked me to tell you that he was a terribly sinful man in the first half of his life, a first-class sinner. Not just little sins either, but big ones. He thought he was a Christian, but he realized later he was just playacting, going through the motions, debating the meaning of Scripture, and pretending to be a righteous man.

"But then, he said, two things happened that saved his life. First, after he hit rock bottom, a friend who stood by him when no one else did helped him find God. He soon realized that his calling was to help others find God, just as his friend had helped him. And then he found Ethel, who gave him the strength and support he needed to do what God had called him to do. During their years together, she packed up and moved with him a dozen times, starting in Santa Anna, Texas, and winding up here in Greenwood, with ten stops in between. Without Ethel, he wanted you to know, he could not have served God as he did.

"Harry also wanted me to tell you that, if God can save a man as sinful as he was, God can save anybody. In fact, God saves everybody who repents and believes in Jesus. And with salvation comes eternal life. We all know the promise from God in the comforting words of John 3:16. 'For God so loved the world, that he gave his only begotten Son, that whosoever believeth in him should not perish, but have everlasting life.'

"The last thing Harry asked me to say is this: You may believe you've committed such terrible sins that you're beyond redemption, beyond salvation, beyond hope. At one time, Harry believed that about himself. But he was wrong, and so are you. Harry wasn't beyond hope, and neither are you. And neither are the people you know and love. You may have a friend who has done such bad things that he believes God can never forgive him. Well, he's wrong too, and you should tell him so. You can be like Harry's friend, the one who led him to Jesus and saved his soul. You can save a soul too.

"When Harry said he was finished telling me what to say, I smiled and put down my pad. 'Harry,' I said to him, 'when I say these words, you'll already be gone. And yet you'll still be working to bring souls to Christ.' 'Amen,' he said, and I said it too. Let us pray.

"Our Father in heaven, watch over this family as they grieve the loss of the fine man who was their husband, father, and grandfather. Watch over the pastors in the Greenwood District as they go forward without his wise counsel and support. And watch over his friends as they miss the man they knew and loved so much. It's a rare man who makes as much difference in as many lives as Harry Brooks did. Thank you, God, for my friend Harry.

He has left us but is now in his new eternal home with You. Thank you for bringing him home. Amen."

At Harry's request, his funeral ended as it had begun, with "Amazing Grace." But this time the congregation sang just the first verse as they filed out of the sanctuary.

Amazing grace, how sweet the sound,
That saved a wretch like me.
I once was lost, but now am found,
Was blind, but now I see.

Former slave trader John Newton wrote these words nearly a century before Harry was born, but they tell the story of his life. He once was lost, but then was found, was blind but then could see. He was a wretch who lost everything, but then he was saved by God's amazing grace.

Harry's obituary, which appeared in the *Greenwood Commonwealth* the next day, noted that he held "many of the leading appointments in his church" and listed them all, beginning with the small church in Santa Anna and continuing to his service as General Superintendent in Greenwood. From his earliest days in Texas, the author wrote, Harry was "recognized as a gifted evangelistic pastor, and his labors bore fruit as his churches went forward."

EPILOGUE

And so, nearly eight decades after his death, what do we really know about Harry Brooks? What is the truth about the man who was a preacher, then a thief and adulterer, then a preacher again? What lessons can we learn from his life?

Harry's obituary was right about the names of the churches he served and his gift for preaching the Gospel, but it was wrong about other things. The author wrote that Harry was sixty-seven years old when he died, but he wasn't sixty-seven based on either his real birthdate or the one he invented for himself. Based on the real one, he was eighty. Based on the one he made up, he was still sixty-six. It was the same mistake that found its way onto the twins' birth certificates two decades earlier.

The obituary also stated that Harry was born near Harrisburg, Kentucky, and that his first appointment after arriving in Texas was to a position at Talpa College. But there has never been a Harrisburg in Kentucky, and there has never been a Talpa College in Texas either. Harry must have made these false claims in the story he invented about his past, and they were then passed along to the newspaper.

Several days after his funeral in Greenwood, Harry was laid to rest beside Ethel's parents in the Carlton Cemetery in Texas. There was no going back to Pennsylvania. The birthdate carved on Harry's gravestone was December 29, 1875. If he ever told Ethel his real birthdate, she didn't share it with the stonemason.

I saw Harry's gravestone for the first and only time when our family drove from Tupelo to Carlton for Ethel's funeral in the summer of 1977, but I didn't learn that the birthdate on it was wrong until more than forty years later. Harry's secret about his age remained a secret until Lee Cheney, with assistance from his daughter Laura, uncovered the truth in 2019. By then, all ten of Harry's children had been dead twenty years or more. Their ten deaths spanned more than a century, from baby Roswell in 1890 to Marjory and then Mama in the summer of 1999.

I know that Harry wasn't born in 1875, but there's a great deal about his life that I will never know. And so I filled in the blanks. For example, I wrote that Rose became depressed and withdrawn after losing three children, which led to Harry's infidelity and other wrongdoing. That seems to be a reasonable explanation, but I don't know if it's the correct one. At his criminal trial, Harry blamed his misdeeds on family problems and intoxicants, but no details about either were revealed in the brief article about his testimony.

Nor do I know if reckless spending while courting Bess was the sole cause of the financial distress that led Harry to embezzle from the schools and take out a loan from Sheriff Kiefer. The amount Harry took and borrowed, $2500, may not seem like much, but it would be worth $75,000 today. Given the amount, it seems likely that Harry's spending on Bess was not the only cause. But if there were others, what were they? The author of the *History of the Church of the Brethren of the Western District of Pennsylvania* wrote of Harry that "moving in high society caused his ruin." Though Harry's ruin and subsequent redemption are well documented, how he moved in high society is unknown.

On Harry's release from Western Pen, he accepted a position as a missionary to Mexicans in Texas for the rest of his life without pay. That documented fact explains what led him to Texas, but whether he ever served as a missionary to Mexicans and, if so, for how long is unknown. If he did, it could not have been for long because he was soon preaching on the circuit, after which he became the pastor of the half dozen churches in Texas, one in Louisiana, and four in Mississippi. How he managed to accomplish all of that—how an ex-con came to hold "many of the leading appointments in his church during a ministry of thirty-four years"—also remains a mystery. I can only surmise that it was because Harry was a gifted and devoted preacher and the church officials making the appointments knew nothing about his past in Pennsylvania.

Why Harry lied about his age is another mystery. Was it, as I concluded, to entice Ethel to marry him? Fear that she would reject him if she knew he was twice her age would be natural, but maybe he had a more honorable motivation. Maybe he did it so he wouldn't be considered too old to preach on the circuit. The circuit was for young men, and Harry turned forty-seven less than a month after he arrived in Texas. Or maybe the motivation for the lie about when he was born, like the one about where, was to make it harder for people to find out what he had done. But if that were the reason, why not adopt an alias? After all, he used an alias when he booked passage to Liverpool.

Finally, did Harry ever tell Ethel the whole truth—or even part of it? I considered different ways of answering this question but ultimately decided not to answer it at all and to leave this blank unfilled. And the reason for my decision is simple: It's because I don't know. I don't know if Harry told Ethel any of it or all of it.

After Triss's surprise visit in the spring of 1937, Ethel remained by Harry's side until his death more than five years later, but that hardly proves he didn't tell her. She would no doubt have felt betrayed if she had learned the whole truth, but what would she have done? Perhaps more important, what *could* she have done? She was a housewife in her fifties with three teenage girls at home. The family lived on Harry's salary, the church provided their home, and Ethel would depend on a pension from the Methodist Church after he was gone. Even if she had learned about Bess and prison and all the rest, what could she have done? She was stuck. In her time and circumstances, her only choice would have been to get on with her life and do the best she could.

Ethel rarely smiled during her many years as a widow, which I always thought was because she was self-conscious about her dentures, which she took out and put in a coffee cup on her bedside table every night. But perhaps she was bitter about devoting her life to a man who deceived her about his age and his past. I hope not. I hope he told her the whole truth from the beginning and that she loved him and married him in spite of it all. I hope she didn't smile because of the false teeth.

So I don't know if Harry told Ethel about his past, but I'm certain that neither of them told others—not church officials, not the members of the churches Harry served, not even their own children. As for the church, there is no way that Harry's years as a preacher in the South would have taken the same course if the leaders in the Methodist Church had known he was a convicted felon. In the Bible Belt in the 1930s, it is inconceivable that a known ex-con and adulterer would have risen to the position of District Superintendent.

As for the family, Mama told me that none of them knew that Harry had been married or had a child before Triss showed up. If Ethel knew, she didn't tell. Then there's my name. That Mama and Daddy would have knowingly named me for a man who did what Harry did, especially if he hid it from Ethel and his children until Triss appeared, is doubtful. There were many relatives they could have named me for who never committed a crime. I don't know what my name would be if Mama had known the whole truth about Harry, but I don't believe it would be Brooks.

A letter to me that was never sent is further evidence that Mama didn't know. A dozen years after she died, Daddy came to live with my wife Carrie and me. While we were going through old papers in Mama and Daddy's house on Rogers Drive in Tupelo, the only house they ever owned, I came across a letter Mama had written twenty-five years earlier. It was in an envelope that was stamped and addressed to me, but she'd never mailed it. She must have decided against it.

Maybe I shouldn't have read the letter, but I did. In five handwritten pages, Mama revealed her feelings about subjects we hardly ever discussed, including Harry. About him, she wrote: "I've never talked much about Daddy because he's been dead so many years, but he was perhaps the most intelligent and certainly the highest educated minister we've ever had in Tupelo. I've always been happy and proud that you take after my side of the family."

Perhaps Mama would have written with such pride in her father even if she had known everything about him, but I doubt it. It's also odd that she wrote that her adopted son took after her side of the family, though I suppose it's possible. Nurture can be as strong as nature, and maybe I learned traits from Mama that she learned from Harry. Could I take after a man whose blood I don't share and who died nearly fifteen years before I was born? Is it possible?

The answer to that question, like so many others, will never be known. But this much is certain: My grandfather Harry Brooks was a fascinating man. He was a thief and adulterer but a man of God. He was cursed with mortal weakness but blessed with towering strength. He sank to the bottom but rose to the top. I wish I could have known him.

So, in the end, even with all that will never be known, what can we learn from Harry Brooks? What does his life teach us?

One lesson is how much the world has changed in the last century. Harry lived at a time when there were trains but no Internet. In his day, a man could escape from his troubles for the price of a westbound ticket. He could stay tucked inside a berth in a sleeping car for twenty-four hours, wake up a thousand miles away, and walk out of the train into a new land where no one knew a thing about him. He could make a new life for himself with little fear that his old one would come back to haunt him. That's what Harry did, and it worked for nearly thirty years. Harry turned seventy-five on New Year's Day 1937. He no doubt believed he'd left his past behind for good. But then came the last Thursday in April, the day Triss knocked on the parsonage door. Compare then to now, when anyone with a laptop could learn more in an afternoon about Harry's past than Ethel learned while sleeping in the same bed with him for more than three decades.

Harry's life also serves as a stark reminder that there is no one among us who is either all good or all bad. We are all made up of both. In the first half of his life, Harry stole from his employer, betrayed his wife, abandoned his family, and tried to escape to another continent. But before he did any of that, he was a respected minister and educator, a good family man, and a community leader. Then, in the second half, though he brought thousands of people to God and lived an upstanding and righteous life, he did not live a perfect one. He lied about his age and his past and concealed his prior sins. I believe, on balance, that Harry was a very good man, but he serves as proof positive that the words of Ecclesiastes are true: "There is not a just man on earth, who doeth good, and sinneth not."

Finally, the most important lesson to be learned from Harry's life, at least for me, is one of perseverance and redemption. How easy it would have been for Harry to wallow in guilt and self-pity after he found himself alone in a prison cell. How easy it would have been to give up on the future after he lost his wife, his family, his job, and his freedom. How easy it would have been to waste away his days, serving neither God nor man.

But Harry did not take the easy path. He came to the South, where he made a new life, raised a new family, and spent the rest of his days preaching the Word of God. He devoted his life to saving souls, just as his own soul had been saved. He was a gifted preacher and received the grace of another gift–a second chance in a second life. He made the most of it, and "his labors bore fruit as his churches went forward."

Harry's fall from grace made him the man that he was. He understood sin. He understood loss and hopelessness. But he also understood forgiveness and redemption. All he achieved in the second half of his life was the result of how far he fell in the first. He lost everything and fell as far as a man can fall. He was lost, but then, through God's grace, he was found.

END NOTES

The known facts about Harry Brooks make for a fascinating story about a fascinating man. Those facts include Harry's embezzlement and infidelity, his betrayal and duplicity, but they also include his strength and determination, his redemption, and his commitment to God and His people. Harry Brooks robbed from the schoolchildren of Uniontown, left his wife for another woman, and abandoned his family when he tried to escape to the country from which his ancestors had sailed to America more than a century before. But Harry also brought thousands of sinners to God in the decades after he was released from prison and came to the South.

Those are the known facts about Harry Brooks but, standing alone, they would not make for much of a book. Had I stuck to a non-fiction biography that included only the facts I could verify, this book would be no more than fifty pages long. So I decided to add what I imagine to be true to what I know to be true. In deciding how to complete Harry's story, I had countless decisions to make: What led to his infidelity? How did he meet Bess? Were they in love? Was she the reason for his financial predicament? How did he meet Ethel? Did she ever know the truth? Why did Triss come to Tupelo? Did Ethel already know about Triss before she arrived?

I did the best I could, but I may have been more generous in my treatment of Harry than the facts warrant. He did terrible things—in addition to his affair and theft, he left a seven-year-old daughter behind when he tried to escape to Liverpool—and he may have engaged in other misconduct that never came to light and is now lost in the mists of time. But I chose to treat Harry's misdeeds in 1905 as the exception—aberrations in what was otherwise an upstanding life. I may have done so because he was my grandfather and because Mama, who was an excellent judge of character, thought so highly of him. But there is evidence that supports my choice.

By all accounts, Harry had an excellent reputation for all his years in Pennsylvania until 1905 and an excellent reputation for all his years in the South after he arrived in Texas in 1908. In the first half of his life, the *Jeannette Dispatch* reported that he was regarded as "a model school man, possessing an exemplary character." In the second, according to the *Greenwood Commonwealth,* he was "recognized as a gifted evangelistic pastor, and his labors bore fruit as his churches went forward." I concluded that Harry was a good man who suffered a catastrophic fall and then achieved an extraordinary recovery.

What follows are my notes about what I know to be true in each chapter as well as my thoughts regarding choices I made about what I don't know to be true.

NOTES ON CHAPTER ONE

The facts about FDR's speech, Harry's invocation, and the 1936 tornado are all based on historical records. I found Harry's essay about the tornado in family papers at my parents' home in Tupelo. Lee Cheney confirmed from genealogical records that Harry's first wife, Rose Cochran Brooks, died in 1916 and that their youngest daughter Katherine died in 1935.

Mama told me when I was young about Triss's surprise appearance at the parsonage in Tupelo. I don't recall her telling me what year it was, but I found Triss's name and address in Harry's handwriting in his pastor's book for 1937. Mama said that nobody in the family knew that Harry had been married or that he had a child before Triss showed up. I don't recall that Mama told me why Triss came, but I know Triss was welcomed by the family because I inherited the family photo at the beginning of the book in which she appears. The photo was taken on the front steps of the parsonage in Tupelo. I also have several other photos of her that were taken in the 1910s and '20s. She must have given them to the family.

NOTES ON CHAPTER TWO

This chapter is based on an excerpt from a Brooks Family History that was published in 1975 and Lee Cheney found on genealogy.com. The excerpt states that John Brooks was a knight but does not say how he came to be one, that the family of seven was immigrating to America from England, and that John and Mary died from an epidemic that broke out aboard ship and from which many adults died. The excerpt does not specify the nature of the epidemic. I chose typhoid fever because it was common aboard ships and was far more likely to be fatal to adults than to children. The excerpt further states that five men who survived the voyage took custody of one Brooks son apiece, that four of the boys were taken to Massachusetts, New York, Maryland, and Virginia, and that Joseph, the youngest, was taken to New Jersey. It also states that the five brothers never saw each other again.

Joseph's age comes from his gravestone, which notes that he was sixty-eight years and twenty-five days old when he died on September 30, 1863. He would thus have been three during the voyage in the summer of 1799. Whether Melchior Entling was aboard the ship or took custody of Joseph later is unknown, but a history of Fayette County, Pennsylvania, states that Joseph was raised as a member of Entling's family. The information about Liverpool's role in the slave trade and conditions in steerage on transatlantic journeys is from publicly available histories of Liverpool, the slave trade, and transatlantic journeys.

NOTES ON CHAPTER THREE

This chapter is based on a short biography of Joseph Brooks that is also from the 1975 Brooks Family History and can be found at findagrave.com. That Joseph and his wife Dorothy had thirteen children who survived to adulthood is from the biography, but the number of their grandchildren is unknown. I chose to give them fifty-eight, which is an average of four and a half children for each child. It was a time of very large families, so they may well have had more.

The biography states that Joseph founded Springfield Township in Fayette County and that he was a large, powerfully built man, six feet tall and 225 pounds, with an impressive and aristocratic bearing; that he was a successful farmer and raiser of stock, one of the wealthiest men of his day, the owner of a number of properties that are still occupied by his descendants, and "an outstanding citizen in every way"; and that he was a Presbyterian, church services were often held in his home, the minister was largely supported by him, and he was one of the largest contributors to the building of a brick church in the township.

The biography also states that Joseph wore a Prince Albert coat and high hat and was buried in the family plot on his land after he died on the last day of September in 1863. I chose to bury him in the coat and high hat and have the funeral on the farmhouse lawn. Records of the Brooks Family Cemetery show that three people are buried in the family plot with Joseph: his wife Dorothy, who outlived him by nearly thirty years and died when she was ninety-four, and two of their grandsons, cousins Abraham and Albert Brooks, who were both born in 1841 and died when they were one and three.

Brooks Funeral Home is still in business in Southwest Pennsylvania, with facilities in Connelsville and Mt. Pleasant. The home's website traces the origin of the business to the early 1850s, when Henry Felgar began a preservation process and manufactured coffins.

NOTES ON CHAPTER FOUR

The information in this chapter about the Lands is based on a family history written by the daughter of one of my great aunts, other family documents, and Civil War records. The dates, including Ethel's birthdate of January 18, 1886, are accurate, but I invented the midwife.

Sources for the second half of this chapter include the cyclopedia cited in the text, a history of the Brethren Church of Western Pennsylvania, Harry and Rose's wedding license, records showing the birth dates of their children, and census and other records showing when Harry's parents died. How Harry and Rose met and the details of their courtship are unknown.

NOTES ON CHAPTER FIVE

Lee Cheney found the dates of the births and deaths of all five of Harry and Rose's children in genealogical records. Nothing is known about what caused the deaths of the three who died in the 1890s. I chose causes that were common for children at the time. Lee also confirmed from findagrave.com that Dorothy died in 1891 and thus outlived her great-great-grandson Roswell. I established from newspaper reports that Harry and Rose moved to McKeesport in 1892 and that he was elected school superintendent in Uniontown in 1902. As for Harry's drinking and his relationship with Rose after George's death, no details are known other than the contents of the newspaper article from Harry's trial in December 1905 stating that he blamed his troubles on family problems and intoxicants.

NOTES ON CHAPTER SIX

I found a number of references supporting the claim that the book of Job was written approximately 1700 years before Christ was born, but Steve Allen, a friend who graciously reviewed the manuscript, told me the consensus now is that Job was written much more recently. Like Harry, Steve decided to seek a divinity degree late in life. As of this writing, he's sixty years old and a student in the Master of Divinity program at Duke, where I attended law school forty years ago. I know far less about the Bible than does Steve and don't dispute what he told me, but when Harry was preaching early in the twentieth century, many biblical scholars believed that Job was written much earlier than what is now believed. Some asserted it was written even before 1700 B.C.

The other known facts in this chapter are from a front-page article in the July 6, 1905, edition of *The Mount Pleasant Journal*, the daily newspaper in Mount Pleasant, Pennsylvania. The article stated that Fayette County Sheriff Mart Kiefer had discovered that Professor H. F. Brooks of

Uniontown had engaged in a romantic relationship with Bess Montgomery of Pittsburgh. The article did not disclose how the relationship began.

NOTES ON CHAPTERS SEVEN AND EIGHT

These chapters are based almost entirely on the front-page article in the July 6, 1905, *Mount Pleasant Journal*. Lee Cheney found the article after he'd told me Harry's story but before he knew Bess Montgomery's role in it. He emailed it to me one night with FLASH REPORT on the subject line. The facts in this chapter that come from the article include the following:

On Saturday, July 1, 1905, the Uniontown School Board met and decided to present information to Justice Dawson accusing Harry of misappropriating more than a thousand dollars in tuition payments that had been paid to him but never turned in to the school district. Harry also owed $475.00 to Fayette County Sheriff Mart Kiefer on a sixty-day promissory note dated April 23, 1905. There were other unpaid creditors in Uniontown as well. Officials had learned that Harry and a woman from Pittsburgh named Bess Montgomery had left the city for Washington. Sheriff Kiefer and Fayette County Detective McBeth followed them there on Saturday night. Sheriff Kiefer found Bess on Monday in Washington. After a "sweating process," she disclosed that she and Harry had gone to New York, where he had persuaded the landlord at a hotel to sell him a ticket to Liverpool on a Cunard liner in the name of H. B. Telfer. Harry had traveled at first as H. B. Felgar, using his middle name. Bess also turned over several letters from Harry.

By the time the article was published three days after Bess's interrogation, Harry was at sea on his way to Liverpool. While on the ship, there was no way for him to learn what the sheriff had learned. The article refers to Bess as "a woman of doubtful repute" but reveals two facts–Harry wrote her a number of letters, and Sheriff Kiefer was forced to subject her to the "sweating process" before she would disclose where Harry was–that make it clear that Bess and Harry almost certainly had a serious, ongoing relationship. It seems likely that Bess was not "a woman of doubtful repute" before she met Harry and that she was characterized that way by the reporter only because she carried on an affair with a married man who was an elected public official and a minister.

The article states that a dress Harry bought Bess "furnished the clue that has led to his detection." The purchase was a seemingly inconsequential act that had enormous consequences. If Harry had not bought Bess the dress, he would have escaped, and he and Ethel never would have met, married, and had five children. But for the dress, Harry and Ethel's children, grandchildren, and the generations that have come after never would have been born. And their descendants who have not yet been born never would be.

Where Harry and Bess stayed and where he bought the dress that led to her discovery are unknown, but I confirmed that all the hotels, restaurants, and other establishments where I placed them in this chapter were in business in 1905. Carlisle's was founded by Sophia Carlisle in 1888 and was still selling bridal gowns and dresses in Pittsburgh in 2020. The store manager was Sophia's great-great-granddaughter. Unfortunately, like many small businesses, it failed as a result of the COVID lockdowns. The Algonquin, on 44th Street in New York, opened in November 1902. Healy's, where O. Henry was a regular from 1903 to 1907, later became Pete's Tavern and is still in business today at the same location on 18th Street. The Auld House in Washington, Pennsylvania, was one of the city's two leading hotels after the turn of the century. It burned on Christmas Day 1963, killing a forty-year-old man who was in town visiting his relatives.

Though the article in the *Mount Pleasant Journal* does not provide the name of the Cunard liner on which Harry made his getaway, I confirmed that the *Carpathia* was assigned the route between New York and Liverpool in 1905. The first subway line in New York, stretching from City Hall in lower Manhattan to 145th Street and Broadway in Harlem, opened on October 27, 1904, the autumn before Harry and Bess visited the city. The Brooks Funeral Home website states that Henry Felgar's grandson Samuel Clymer Brooks began embalming as we know it today. It does not mention that Harry was Samuel's older brother.

Harry, Bess, Rose, Justice Dawson, Sheriff Kiefer, Detective McBeth, and Harry's brothers are the people in the chapter whose names are known. The identity of the school board president is unknown. I decided to name him Mark Shepard in honor of a good friend and classmate of the same name who practices law in Pittsburgh and goes by Shep.

NOTES ON CHAPTERS NINE AND TEN

A 1903 brochure advertising trips on the *Carpathia* stated that the fare from Liverpool to New York was five pounds, fifteen shillings. Based on the exchange rate at the time, the fare in dollars would have been nearly thirty. The brochure included a photo of a third-class cabin for four, with two stacked berths along either side and a lavatory in between.

Nearly all the facts in these chapters are based on a series of newspaper articles. The July 6 *Mt. Pleasant Journal* article, published while Harry was still at sea, stated that detectives from Scotland Yard would be waiting for him in Queenstown. Other articles reported on Harry's incarceration in London, his extradition, and his return from London to Pennsylvania with Sheriff Kiefer and Detective McBeth. One of the articles disclosed that Harry had grown a beard and become seasick on the way home, that they were arriving on the *Duquesne Limited*, and that Harry expected one of his brothers to post bond, but neither of them did. I found the information about the terrible train wreck while reading about the history of the *Duquesne Limited*.

Two short newspaper articles reported on Harry's trial in December. The first provided the gist of his testimony, the second his reaction to the jury verdict. There was no mention of prosecution witnesses in either one. The article headlined "BROOKS WAS SORRY" about his sentencing appeared in the January 5, 1906, issue of Uniontown's *Weekly News Standard*. Harry's remarks at the sentencing and Judge Reppert's response are from the article. Rose's divorce filing was also reported in the paper. The date of Harry's transfer to Western Penitentiary is reflected on his prison intake form.

NOTES ON CHAPTER ELEVEN

The Hotel Tupelo was built in 1917 and demolished forty-five years later. On special occasions, my paternal grandparents Cliff and Margaret Eason took their children, sons- and daughters-in-law, and grandchildren there. I have a photo of twenty of us that was taken at the Hotel Tupelo on Mother's Day 1965 when I was seven. Ethel, who was included in the gathering, had been a widow for more than twenty years by then.

My father Paul Eason, the finest man I've ever known, was a Boy Scout leader in Tupelo for sixty years. Clark Burnett, whose father was the manager of the Hotel Tupelo, was one of the hundreds of boys who became Eagle Scouts under Daddy's leadership. Clark responded to my request for assistance in writing this chapter by sending me a photo of the lobby of the hotel and a Blue Room menu from 1937. A filet with mushrooms was seventy-five cents, a BLT twenty.

The facts about Frank Soles's career at Talon, the YMCA camp he established, and Triss Lake are from historical records that Lee Cheney found. The YMCA announced in early 2021 that the camp was closing permanently because of the pandemic. Triss married Frank in June 1909. There is no mention of Harry in the wedding announcement. He had left for Texas by then. Lee also found the birth dates of Triss's two children. Dorothy, nicknamed Dottie, was born in 1920, John in 1922. Mama and Marjory were born in March 1921.

Harry lied about his age by fourteen years less three days. Lee and his daughter found a number of census and other records confirming that Harry was born on New Year's Day 1862. Lee became suspicious about Harry's purported birthdate of December 29, 1875, because of records showing that his father Milton died in 1871. The subsequent investigation turned up Harry's actual birthdate as well as the other details of his story. I have Mama's birth certificate, which says that Harry was born in Kentucky and was forty-six years old when she was born. If he had been born in December 1875, he would have been forty-five.

Other than his false claims about his date and place of birth, I know little about the past life Harry invented for himself or his communications with Triss when she showed up in Tupelo. Exactly how they sorted things out will always be a mystery, but they must have found a way to sort them out because Triss stayed and was embraced by the family and the details of Harry's misdeeds never came to light. My older cousins heard rumors but nothing specific. To my knowledge, nobody ever found out that the upstanding minister and family patriarch had served time in the penitentiary for embezzlement.

As for Harry's birthplace, all the records from the first half of his life state truthfully that he was born in Pennsylvania, but all the records from the second half state falsely that he was born in Kentucky. These records include census reports, Mama's birth certificate, and the Land Family History written by one of Harry and Ethel's nieces. In that history, Harry's birthplace is recorded as Courtney, Kentucky, but I found no proof that there's ever been a Courtney, Kentucky. Harry's obituary states that he was born near Harrisburg, Kentucky. I found no indication that there's ever been a Harrisburg, Kentucky, either.

TKE was a popular drugstore and restaurant on the corner of Spring and Main Streets in Tupelo. I had lunch and ice cream at the soda counter many times while I was growing up. Finally, Mama really could wiggle her ears. Maybe Marjory could too, but I never saw her do it.

NOTES ON CHAPTER TWELVE

This chapter is almost entirely fictional. I invented the character of Harrison Matheny. My daughter has a friend with that name, it sounded like a good turn-of-the-century name, and I borrowed it with the real Harrison Matheny's permission. I used the fictional Reverend Matheny to explain Harry's decision to leave the German Baptist Church to become a Methodist because the real explanation is unknown.

From historical records, three things are known about Harry's religious affiliation during these years. The 1890 history of Westmoreland County states that Harry was a member of the German Baptist Church. The German Baptist Church changed its name to the Church of the Brethren in 1909. According to the 1916 history of the church, Harry was called into the ministry in the Indian Creek congregation of the church. When Harry became a minister, it was still the German Baptist Church. Indian Creek is in Fayette County, which means that Harry almost certainly began preaching in the Baptist Church before he and Rose moved to McKeesport in 1892. Like Pittsburgh, McKeesport is in Allegheny County, two counties north of Indian River. Third, Harry was listed as a Methodist on the intake form when he was transferred to Western Penitentiary in March 1906. Harry thus left the German Baptist Church and became a Methodist sometime between 1890 and 1906. When, where, and why are unknown.

I found the article from the December 3, 1908, *Jeannette Dispatch* about Harry's position as a missionary in Texas while doing additional research to supplement the wealth of materials Lee Cheney provided me. The article supplied the answer to the question: Why Texas? Harry's motives for leaving Pennsylvania were obvious, but until I found the December 3 article, I didn't know why he chose a new home 1400 miles from his old one.

The other part of the chapter that has some basis in fact concerns Dr. Edwin Mouzon, who received his Doctor of Divinity degree from Southwestern University in 1905 and became the dean of the theology department shortly before Harry arrived in Texas. Dr. Mouzon later became a prominent leader in the Methodist Church, serving as a bishop for many years. What role he played in Harry's life after Harry got to Texas is unknown, but when Harry and Ethel's second child and only son was born in Cleburne, Texas, in the fall of 1912, they named him Edwin Mouzon Brooks. Their new son, my uncle, was Lee Cheney's biological father.

I don't know if Harry's brothers sent him a letter disowning him while he was in prison, but they definitely severed all ties with him. Not only did they decline his request to post bond, but when they died years later, Harry was not mentioned in their obituaries.

NOTES ON CHAPTER THIRTEEN

There are few confirmed facts that have any bearing on this chapter. First, Harry accepted the position as an unpaid missionary in Texas when he was released from prison in December 1908. Second, when Harry got to Texas, Edwin Mouzon had recently become the dean of the school of theology at Southwestern University. Third, Harry and Ethel named their only son Edwin Mouzon Brooks.

As for the two buildings, the courthouse in Uniontown was built in 1892. In its early years, prisoners condemned to death were hanged from the clock tower. Legend has it that one of them cursed the tower so that the four clocks facing in the four directions would never show the same time again. The Administration Building at Southwestern, now called the Cullen Building, was constructed in 1900. Southwestern is the successor to the oldest university in Texas and traces its origin to 1840.

NOTES ON CHAPTER FOURTEEN

How Harry and Ethel met is unknown, but documented facts make the explanation for their meeting in this chapter as plausible as any other. I know that Harry preached on the circuit. In a report to the General Conference when he was serving as the minister of the First Methodist Church in Starkville, Mississippi, he wrote that he had "served in pastorates from the circuit to what may be called some of the leading stations of five conferences in three states." Riding the circuit almost certainly would have preceded his being assigned to a church of his own. Second, I found records showing that Methodist circuit riders preached in the tiny church in Carlton.

The Lands lived just outside Carlton, but presumably Ethel no longer lived at home in 1909. She turned twenty-three in January of that year. Land family records state that she went to business school in Tyler and then worked for a judge in Ft. Worth.

My family and I went to Carlton in the summer of 1977 for Ethel's funeral in the old Methodist church there. Ethel was buried beside Harry, who had died nearly thirty-five years earlier. We had no reason to suspect that the birthdate on his gravestone was wrong by nearly fourteen years. Carlton is all but gone now. Its population peaked at 750 in 1910, shortly after the railway was routed through town, and has been shrinking ever since. No more than seventy people live there now.

Harry's obituary in the *Greenwood Commonwealth* in December 1942 states that he worked as a schoolteacher and traveling salesman before entering the ministry. Harry began teaching school when he was only seventeen. I found no evidence that he was ever a traveling salesman, but maybe he was.

Harry's two wedding dates are based on his two wedding licenses as well as family records. He married Rose on February 18, 1886, Ethel on February 17, 1910. He also represented to the world from the time he arrived in Texas until his death that he was born on December 29, 1875. Harry likely got away with the lie because he had a full head of hair and looked younger than he was. I have a photo of him with Ethel and their two oldest children that was likely taken in 1914. He was fifty-two then but looked no older than forty-five. Based on the new birthdate he invented for himself, he claimed to be thirty-eight.

NOTES ON CHAPTER FIFTEEN

The churches where Harry was assigned in Texas are listed in his obituary and are consistent with Texas Methodist conference records that I reviewed. The birthdates and birthplaces of Harry and Ethel's children are from the Land Family History and other family records. I don't know what led the family to move 500 miles east to Shreveport shortly after the twins were born and then another 200 miles to Jackson two years later, but the transfers are confirmed by Harry's obituary as well as family records and photographs. The information about the success of Capitol Street Methodist Church under Harry's leadership is from the April 17, 1925, issue of the *Christian Advocate*.

Harry received a Doctor of Divinity degree from Asbury College in Wilmore, Kentucky, in 1923, the year he turned sixty-one. It was the same year he became the minister of Capitol Street Methodist Church. He may have obtained the degree through a correspondence program, but he may have spent time on campus before beginning his ministry in Jackson in November of that year.

I discovered with an Internet search for Henry Felgar Brooks that Harry gave the invocation and served as a delegate to the annual Congress of the American Prison Association in Jackson during the second week of November 1925. Whether he was chosen to be a delegate because he was the pastor of a dynamic church in the host city or because he was an ex-con with first-hand knowledge and unique insights is unknown. Whether Harry disclosed the basis for his knowledge about prison life is also unknown, but it's very unlikely. Harry is not listed among those who attended the Congress held the following year in Pittsburgh. I found no evidence that Harry ever returned to Pennsylvania after he left in December 1908.

NOTES ON CHAPTER SIXTEEN

The conversations that Harry had with Ethel and others when Triss appeared in Tupelo can only be imagined, and the extent to which Triss may have agreed to protect Harry is also unknown. But I concluded that it's very unlikely that Triss disclosed Harry's age or his incarceration in Pennsylvania to anyone for a number of reasons. First, Harry was promoted to the position of District Superintendent in Greenwood in 1938, which would have been inconceivable if his past had come to light before then. Second, I'm sure that Mama never knew her father was a felon. Finally, Harry's false birthdate of December 29, 1875, was carved on his gravestone. If others knew his real birthdate, they kept it a secret.

NOTES ON CHAPTER SEVENTEEN

Information about the service Harry led encouraging generosity to victims of the 1927 flood is from an article in the Clarksdale newspaper. The facts about Roosevelt's visit to Tupelo in November 1934 are from numerous press reports. How Harry was chosen to give the invocation is unknown, but he was definitely chosen to give it. Not only did he refer to the invocation in his 1935 letter to the president, but I inherited a photo of him standing at the lectern with Roosevelt behind him. A note on the photo says there were "acres of people" present.

The text of FDR's speech that he said was not a speech is available from multiple sources, but I was unable to find the text of Harry's invocation. The last line of the invocation that Harry gave but I wrote is a tribute to the wonderful song about the TVA and Wilson Dam written by Jason Isbell. George Booth's account of his experience helping the president into his car is from a podcast. Harry's 1935 letter is quoted in a book by Fred C. Smith entitled *Trouble in Goshen: Plain Folk, Roosevelt, Jesus, and Marx in the Great Depression South.*

NOTES ON CHAPTER EIGHTEEN

I found the stack of envelopes covered with the notes Harry used to give his sermons among family papers long after I started writing this book. His trip on the Ohio River is in the notes. The Ohio begins in Pittsburgh, where the Allegheny and Monongahela merge to form it, but it also serves as the northern border of Kentucky. Preaching about a trip on the river thus would not have revealed that Harry was from Pennsylvania.

The Bible verses, books, and poems, and the references to Roosevelt, York, and Lindbergh are all in Harry's notes, as is his advice for how to rid the world of harlots and libertines. I was delighted to see the reference to *Huckleberry Finn* in the notes for Harry's sermon about boys months after I wrote, with no basis in fact, that Harry and Bess agreed that Twain was their favorite author and *Huckleberry Finn* his finest work.

I don't know if Harry ever spoke at a conference on preaching, at Asbury or anywhere else, but all the rest of this chapter comes from Harry's notes. The notes my grandfather used to preach his sermons are a treasure.

NOTES ON CHAPTER NINETEEN

Most of the details and stories in this chapter are from an excellent history of the 1936 tornado compiled by Martis D. Ramage Jr. that was published in 1997, but friends shared some of them directly with me. I posted a draft of part of the chapter on Facebook on the eighty-fifth anniversary of the tornado, and friends from Tupelo responded with stories about the storm that had been passed down through the generations. I added several of them to the chapter.

Death counts from the storm have varied over the years. Early reports inexcusably and significantly undercounted the death toll among the black residents of Tupelo, and the official death toll of 216 omitted most of them. The 1997 Ramage history attempted to correct the error and listed 275 victims by name. No tornado in America since 1936 has killed nearly as many.

A history of the First United Methodist Church in Tupelo prepared for its sesquicentennial in 2017 revealed that replacement of the roof on the parsonage was completed the day before the tornado and that Harry conducted more than sixty funerals for its victims in the days after. I found the names of the dead church members written in Harry's hand in his 1936 pastor book as well as the numbers of the injured and the homes that were damaged or destroyed. I discovered Harry's essay about the tornado among family papers in my parents' home and sent a copy to a museum in Tupelo.

Mama told me about the organist's car trapped between two fallen trees, and Daddy told me about the destruction of Church Street School and the woman with the broken back at the hospital. Mama and Daddy were both in the ninth grade in April 1936. The tornado went right between their homes. Had its path varied slightly in either direction, one of them could have been among the hundreds of fatalities.

Mama and Daddy graduated from Tupelo High School three years after the tornado struck. They went away to different colleges in the fall of 1939 and didn't see each other for years. Daddy was in the Naval Air Corps during the war and was discharged in 1946. They reconnected when Mama moved back to Tupelo in the late 1940s and married in January 1950. They adopted my sister Margie in 1955 and me two years later.

Postscript: The tornado struck on a Sunday night. On another Sunday night many years later, May 2, 2021, I was on my screened porch in Madison, Mississippi, working on this chapter. The air outside grew still, and the local tornado alarm sounded. A man's voice came over a loudspeaker, reported that a tornado had been sighted, and urged everyone to take cover. Later that night, a different tornado passed through Tupelo, following almost the same path as the terrible tornado eighty-five years earlier. This time, fortunately, the damage was limited, and no one in Madison or Tupelo was killed or injured by either tornado. There were no warning systems in 1936.

NOTES ON CHAPTER TWENTY

There is little in this chapter that I know to be true other than details about the people and places. Ethel, whom I called Grandma, was quiet but very observant. She always beat me at checkers, and I loved her home-made bread. Danny did have a sharp tongue and a great sense of humor. Unlike Grandma, she was not quiet. Mama and Marjory were both bright and excellent students, but they took different paths after college. Mama married Daddy, they stayed in Tupelo, and she never had a job that truly challenged her. Marjory, who never married, earned a PhD from Ohio State and served as a professor and dean at universities all over the country. When she retired from New Mexico State, she moved back to Tupelo and bought a house down the street from the house where I grew up and Mama and Daddy still lived. The twins died two months apart in the summer of 1999.

Daddy was handsome but shy, at least when he was young. He rarely dated. Mama loved to sing and dance. Daddy's singing was limited to hymns in church. I never saw him dance and would have been astonished if he ever did.

I mentioned Harry's clock because it was passed down from him to Grandma to Mama to me. A neighbor who grew up in Switzerland and is a clock expert told me it was made around 1880. It sits on the buffet in our dining room and keeps perfect time.

NOTES ON CHAPTER TWENTY-ONE

Harry's pastor's book for each of his years at the First Methodist Church in Tupelo lists the new members who joined the church that year. The total for the five years was more than 600.

I found Harry's letter complaining about the time and money the church spent on administration among family papers. It was written while he was the minister of the First Methodist Church in Starkville. In the letter, Harry wrote that "we are fast becoming head developed and soul shriveled. The head and the heart must go together. We are losing the power to stir the souls of men. We must have more time for soul development."

A woman at the First United Methodist Church in Fort Worth sent me Harry's obituary, which had not turned up in my searches or Lee Cheney's. The obituary stated that Reverend Lott conducted the service with assistance from Reverend Ward and Dr. Chappell. The quote that ends the chapter is from the obituary as well.

The three grandchildren referred to in the obituary are the oldest of Harry and Ethel's eleven and the only ones who were alive in December 1942. Andy and Brooks Anderson were my Aunt Elizabeth's two oldest children, and Betty Brooks was my uncle Edwin's oldest. I am Harry and Ethel's youngest grandchild. Lee Cheney, who learned he was their grandson shortly before discovering the story of the first half of Harry's life, is their second youngest.

ACKNOWLEDGMENTS

I am grateful to my friends Michael de Leeuw and Steve Allen and my wife Carrie for reading the manuscript that became this book and providing valuable insights and suggestions. Michael has now volunteered to serve in this role for all four of my books and has made all of them better.

I appreciate all of my friends who've taken an interest in the book and given me suggestions about the title, the cover, and the story, especially Tom Wicker, who offered valuable advice about all three.

I am also grateful to the team at Morgan James for their faith in me and their hard work to make the book a success.

Finally, I am thankful most of all to Lee Cheney, without whom there would have been no book to write. But for Lee's curiosity and research, aided by his wife Linda and daughter Laura, the story of the first half of Harry's life would have been lost forever. Are Harry's accomplishments in the second half of his life more impressive because of his misdeeds and the consequences he suffered in the first? To me, the answer is clear.

ABOUT THE AUTHOR

Brooks Eason is the author of *Travels with Bobby*, a travelogue about hiking trips with his best friend; *Fortunate Son*, a memoir about his adoption as an infant and discovery of his birth mother's identity when he was nearly fifty; and *Bedtime with Buster*, which consists entirely of conversations between him and his beloved mixed-breed dog. *Fortunate Son* was nominated for best nonfiction work by a Mississippi author in 2020. Eason has an undergraduate degree from the University of Mississippi and a law degree from Duke and is a mostly retired lawyer. He grew up in Tupelo, Mississippi, and lives in Madison, Mississippi, with his wife Carrie, their two dogs, and a cat. He has three children and five grandchildren.

A free ebook edition is available with the purchase of this book.

To claim your free ebook edition:

1. Visit MorganJamesBOGO.com
2. Sign your name CLEARLY in the space
3. Complete the form and submit a photo of the entire copyright page
4. You or your friend can download the ebook to your preferred device

Morgan James BOGO™

A **FREE** ebook edition is available for you or a friend with the purchase of this print book.

CLEARLY SIGN YOUR NAME ABOVE

Instructions to claim your free ebook edition:
1. Visit MorganJamesBOGO.com
2. Sign your name CLEARLY in the space above
3. Complete the form and submit a photo of this entire page
4. You or your friend can download the ebook to your preferred device

Print & Digital Together Forever.

Snap a photo

Free ebook

Read anywhere

CPSIA information can be obtained
at www.ICGtesting.com
Printed in the USA
JSHW050407010622
26543JS00001B/1